Between Friends

Jenny Harper

Published by Accent Press Ltd 2016

ISBN: 9781783757473

Additional typesetting by Head & Heart Publishing Services.

Acknowledgements

When I was writing *Between Friends*, I was fascinated by the idea of how female friendships might be threatened by the re-emergence of dark secrets from the past. However, the book went through a number of drafts before it finally took flight and I am incredibly grateful for the wisdom and encouragement I received from the late Dorothy Lumley. I wish she could read the book now.

I also owe a huge debt to my editor, Rebecca Lloyd, whose insights and observations have been invaluable – as is, also, her faith in my writing.

Thanks to my writing buddies for their endless encouragement and suggestions, and to Jane Knights for her proof reading of my manuscript. Finally, to my husband, who tolerates my constant withdrawal to my computer without complaint and handles my often bizarre requests for information, character insights or responses to my work with great patience and good humour.

Chapter One

Sometimes Marta wondered how different her days might be if they were a family rather than a couple. If, instead of putting on a business suit at the sound of the alarm, she were to wake to the snuffling cries of a baby and pad across the carpet in the bedroom she shared with Jake to a cot in the corner. She imagined the feeling of picking it up, this squalling infant, of holding it to her breast and hushing it with love and milk.

She picked up her coffee from the counter of the small café, filled with a disappointment so profound that for a moment she thought it might set her weeping. This morning, again, her hopes had been dashed.

Still – she placed the cup on the table in the window and dropped her briefcase on the floor – it was a day of rare promise. She could see it in the slant of the morning light hitting the chiselled stone of the Georgian tenements across the road, and feel it in the warmth of the sun already beating through the window. It was going to be hot, a day for walking the beaches from Silverknowes to Cramond Island or strolling up the Pentland Hills with a flask of tea and a pack of sandwiches. A day not to be wasted.

By nature cheerful, she allowed her spirits to lift.

Across the road, sun hit glass as a door opened, reflecting low rays of light sharply into her eyes. A man emerged and stood, undecided, as the door swung to behind him. Was he a celebrity? It was August, and Edinburgh was teeming with personalities and stars, real and wannabe. Authors were here for the Book Festival, jazz musicians were opening their souls

1

for the world's inspection, dancers, actors, comedians and television personalities were vying with each other for attention and audiences.

She watched as the lights changed and the man crossed the road. He was tall and slim, stylishly dressed with well-cut jeans, brown loafers, a crisp white shirt and a grey sweater tied loosely round his neck. A battered brown fedora sat jauntily on his head and he carried a brown leather holdall over one shoulder. He was heading straight towards her.

Surely she knew him? The café door opened and she tried not to stare as she scanned her memory bank. Maybe she had just seen him on television. It was rude to stare. She dropped her gaze, dipped into her briefcase, spread notes on the table in front of her.

'Americano, please.'

The two words did what Marta's eyes had failed to do – now she knew. 'Hello, Tom,' she said.

The hat spun round and a pair of quicksilver eyes regarded her questioningly.

'It *is* Tom Vallely, isn't it?'

The man threw down some coins, picked up his coffee and crossed the floor to where she was sitting.

'I'm afraid I can't quite—'

'Marta Davidson.' She stuck out her hand. He took it and held it. 'I was still Marta Henkel when we met, though.'

'Remind me?'

'We met in London a few times. You were living with my friend, Jane. Jane Porter?'

He swung the leather holdall from his shoulder and let it slide to the floor, then removed his hat, revealing the floppy black hair she now remembered – perhaps just a shade thinner? And maybe with a strand of grey? Marta wondered how she could ever have forgotten the beautiful symmetrical features or the mercury eyes.

'You do remember Jane, I suppose?' she teased. Jane and Tom had been together for years, a pairing she and Carrie had always found odd, but which had nevertheless seemed set to last.

He smiled, a flash of brilliance that illuminated his face.

'Dear Janie. How could I forget? Are you still in touch?'

'Of course.'

'How is she? Is she happy?'

As he pulled out a chair and sank onto it, Marta was thrown back into her past by Tom's unexpected appearance.

Jane, Carrie and Marta. Marta, Jane and Carrie. Put them in any order, they'd always been inseparable – an unlikely trio, but always close. Carrie was ambitious, materialistic, driven: Jane family-focused and budget-conscious. As for herself – Marta liked to think that she slotted comfortably in the middle, relating to career on the one side and family on the other. She thought of Jane, always so busy – secretary of her local choir, keeping an eye on her aging mother, walking the dog, supervising the many activities of her three lively children. Was she happy? Marta had always assumed so.

'Oh yes, very happy,' she said at length, in reply to Tom's question.

'I suppose she's still in London? Still playing the cello?'

'No, she's right here. In Edinburgh. And she gave up the cello years ago. Oh, sorry—' in her handbag, her mobile was shrilling for attention, 'I'd better take this. Hello? Mr Morrison, hello... you can't? – but everything's ready for you... What? ...Well, when can you? ... Oh. I see. No, I suppose we'll have to manage... yes, yes, I understand. You will call when... Yes... yes, thank you. Yes, goodbye.'

She ended the call and dropped the phone back into her bag with a tut of exasperation.

'A problem?'

'My plumber. Our washing machine is leaking. He promised

to come today to fix it, but his wife's mother's had a turn, apparently, and he's got to drive up to Inverness.'

'Can you get another one?'

'Washing machine?'

'Plumber.'

'Oh. No, well Mr Morrison's been our man for ages. I think we'll just have to wait.' Marta glanced at her watch.

'Are you in a hurry?'

'I've got a meeting in twenty minutes.'

'Are you still in tourism?'

'You remembered! Yes, I work for a small company, Tartan Ribbon Tours. I've moved around a fair bit but I've been back in Edinburgh a few years now. I went to school here,' she added, by way of explanation.

'So that's how you know Jane.'

'Yes. And Carrie, of course. Did you ever meet Carrie Edwards?'

Tom's smile was a lesson in engagement.

'Now who could forget Caroline? I expect she's still in London?'

'Oh no. Carrie's here too. We're all here.'

Tom looked surprised. 'She was so ambitious.'

'She still is. She hasn't changed a bit.'

'Really?' Tom looked thoughtful. 'Now that is good to know. Married?'

'Nope. Career woman, that's our Carrie. I keep telling her what she needs is a good man, but she just laughs. Listen, what about you, Tom? What are you doing these days?'

Tom drained his coffee.

'Still acting. I'm doing a play on the Fringe – you must come and see it, it's only on for another week. My agent told me there are some big scouts in town. Theatre's fine, but I'd really like a big film or television role again.'

'I'd love to come. I'll tell Jake – my husband – but he works late most nights. Where are you staying?'

4

'Actually, that's a bit of a problem.' He gestured at the brown holdall on the floor. 'Just got thrown out.'

'For misbehaving?' Marta teased.

'Friend's mother landed on her unexpectedly. She needed the room.' He looked rueful. 'Bit of a problem, though, I hadn't budgeted on a hotel. You know what it's like for us actors – always juggling things between jobs. The Festival's terrific, but it hardly pays the bills.'

'What are you going to do?'

'Make a few calls, I guess. See if I can fix something else up. I haven't got a lot of time, though, the play's on at five thirty.'

'We've got a spare room,' Marta blurted out, surprising herself because Jake, teetering on the edge of depression since losing his job, had become something of a hermit.

Tom's eyebrows rose a fraction.

Thinking of Jake, Marta's generosity wavered before her irrepressible good nature won.

'You won't be here for long, I guess?'

'A week at most.'

'Well, I don't see why you couldn't stay with us, then. In fact, I can even give you a key.' Marta picked up her handbag again. 'This was obviously *meant*, Tom. The plumber not being able to come, I mean, and meeting you like this. Here,' she held out a set of keys, 'I don't normally carry spares, but I was going to give them to Mr Morrison.'

She dropped them into Tom's outstretched hand.

'Darling. This is extraordinarily generous. Are you sure? What will your husband say about a complete stranger landing on you?'

'Jake'll be fine,' Marta said with conviction. 'He's used to me and my good deeds. I'm just pleased to be able to help. You can go there right away to drop your bag. The spare room's upstairs, at the front. Jake will probably still be asleep, but I'll call and let him know you're coming.'

Tom bent forward and kissed her cheek, making Marta blush. 'Are you an angel sent from heaven?'

'That's me. Now, here's how you get to my place—'

Five minutes later, Marta shoved her unread notes in her briefcase and said a hurried goodbye.

Tom Vallely.

Amazing.

At the door to the street she half turned, waved, and was rewarded with another of his life-affirming smiles.

Good deed for the day.

Tick.

Some hours later, her hands full of shopping bags, Marta barged open the gate to their cottage in the seaside suburb of Portobello. Inviting Jane and Carrie for supper had seemed a good idea earlier, but now...

'Hi!'

She paused at the foot of the stairs and called up to Jake. He'd be in his study going over job applications. Shifts in the bar at the Assembly Rooms brought in some cash but was hardly what he was qualified for.

'Hi, Jake?'

There was no reply. He must be plugged into some music.

Marta unpacked her shopping methodically, leaving the ingredients for the main course by the sink, and those for the dessert on the worktop by the mixer. Absorbed in her preparations, she didn't hear Jake come downstairs.

'I broke a plate.'

'What?' Marta, concentrating on dicing lamb, jumped at the sound of Jake's voice. 'Which one?'

'One of the kitchen set.'

'Oh. Not so bad then.'

Jake leant against the sink and crossed his arms. 'I don't know what's got into me.'

'It really doesn't matter, love.'

'It's not like me to be so bloody careless.'

Marta stopped chopping and glanced at him sympathetically. 'Bad day, sweetheart?'

'The plumber never arrived. I broke a plate. And I came down half an hour later to find a complete stranger making himself a sandwich and raiding my beer. Oh, and there were two more rejections in the post. Thanks, Mr Davidson, but no thanks. Bad day?' His lips tightened. 'You could say, yes.'

'Christ.' She dropped the knife with a clatter and clapped a hand over her mouth. 'I forgot to call you about Tom. No wonder you're cross. Oh Jake, *sorry*.'

'Tom. Let me see. Tom.' He ran a hand through his short brown hair and scratched his head. 'Could he be the sandwich-making, beer-drinking, key-holding thespian?'

Marta wiped her hands on her apron and crossed the kitchen to smooth down his hair. 'I said sorry. I meant to call. Honest.' She kissed him gently. 'He's an old friend of Jane's. I bumped into him and he needs somewhere to stay for a few days. The plumber had to call off so I gave Tom the key.'

'So I understand.' His arms, still crossed, excluded her.

'Don't be cross, love, it's only for a few days. He's in something in the Festival.'

There was a small sigh, then his arms came around her, his head buried itself into her hair, and his body slotted into comfortable, familiar places.

'Forgiven?' she mumbled into the warm flatness of his chest.

'Always forgiven, Pollyanna.'

She loved Jake for many things, but his unwavering love was top of the list.

'What are you cooking?' he asked as he released her.

'Oh God, I'd better get on! Nigella's lamb. I've asked Carrie round, and the Harvies. It's a surprise. I thought they'd like to see Tom again.'

'Really? Didn't he used to live with Jane? I seem to remember you telling me he left her for some actress.'

Marta threw the last of the lamb into the casserole and opened a jar of caramelised onion. 'Serena Swift. It didn't last long. But the breakup with Jane was all very amicable. I was in South Africa at the time, but Jane wrote to me about it.'

'You mean, there were no hard feelings?'

'She was cool about everything.'

'So she's going to be delighted to see this man again tonight, is she?'

'Yes. Don't be such a cynic.'

'You always look on the bright side.'

'And you're always pessimistic. It was seventeen years ago, for heaven's sake. We've all moved on.'

She opened the oven door and put the casserole inside, then poured the cream into a bowl and started beating it, watching as the pale liquid began to froth and thicken.

'Are you expecting me to join you?'

'Aren't you working tonight?'

'Nope. Andrew messed up the rota.'

'Fantastic! I mean, I'm sorry about that, but I'm pleased you'll be here.'

Jake grunted.

Marta glanced at him sharply. 'What? It's lamb and cheesecake.'

'It means I'll have to be sociable.'

'Oh Jake, don't be grumpy. You like Neal, you know you do. And you've always adored Jane and Carrie. What's the problem?'

A small smile softened his mouth and he held out his hand.

'Give me the scrapings and I promise I'll be nice.'

Marta laughed, pleased. 'Here. A cheap victory.' She grew serious. 'I forgot to say, I got the curse this morning.'

His hand, half way to his mouth with a spoon laden with cheesecake mix, froze in mid-air. 'Oh.'

'I know. We just need to keep trying.' Again that gnawing emptiness inside her. Every month she had to battle it, every month came the struggle to remain optimistic. 'Don't be down about it, Jake, I'm trying not to be.'

He handed her the bowl. He hadn't eaten a mouthful.

Chapter Two

In her stylishly minimalist flat in the Quartermile, Carrie Edwards opened her sports bag and threw her kit into the washing machine. Her face was still scarlet after forty minutes on the treadmill and a further twenty on the rowing machine, but she felt virtuous. Carrie never did anything by halves. Work hard, play hard was her motto.

A flick of the dial and the load started to turn. Another click on her docked iPod and music filled the large open-plan living space, filtering through the eight cream micro-speakers placed discreetly near ceiling height and pointing at a space right in the centre of the room. Sometimes Carrie just threw herself on the thick pile rug right at the heart of the sound, lay back, closed her eyes and let it all wash over her. Tonight there was no time for such luxury. She had precisely fifteen minutes to change and get out. Thank goodness she'd showered at the gym because the traffic on the way home had been knuckle-chewingly slow.

Why had she agreed to Marta's invitation? It had already been a long day because she was intent on proving herself at her law firm, and with a partnership review coming up in the next month or two, that meant getting in before the boss and leaving after him. But Marta had been insistent. Anyway, who was the 'mystery guest' she'd said would be there?

She stepped into a Ted Baker silk shift in bright colours, teamed with Marc Jacobs satin peep toes. Keep it simple. This was supper with Marta, not dinner at the Balmoral.

Carrie pulled a sheaf of papers out of her briefcase, shuffled through them to check that everything was in order for the morning, and fired up her personal laptop. She clicked on to her favourite site and watched the icon – a red satin sheet, silky and sensual – float and settle into place. Just seeing the fabric swirling made her shiver with pleasurable anticipation. Another click of the mouse and the sheet was drawn back, allowing her to log in.

Bed Buddies welcomes D.A. Delight

This was Carrie's secret indulgence – a site for commitment-free sex. Many subscribers were married and looking for excitement, others were lonely or sexually unfulfilled within marriage or without. Whatever ... Carrie took the view that it wasn't up to her to judge them. She was single and owed no-one anything, and she chose her companions with care.

She clicked into her space and scrolled down the messages. Seven today, the usual suspects.

<Hi D.A. High Five is free on Friday, midday, for fast fun.>

<Hello D.A. Delight, how are things with my favourite buddy? Can you make Thursday at seven? Jury Service>

<Darling Delight, I'm yours tonight. The Big Man>

And so it went on. Seven messages, all from buddies she knew and trusted. High Five was a father of two from Livingston. His wife had lost her libido after the birth of their second child and he was desperate, poor guy – but loyal to his wife. The Big Man was a director of a FTSE 100 business, always under pressure, often away from his family, very much in need of trustworthy company.

Carrie never discussed Bed Buddies with anyone, not even with Jane and Marta – *particularly* not with Jane and Marta. What

12

would earnest Jane with her serious man and her precious kids say if she knew Carrie's secret? Would she be shocked? Judgmental? Condemnatory? Marta might be more understanding, but under the happy-go-lucky exterior she suspected that Marta was rather proper and Carrie wasn't prepared to risk a confidence.

She clicked on the message from Jury Service, an eminent judge. The first time Carrie met him, he'd been very nervous at the risk he was taking. Bed Buddies relied heavily on trust and it worked because that was the basis of membership for all parties. Jury Service was a kind and honest man, but a widower and lonely. He was undemanding, uncomplicated, and surprisingly good company.

<Thursday works for me, Jury. Usual place. You book.>

Click. The message was sent. Something to look forward to. She sent brief responses to the others, putting them on hold. It was nice to be popular. Bed Buddies had been the safe, reliable basis of her sex life for some years now and it suited her fine – no names, safety in anonymity. A long time ago, Carrie had taken the decision that relationships, with all their complications and heartaches, were not for her. But she enjoyed sex, and by using the bed-buddies.net site she could get it whenever she wanted it, in the certain knowledge that the other members were as concerned to keep their business as private as she was.

Log off.

Follow the red sheet as it floats into the darkness.

Watch the site close down.

Time to go.

Chapter Three

At Jane Harvie's small semi near Blackford Hill, her husband Neal was producing order out of the trail of chaos that always followed their family while, in the kitchen, Jane concentrated on getting a meal together and directing from the sidelines.

'Come on, Ian,' she urged her youngest, 'you know you have to wash up the pans you use when you're baking. Here, get these rinsed.'

She scoured out the last remains of his baking experiment and consigned them to the bin, then stacked the bowls and whisks, spoons and muffin tins next to the sink. Ian was still only eight and she didn't know yet how he would develop or where his true passions might lie. One day he wanted to be a pastry chef, the next a marine scientist. She still felt the need to protect him, although if she was honest with herself, Ian was like his father in his general cheerfulness and sailed through life with an ease she envied.

Her middle child, Ross – thirteen and already inhabiting his teenage years as though he owned them – said, 'Can I nick one?', reaching to the plate where Ian had stacked his raspberry and fudge muffins.

'No! They're for Granny,' Ian yelped crossly, up to his elbows in suds.

'So? There's plenty.'

Ross ignored his small brother and helped himself anyway.

'*Mum!* Tell him,' Ian cried, furious.

Exerting control over Ross was getting ever more difficult. Jane thought, *I have to learn to grow with him, he's no longer my*

15

baby. Already he was edging away from her. He was embarrassed if she tried to cuddle him even at home and a hug in public was certainly taboo. She remembered with wistfulness the baby he'd once been – the clarity of his skin and the way his hair had curled in a long, soft strand down the nape of his neck, blond and downy. It was scraped to the skull now, and no longer blond but mousey and brown. He would probably darken further, like her and Neal.

Emily, a week or two short of sixteen and all legs and arms, walked into the kitchen and yanked open the fridge. She had just finished her cello practice, something she never needed to be nagged about. Soon she'd be taking her Grade Eight examination, which Jane was confident she would pass with distinction. Pride bubbled in her head when she thought about Emily's musicality, but why, why, why the cello? The old question brought with it the familiar counterweight of sheer, desperate panic – controllable now, but still there, even after all these years.

Emily's voice brought her back.

'There's no lemon yoggie, Mum.'

'You don't need yogurt now, Emily. Gran'll be here in a minute and supper's almost ready.'

Emily was scowling. When she'd started the cello, she'd been such a sweet, docile child.

'I've bagged the strawberry,' said Ian from the sink. He had learned toughness in the hard school of sibling rivalry.

'I'm having the strawberry,' Emily said, extracting it. 'You can have the toffee.'

'I hate toffee.'

'Me too. That's why I'm having the strawberry.'

'Mum – tell her she can't.'

'Can.'

'Can't.'

Jane sighed. 'Do stop bickering. Emily, put that back in the fridge. Now.'

Neal came in from the hall, sized up the situation, took the yogurt from his daughter and returned it to the fridge, the muffin from Ross and replaced it on the plate, and a saucepan from where Ian was waving the dripping pan uncertainly in the air because the draining rack was full.

'I'll dry this one. Emily, get the table set please. Ross, you can get out pasta bowls. No, no arguing.' He held up a hand in warning. 'Jane, your mother's just arrived, we should get going.'

Jane looked around at the untidy kitchen and her bickering children. The prospect of escape was enticing.

'Hi Mum. Will you be all right?'

'Fine. You just go and enjoy yourselves.'

One day she would have to take care of her mother, and when she did, Jane hoped she would do it with the same unshakeable willingness her mother showed when taking care of the grandchildren.

'We won't be late. Thanks for this, Mum. You're a star. Supper's all ready and Ian has baked a treat for afters. Ross has eaten half his share already.'

'*Mum—*'

Neal pulled the front door behind them, smiling.

'Rare to be out like this mid-week.'

'Yes. Quite fun.'

Looking back later, it seemed an odd thing to say – and, as it turned out, horribly wrong.

Chapter Four

Each of the friends was rooted in her own neighbourhood. Jane was surrounded by other mothers and other young families – a desirable and indispensable support system. Carrie was city girl personified, modern and stylish, at the centre of the action. From her apartment, the city-centre stores were a mere ten-minute stroll, the taxi ride home from the clubs at night was speedy and affordable. Marta loved the freshness of the Portobello air, the quirkiness of the architecture, the feeling of escape from the confines of the city.

One particular benefit Marta enjoyed was easy parking. The city's swingeing parking restrictions hadn't yet extended to the street outside the Davidsons' cottage near the sea, so Carrie – who had to pay extravagantly for a parking space underneath her apartment block – was able to pull up her Mercedes convertible almost right outside. Jane and Neal, arriving at almost the same moment from the other direction in their battered estate car, were less fortunate and had to drive further down the street.

'Hi!'

'Hi Carrie, you look fab, as ever.'

Jane wasn't really envious of Carrie's extravagant wardrobe, but she did occasionally look at her own High Street store clothes a little critically after an evening with Caroline Edwards.

'You're looking great too.' Carrie patted Jane's red shrug. 'Love the colour. Suits you.'

'Thanks.' They swung through Marta's gate and threaded their way along the path, through the rose bushes and clumps of

19

lavender, still fragrant after a long day of sunshine. 'Did Marta tell you who her mystery guest is?'

'Wouldn't be drawn on the matter. You?'

'Not a chance.'

'Hope she's not trying to set me up again.' Carrie lifted the heavy iron knocker and allowed it to drop back against its plate with a loud thud. She grinned at Jane. 'One of these days, honest to God, I'll clock her.'

'Clock who?' Jake had opened the door and was smiling at them, his face friendly. He held out his hand and drew Carrie close to kiss her cheek. 'Who's inspiring these violent thoughts?'

'Your wife,' Carrie said unrepentantly. 'I don't trust her.'

Jake laughed. 'What's she done now?'

Jane said, 'She's being mysterious.'

'Hi Jane, hi Neal, come in all of you.'

Jake ushered them through the hallway into the snug living room, which Marta had filled with flowers. The scent of lilies was cloying, but they looked magnificent on the small chest in front of the window. On the mantelpiece was a small vase of lavender, clearly picked from the garden. A bowl of roses, packed thick and short into a crystal bowl sat in the centre of the coffee table. Flowers everywhere. So pretty, so Marta.

'Oh dear. Maybe I should have brought wine,' Jane handed a bunch of chrysanthemums over to Jake doubtfully.

'They're lovely.' Marta, still wearing an apron, appeared in the doorway. 'Thanks, Jane, they'll be great in the dining room.'

'I brought wine. And chocolate.' Carrie handed her bag over. 'I was just saying, Marta, that one of these days I'll cheerfully strangle you.'

'Thanks,' Marta took her gifts, 'but why the death threat?'

'You know damn well. Mysteries. Secrets. Mid-week dinner invitations at short notice. I'm deeply suspicious.'

'Me too,' Jane sank down onto the cream sofa, straightened her skirt and crossed her neat ankles. 'Do tell us, Marta.'

'You're so right not to trust my wife,' Jake said with a trace of the wry humour Jane remembered from before he'd lost his job. 'What will you drink? Jane? Carrie? Neal? Glass of wine?'

Jane said, 'Perfect. White please, if that's okay.'

'White's fine by me,' Neal agreed.

'Could I have red please, Jake?' Carrie said.

Jane looked round the room. She hadn't been to the house in an age. The cottage had real character, not like her 1960's house, cheap when it was built and even less desirable now. Hard as she tried, her own living room looked dull at best, a shambles at worst. What with the toys, clothes, dog hair, books and games, forever being discarded at random, simply keeping the place tidy was a constant struggle. Marta's living room, though, could be out of the pages of a magazine.

She heard a rattle, then a slight creak, then felt the faintest of draughts. Someone had opened the front door.

There was no time to wonder, no time to consider why someone might be letting themselves in rather than ringing the bell. No time to think that her life might be about to change dramatically. Yet a few seconds later, Jane knew with a horrible dark certainty that nothing would ever be quite the same again – not her marriage, not her friendships, nothing. She'd thought she had her life under control. Now she realised just how wrong she'd been.

Her nightmare had returned in the flesh. He was standing with the heavy jambs of the doorway framing his body. Even with the light from the hallway behind him, there was something about the set of his bones, the tilt of his hips, the angle of his arms, the fineness of his fingers that brought everything flooding back. He loomed there, tall but slender, a brown fedora covering his hair, a sweater slung casually round his shoulders, his body so long untouched and yet so instantly, so terribly recognised.

Tom.
Vallely.
Oh.
My.
God.

Carrie, flying high in blue skies, knew at once that she had entered a cloud of ash that would bring her down. The slow, spiralling descent had already begun.

Light streamed in from the hallway so that the man's features were shaded, his eyes almost invisible in the shadow under the broad brim of the hat. She hadn't seen him for seventeen years, but she would know him anywhere.

Her hand clenched in an involuntary movement round the stem of her wine glass.

'*Shit!*'

The glass splintered, splashing red wine across the pristine cream carpet and down her dress. There was a different red there too – blood.

The wine looked more dramatic, she thought dispassionately, staring wide-eyed at the carpet.

'You've cut yourself!'

Pain bit in.

'Hell, Marta, I'm so sorry. Oh God, look at the mess.'

'Don't worry about that, give me your hand.'

'You all right, Carrie?'

'I'll get a cloth.'

'Come on through to the kitchen, Carrie. Let's get that wine off your dress.'

'I had to pick red, didn't I?'

She laughed, tried to keep her voice light, couldn't quite keep out the tremor.

It was crazy. One minute all was tranquility and politeness and small talk, the next, pandemonium. And through it all, Carrie realised, Tom Vallely had simply stood and watched, a twist of amusement playing round that beautiful mouth.

He took his hat off as she passed.

'Hello Carrie,' he said, his voice low, the deep, entrancing timbre unchanged across the years.

She glimpsed his eyes for a second, registered once more their astonishing pale grey and their cool, critical way of assessing the scene. She was so close she could smell him. She had to shut her eyes as the crisp scent of him lit a flame inside her that she had thought long dead. The brush of his fingers on her arm sent a thrill through her core.

He's here.

And so is Jane.

Chapter Five

Tom Vallely took in the room at a glance. Marta Davidson had stitched him up. He should have realised she might do something of this sort.

Jane. And, bloody hell, Carrie Edwards. Now that brought back a memory or two.

'Janie. Darling. As beautiful as ever.'

In two relaxed, lazy strides he crossed the room, pulled Jane to her feet, cupped her face between his hands to examine it, then ceremoniously, gently, kissed first her right cheek, then her left, before relinquishing his grasp.

'Hello Tom.'

Still the same diffident voice. She never had had any spark – what the hell had he seen in her? Except that she'd been delightfully easy to dominate, of course.

'Isn't this lovely? And this must be—?'

He turned to the man next to Jane, who had also risen. Balding, stocky, flat-featured, dull.

'I'm guessing you must be the lovely Jane's husband?' He smiled his best smile and stuck out his right hand, reaching to grasp Neal's shoulder with his left in his best hail-fellow-well-met gesture, inclusive, warm, friendly.

She hadn't told the husband about him, that was clear. She'd airbrushed him out of her past. Not good enough, Janie.

'Neal, this is Tom.' Jane's smile fluttered on her lips uncertainly. 'In another life, Tom and I—' she hesitated, as if unsure how to describe the relationship.

'Jane was the light of my life, Neal mate, for a year or two, back in the Dark Ages. Before she found you, of course, you lucky dog.'

'Right. Okay. Well.'

Neal looked awkward.

'How long have you two been married, then? Few years, huh? You never sent me an invitation to the wedding, Janie.'

There it was, surely? A glimmer of panic in her eyes, sensed more than observed.

'Just joking. Waters long flowed past. Hey, I believe you have kids?'

Marta, coming back into the room with Carrie, said, 'Heavens, you're all standing up! Sit, look, there's plenty of space.'

Carrie looked pale, but she was a different sort from Jane. Carrie had spirit. Carrie didn't give a damn. Perhaps he'd made a mistake, choosing Serena. Well of course he had, Serena was nothing but a fame-seeking bitch, it had taken him ages to get out of her clutches and he didn't got much out of the divorce deal either. He'd misjudged her. Or rather, he'd miscalculated what he would get out of the relationship against what he would have to put in. Lesson learned.

'Jane and I have three children,' Neal said.

'Fantastic,' Tom murmured, looking at Jane. 'Fantastic.'

He sank into a chair and watched as the others shuffled and rearranged themselves and slotted back onto sofas and chairs and stools, leaving Marta standing.

'Jane's children are adorable,' Marta said enthusiastically. 'Listen, I'll just finish getting supper ready, you keep talking. Tom what are you drinking?'

'If there's any red left that doesn't require me sucking it off the carpet with a straw, I'll go for that.'

'It was an accident,' Carrie said belligerently. 'You gave me a shock. And I'm tired. Things are really busy at work.'

She pushed at her hair with her hand, now bandaged. Her other hand, holding a glass again, was trembling slightly.

Tom watched the surface of the wine ripple and tip up the sides so that viscous legs formed and ran down. She'd be spilling it again if she wasn't careful. Caroline Edwards was nervous. Now why would that be?

'You never used to get tired.'

Was that a blush? Tom settled down into the chair luxuriously. He was beginning to enjoy himself.

Marta, presiding cheerfully over her guests, looked round the table. Jake's warnings had been quite unnecessary – Jane was smiling quietly, a fraction quieter than usual perhaps, but relaxed. She'd forgotten to factor in that Jane might never have told Neal about Tom. Perhaps it had been unfair to spring this on everyone.

'More lamb?'

'N-no thanks.' Jane raised a thin hand protectively over her plate to ward off Jake's hovering ladle.

Was that a stammer? Marta couldn't remember Jane stammering for twenty years or more. Those special lessons from Ann Playfair, their English teacher at school, had dealt with the problem most effectively. That, and Jane's gradual realisation that her talent as a cellist was prodigious.

Maybe she'd imagined the stammer.

Tom laid down his fork and knife with a flourish. 'You used to love lamb.'

'I did. I d-do. I'm just full.'

There it was again. Curious.

'Remember when you tried that tagine thing with the apricots but you forgot to put any stock in?' Tom laughed loudly. 'Took me a week to scour out the bloody pot. Talk about charcoal.'

Jane coloured and looked at the table.

Marta laughed. 'Jane's cooking disasters are legendary,' she said cheerfully. 'Ian now, that's her youngest son, he's an amazing cook, isn't he, Jane?'

'Neal? Can I persuade you to have some more?'

Jake's interruption moved attention back to the circulating casserole.

'Please. It's really tasty.'

'I'd love some, if there's any left.' Tom pushed his plate towards Jake. 'Cheers mate. Thank heaven there was a Turkish takeaway at the bottom of the street, hey Janie?' Tom glanced around the table, smiling broadly, 'or we'd have starved many a time.'

'Are you married, Tom?' Neal asked, scraping his plate.

Tom shook his head. There was a thread of grey at his temples, Marta could see it gleaming in the soft light from the candles. It made him look rather distinguished.

'As the great Mae West once said,' Tom turned on a stage voice and declaimed in a drawling falsetto, '"Marriage is an institution – and I'm not ready for an institution yet".'

Neal guffawed, Marta laughed, Jake looked amused. Jane's mouth pulled into a crooked half smile and she started to twist a strand of her hair between her fingers.

Carrie said drily, 'On that we agree.'

'But what about Serena Swift?' Jake asked.

'Just makes my point, mate. Yeah, it's true. I was married briefly, a long time ago. But I was on the rebound—' he looked pointedly at Jane, who flushed and hastily resumed her minute scrutiny of some small mark on the table, scratching at it with her nail, '—and my view of marriage was coloured by the experience.'

'No children then?'

Jane abandoned her scraping and started to cough, with a disconcerting dry hiccup.

'Sorry,' she gasped, 'something must have down the wrong way.'

It was Tom who thought to pour her a glass of water. 'No children. Not that I know of anyway, mate,' he said, staring into Jane's eyes as he spoke. She sipped at the water and looked away. 'See me as a father? Still a child myself, I confess it. I'm hopeless at responsibility.'

'What are you doing in Edinburgh, Tom?' Neal asked in the pause that followed this pronouncement.

'I'm in a play on the Fringe, *The Glass Ornament*. You should come and see it; it's been getting good reviews.'

'Not a great time for me,' Jake said. 'I'm usually working. What's it about?'

Tom settled back in his chair and checked he had the attention of his audience.

'You know the old saying, "Friendship is like a glass ornament – once it's broken it can rarely be put back together again exactly the same way"? Well, that's the premise. It's a sticky situation, relationships are strained to the utmost.'

'I think if your friendship's strong enough, nothing will break it,' Marta said, looking at Carrie and Jane. 'Don't you agree, girls?'

'Sure,' Carrie said.

'I mean, look at the three of us – we're all very different, but we still value our friendship above everything.'

'Yeah, and your phone bills prove it,' groaned Jake, amid laughter.

Neal, his voice thoughtful, said, 'I'm sure I saw you in that docu-drama on television, what was it called, *Mary's Child*?'

'I played one of the lawyers. Small part.'

Neal leant forward. 'Was it true, that story? I thought it was rather extreme. Did they doctor it up to make it more dramatic?'

Tom shook his head. 'On the contrary, they had to underplay the true facts. The actual rape of the woman was quite horrific. I'll spare you the details, but her ordeal actually went on for days, not hours and—'

'Yes, thank you Tom, please do spare us,' said Marta hastily. 'I've eaten far too much cheesecake, it's sitting on my stomach. I really don't need to be made to feel even more queasy.'

'Even so,' Neal said forcefully, 'she should not have had the abortion. Abortion's murder.'

'Surely in the circumstances—'

'There are no circumstances that justify abortion.'

'Come on, mate,' Tom said. 'It's only cells if you do it early enough, isn't it?'

Marta placed her hand on her stomach. Only cells, she thought, coming together to form a life. The most precious miracle on earth – and one that just wasn't happening for her.

Across the room, she noticed that Jane had placed her hand on her stomach too. The gesture was sweetly protective – Jane really loved her kids. Neal too. Perhaps his vehemence wasn't surprising.

'Well, that went well, don't you think?' Marta said as she climbed into bed next to Jake.

'You think?'

'Everyone seemed to enjoy themselves.'

He rolled over to look at her.

'Marta, my sweet, naive wife, there was blood everywhere – literally and metaphorically, spilled wine, hurt feelings, old wounds opened and an argument fit to start World War Three and you think it was a good evening? Only Pollyanna—'

'Oh really, Jake?' Marta instantly became anxious. 'I thought people—'

'The food was great.' He rolled away from her, then turned back to give her a kiss. 'Goodnight, sweetheart.'

'Night.'

Marta lay awake, thinking and worrying until, lulled by the steady tick of the clock and the effects of the wine she had drunk, she drifted off into a dreamless sleep.

Chapter Six

Sight, sound, touch, smell. There were five senses, weren't there? What was the other one?

Sight, sound, touch, smell ... ah yes, *taste*.

Carrie stood in her marble-tiled bathroom gazing at her funny lopsided face, with its oversized mouth and large eyes. Her skin looked almost grey and there were dark rings under her eyes – shock, she supposed. But was it the shock of cutting herself, or the shock of seeing Tom again?

Her palm was throbbing and felt swollen and painful. She stared at the bandage round her hand and tried to decide whether to take it off and wash the cut, or leave well alone.

Leave it. Take a painkiller instead.

She reached up to open the bathroom cabinet where she kept the ibuprofen and was met again by the ghost of herself. Not a pretty sight. What must Tom have thought?

Why did she care what Tom thought?

Sight, sound, touch, smell, taste. Five senses, each one aflame.

She cared. Oh God damn it, she cared! Not with her head, perhaps, but with her body, if you can care with your body. Seventeen years and the man turned her on just as wickedly as he ever had.

Tom Vallely.

He hadn't changed a bit. Still handsome, a dish of pure temptation laced with poison but oh ... so ... seductive. His hair had a touch of grey, but it suited him – gave him an air of distinction, as if he'd seen things, experienced things, learned from them and come back primed with judgement and wisdom and ... skill. And his voice! Still the same Tom voice, spice and sugar and honey, a voice to lose yourself in. She could hear his words in her head, whirling round and round, irresistible.

'Hello Carrie.' ... *'Marriage is an institution – and I'm not ready for an institution yet.'* ... *'Come and see the show.'*

Several times across the hours at Marta's she'd found herself drifting into a fantasy sparked by that voice. *'Come and see the show.'* Maybe she would. Maybe she just would.

He'd touched her arm as she passed him at the door. The merest brush, no more, yet she felt the trace of his fingers like a thousand volts, crackling and sparking the length of her limb. He'd seen the response, too, she knew it. A touch was all it had taken, the slightest graze and he'd rolled back the years and claimed her for his own once more. She inhaled sharply and caught the smell of him, the faintest whisper of wood smoke and nicotine laced with Roger et Gallet's cedar soap – and now she was his again.

Carrie unscrewed the top of the medicine bottle, shook out two pills and swallowed them with some water. The throbbing would subside soon and she could forget about her hand and go to sleep. Except that she knew sleep was not likely to come easily to her tonight and she was furious because tomorrow was an exceptionally demanding working day, and she needed to be on top of her brief.

Carrie had always known what she wanted – success. Money was a given, but it was a by-product. Or was it the other way round? She mulled the point over, her brain so tired it almost refused to function – not a good sign.

Did she want money more than anything? She liked it, of course. She liked being able to buy what she wanted, the Mercedes roadster, her brand new penthouse in the Quartermile, the designer clothes and luxury holidays. She liked not having to think about what she spent – not like Jane, perpetually having to budget, with Neal's modest income and three children to provide for, nor like Marta, who was having to take on all the expenses right now, with Jake being out of work. Thinking of her friends and their marriages created in Carrie a sense of satisfied complacency that displaced pain for a few welcome moments. She didn't envy them their families.

Could you ever judge yourself to be successful? If you achieved one goal, wouldn't you simply accept success and aim for the next goal, the next objective, the bigger purpose, the higher aim?

Carrie had her own hierarchy of goals. The most achievable – and surely it would happen soon – was a partnership. She'd been working for more than ten years for Ascher Frew, a sizeable law firm in Edinburgh, with partner firms in London and New York, but the accolade of partner status, which she craved more than anything, had been elusive. Henry Frew, the managing partner, was an affable man but from another age. If challenged, he would vehemently deny any accusation of gender prejudice, but time and again Carrie had seen younger men promoted before her. She'd chosen to bide her time. There was nothing to be gained by whining but she did need to be more aggressive about her abilities, not sell herself short.

Another round of reviews was due shortly and this time all her performance appraisals indicated she'd get what she so longed for. Carrie had chosen to renounce the restraints and responsibilities of relationships because sex without tears was much simpler – and it allowed her to pursue her career untroubled.

Career? Untroubled sex? Simple?

That's the way it had seemed – until tonight.

Tom effing Vallely.

Her instincts proved to be right. With thoughts of Tom filling her head, sleep wouldn't come. She tossed and stared into the darkness, rewinding her life and watching as scenes from her past played out in front of her.

The only thing she could remember of that fateful night was that the Proclaimers had been pounding out their beat on the CD player in the corner of the room.

No, wait ... she'd been clutching a glass of indifferent wine – red of course, even back then, she'd always preferred red – and staring down at her black leather mini skirt, wishing she hadn't bothered coming, despite her promise to Jane. She didn't see a great deal of Jane back then, even though they were both living in London. She was working all hours at Ascher Frew, excited by her first real job after graduating and exhilarated by the buzz of the Big Smoke, and Jane was away a lot on tour with the orchestra.

'Please go. Look after Tom for me.'

'It's Friday night, Jane. I'll be wrecked after a week at work.'

'Listen to yourself, Caroline Edwards. Are you nineteen or ninety?'

'Neither. I'm twenty-two, broke, single, and by Friday, shattered.'

'That's rubbish and you know it. Go. You never know, you might meet the man of your dreams.'

'Hardly likely.'

'I'll still be in Cardiff. We're giving a concert on Friday, another one on Saturday, I can't get home till Sunday and Tom's not working at the moment. He's bored, Carrie. Do me a favour, chum him?'

She'd sighed, decided it might be quite fun – after all, she'd never been to Richmond – and agreed. Tom Vallely was such a chancer, she'd never understood how Jane couldn't see it. Devastatingly good-looking, of course, but most certainly not to be trusted. If she were Jane ... Well, she'd go and keep an eye on the guy, if it kept her friend happy.

She had arranged to meet him at this small terraced house where she knew she'd know no-one, and already she'd been at the party long enough to decide that she really didn't want to get to know any of them. Posers and ponces. God knows what these people did for a living. A lot of them were clearly luvvies, which must be how Tom knew them.

She watched a slim blonde with a Rachel haircut leaning against the sink in the pokey kitchen. She was holding her wine glass ostentatiously by the stem and drawing on her cigarette in an affected way, batting her eyelashes at a giant of a man with a grunge shirt and designer stubble. Probably someone famous, Carrie hadn't a clue.

Where *was* Tom? Carrie glanced at her watch. Ten o'clock already. Why had she agreed to meet him here? A gentleman would have collected her. Even a guy with a half-decent sense of etiquette would have met her at the Tube station and walked her to the party, which just went to prove what a ratfink Tom was.

The Proclaimers were still pounding away – 'I'm Gonna Be (500 miles)' – and the room was ringing with an unfettered, shouted accompaniment to the chorus, feet stamping, people clapping and chanting to the beat. Then there was a voice, in her ear. She whirled round.

Tom Vallely was standing there, inches from her, grinning all over his face.

'Hi.'

'Hello Carrie. Sorry I'm late.'

He didn't look sorry, but somehow the perfect symmetry of his smile was some kind of compensation. His gunmetal eyes were on her, their clarity rimmed with a hardness that was impossible to define but that had an edge to it that promised thrills. In that instant, Carrie understood how compelling this man was, and why Jane was so bound to him.

'You're forgiven. Have you got a drink?' she shouted back.

He lifted a can of beer in a toast. It was cold, she could see the condensation running down the sides. Knowing Tom, he had simply ignored the tepid offerings piled on the worktop and reached right into the fridge to help himself.

The next moment, he placed the can on the small of her back. She felt the icy coldness of it sear into her hot skin and arched away from it, exclaiming – and found herself in his arms.

'What the...?'

And then her outrage was overtaken by sheer lust as his mouth came down on hers, hard and commanding, his tongue working its way round her teeth, his lips by turns gentle, teasing and then passionate. The Proclaimers' insistent lyrics went round and round in her head: with their certainty that these two lives were inextricably linked, their conviction that the next morning the lovers would wake up together.

Damn it. That night, that first time, she'd been flooded by certainty too. There was never a moment from the second he'd started to kiss her that she had doubted they would spend the night together. She hadn't stopped to think of Jane, her best friend, her friend for life, who had asked her to keep an eye on her man. She'd succumbed to the irresistible tide of sexual desire that had swept over her, and she'd betrayed every rule of friendship since the beginnings of time.

Such overwhelming lust.

Her first illicit affair.

She'd stared in disbelief at the provocative MX-5 convertible he had purloined from somewhere, but when he opened the door for her, she slipped right inside. *It'll be all right. Jane will never know. Just this once. It can't hurt.* She used all the clichés in the book to justify her actions.

Later, she realised he must have borrowed the car and the posh flat for the evening with the deliberate aim of seducing her. Tom knew how to set a scene, it was his skill, he was a consummate actor – and, boy, could he play a great lover. But eight weeks later – eight weeks of avoiding Jane as much as humanly possible, of pretending to be too busy to meet her for drinks, of being wracked with guilt – and Carrie's conscience caught up with her. One day, lying next to him in her barely private room in her shared flat, she said, 'I can't do this, Tom.'

'Can't do what?'

He squinted down at her, his grey eyes hooded.

'You know. Betray Jane. And I don't know how you can.'

'Carrie. Sweetheart. Look at me.'

He tilted her chin up so that she was forced to look into his eyes.

'What?'

'I don't love Jane any more. It's hard to say it, I hate saying it, she's such a dear, but there, it's out. That's the truth of it. I just need to find the right time to tell her and then I'll be out of there.'

'Isn't it a bit unkind, staying with her if that's how you feel?'

'Unkind? How can you think that of me, sweetie? It's because I think so highly of Janie that I don't want to hurt her. I need to find the right moment to tell her, that's all.'

'And then what?'

'And then—' he rolled over so that his splendid naked torso was inches above Carrie's breasts, '—and then, Carrie my love, we can be together.'

They sealed the suggestion with the kind of all-consuming sex to which Carrie became addicted. And although she was uneasy at the notion of Tom leaving Jane and coming straight into her arms – surely their friendship couldn't survive such an event? – she justified her perfidy by convincing herself that Tom really had stopped loving Jane, that she wasn't breaking anything up.

Sleepless, Carrie turned onto her other side so that she faced the window. Instantly, the drawn curtains infuriated her. Why shut out the sky? Hopelessly restless, she swung her legs out of bed and yanked them back.

Scotland in summer. The sky was barely dark and she could make out the silhouette of the buildings on the far side of the

Meadows. Soon, people would be stirring, rising sleepily, going about their business. Soon, she would have to do the same.

Tom did leave Jane, but it turned out that all the time he'd been sleeping with Carrie, he'd also been having an affair with a young starlet called Serena Swift. Soon after that, Jane had gone off radar – chucked in her place in the orchestra and simply disappeared.

Inside Carrie, guilt and fury had blended in almost equal measure, and boiled over. How could he have done that? For a whole year after Jane had vanished she had been wracked by anxiety. Where had she gone? What was she doing? Was she even still alive? She'd itched to tell Serena the grubby truth about the man she had married, and she'd very nearly gone to the press to give them the whole story – but she'd lacked the courage to do either. Or perhaps a sense of self-preservation had kicked in. She was glad now that she'd held her tongue, but it was more than Tom Vallely deserved.

She tugged the curtains back across the window with vicious ferocity. Dammit. She shouldn't blame Marta for bringing Tom back into their lives. She'd been in South Africa, and couldn't have known.

Chapter Seven

'Here Benji! Walkies!'

The day after Marta's dinner party was dull, verging on damp. Jane reached for the lead, which was hanging on the coatstand in the cluttered hallway. The mirror's streaky glass was almost covered by the many coats bundled on hooks and by assorted hats and scarves thrown carelessly on top of them. She pushed aside a lank furry monkey of Ian's that was supposed to double as a backpack to peer at her reflection, and scraped at her tangled locks. Useless. Why bother? It was unseasonably windy outside and anything she achieved now by way of improvement would be destroyed as soon as she was past the porch.

She reached instead for one of the hats, a droopy beanie in kingfisher blue that had been Emily's first attempt at knitting. It sat on her head uncertainly. It was unlikely it would do anything to control her hair and, indeed, it was in danger of being blown away, so she pulled it further down over her ears. Now it looked even odder, but vanity was not one of Jane's vices so she turned away, shouting again for their little spaniel, who this time came bounding through the hall and skidded to a stop at her feet.

'Good boy.' Jane bent and fastened the lead to his collar, feeling through his grey-speckled hair for the clip. Benji was spoiled by every member of the Harvie family so that he'd become quite plump. He gazed up at her excitedly, his bottom waggling, his feet scrabbling on the wooden floor. She knew he hoped that 'walkies' meant 'rabbits', which it would do if she went up Blackford Hill.

On the hill, there was only one thing she could think about. One person and a necklace of memories.

Tom Vallely had walked into her life when she was eighteen years old. Her over-anxious mother had driven her all the way from Edinburgh to London to audition for Guildhall. 'You can't travel alone, darling,' she'd said. Secretly, Jane had been glad of her mother's company, despite her constant fussing. London seemed vast compared with Edinburgh; she'd never seen so many people in her life; and though she'd never confess to it, she'd been terrified about the forthcoming ordeal of the audition.

It was a day she'd never forget. She remembered standing at the doorway of the huge hall where hundreds of young hopefuls were waiting for their turn to perform. She had clasped her cello to her chest.

'I'll wait with you,' her mother said, starting to move forwards.

Behind them, a youth said, 'Excuse me please,' in a polite voice and Jane stood aside self-consciously, eyeing the dark-haired boy with awe. He'll get in, she thought, he's tailor-made for stardom.

'*No*,' she said emphatically.

She'd feel like a baby with her mother there. This was her first step into the big, exciting world of adulthood. She was standing on a threshold, literally and metaphorically, and she needed to cross over it by herself.

'No, thank you, Mum,' she said more quietly. 'I really appreciate it, but honestly, I need to concentrate and think about my music. I'd much rather be on my own. You don't mind, do you? Tell you what, I'll drop my cello at the hotel after I've finished, then I can meet you somewhere and we'll do something special. Okay?'

'All right, darling,' her mother conceded, perhaps understanding, possibly merely relieved.

Jane watched her depart with a mixture of love and embarrassment. She was alone and nervous, but also excited and energised. Around her, some applicants stood in groups or sat chatting animatedly. Too shy to approach anyone, she pulled out her Walkman, put on the headphones and immersed herself in the concerto she was going to play as one of her audition pieces. All around her she sensed the crackling electricity of anticipation. A blonde girl, with skin so delicate it was almost translucent, sat cross-legged on the floor, trying to calm herself by doing yoga. Nearby, one girl was biting her nails; another had streaked her hair purple and outlined her eyes heavily with kohl; a third was wearing skin-tight leather trousers and a coral spandex top that barely reached her waist. Everywhere, she could see aspiring Jennifer Anistons with shoulder-length bobs and Meg Ryan lookalikes, hair bleached, cut short and tousled.

Jane felt horribly dowdy in her neat skirt and blouse. These kids were fashionable, confident, extrovert. They already looked like drama and music students. They were hip, trendy, cool, all the things she wasn't. She turned up the volume and sank back into the music. With that, at least, she was safe.

A hand tapped her arm and she looked up, startled. The young man they'd bumped into at the doorway was looking down at her, his mouth moving. For a few seconds she was too riveted by his good looks to realise that he was trying to talk to her. His black hair was thick and floppy, falling into his eyes. Compelling eyes – metallic grey, almost silver, and hooded, like a falcon's. He was wearing a grandpa shirt, collarless and striped, tucked into wide-legged trousers held up by broad braces. It was an unusual look, not fashionable, but a powerful statement.

What did he want?

'Anybody in?'

She slipped the headphones off so that they fell round her neck.

'Hi.' Her mouth felt dry.

'Are you for acting? Or music?'

'Oh. Music.' Jane gestured at her cello, propped up in a nearby corner. 'You?'

'Acting. Scary, isn't it?'

He looked friendly.

He was speaking to her like an equal.

He admitted to nerves.

He was beautiful.

It took Jane about three seconds to fall wildly in love.

She nodded and bit her lip, longing for this boy to fall for her, too, though she knew it would never happen.

'Tom.' He stuck out his hand and she took it gingerly, feeling the connection like an electric shock. 'Tom Vallely. Hi.'

'Jane Porter.' It sounded so boring. 'Good luck.'

'What are you listening to?'

She wished she could say Bryan Adams or Madonna, but she had to admit to Dvorjàk's Cello Concerto. She could almost see his eyes glazing over.

'Well, nice to meet you. Good luck.'

He smiled an easy, natural smile as he turned away.

Jane put her headphones back on, turned up the volume and, this time, closed her eyes.

'Benji! Here boy!' Jane had been so engrossed in her memories that she'd lost sight of the dog. 'Benji!'

There was a scuffle and a whisper of movement in the undergrowth and the dog appeared, trailing sticky-willy from his coat. She picked it off, cradled the trusting little face in her hands and stroked the dog's head affectionately. 'Silly boy. Be good now.'

He shot off towards the top of the hill and Jane plodded behind him, scenes from long past still replaying in her head.

She'd spent the best part of the first year at Guildhall not learning music, but learning how to be a student. She'd never adopted the razzmatazz style favoured by many of the acting students, but she had metamorphosed from the dowdy schoolgirl who had attended the audition into someone who felt comfortable in her own skin. She wore stone-washed jeans and white trainers most of the time, teamed with skinny white cotton T-shirts. She had always been slim and it was a look that did her no disservice. She liked big jackets and scoured the vintage and charity stalls in Camden market for affordable ones.

She came across Tom Vallely frequently. He was always charming, always surrounded by eager women, always friendly, but no more than that. He seemed to go through money at a ripping pace, there were countless tales told by people he'd borrowed from.

One exceptionally sunny day in March, she was sitting on a bench in a small square near the School, her eyes closed, her head back, enjoying the warmth on her face.

'Hi.'

A body landed on the bench near her.

She opened her eyes. Tom was sprawled a yard away from her, his arms draped over the back of the bench, his legs crossed casually, his face creased into a friendly smile.

'Hi Tom. Isn't this fab?'

He looked startlingly attractive, as always. His hair, shining in the sun, fell softly over his left eye so that he had to peer through the long fringe. He was wearing baggy tweed trousers and a chunky dark green sweater, pushed up to his elbows. Tom Vallely had style.

'How's the music?'

'Fine, thanks. How's the acting?'

'Oh, you know. Bit of declamation, bit of interpretation and a great deal of boring line learning.'

'Boring? Aren't you enjoying it?'

'I love it. Can't imagine myself doing anything else. To be honest, I don't think I'm bright enough to do anything else. I'm going to have to rely on my looks to earn me some money.'

'At least you have looks.'

'You don't flatter to deceive do you? You didn't have to agree that I'm stupid.'

'I didn't mean ... sorry, I ... I only meant...'

He laughed.

'You're delightfully easy to tease, Jane. Are you giving a concert?'

'Just before we break for Easter.'

'Can I come?'

'Of course.' Jane was astonished. She hadn't imagined that classical music would be Tom's bag. 'I've got a solo,' she said shyly.

'Then I'll definitely come. Can you get me a ticket?'

'I will.'

They were expensive, but he didn't offer her money. Maybe he'd do that later. It was enough that he wanted to hear her.

Tom dug in his pocket and pulled out a bag of brightly coloured boiled sweets.

'Fancy one?'

They were sugary and yet sharp, red and round, like little cherries. They sat and sucked in silence for a few minutes, then Tom said, 'You couldn't lend me some cash could you, Jane? Just till Easter? I'll get my new allowance then.'

So that was it after all. Having borrowed from every other person in college, he had at last turned to her. Did he think she was such a sucker that she'd simply say yes?

'No problem,' she heard herself saying. 'How much?'

It had been more than she could easily afford, so that she had to go without things herself over the next few weeks. She didn't mind, nor did she expect to get her money back. Giving had been an impulse, but it wasn't one she regretted.

Tom did come to the concert – she spotted him sitting near the back – but afterwards, he'd been surrounded by admiring girls, each flattered by his attendance, and he didn't bother to come and say hi.

So much for getting him a ticket. So much for the loan.

One night there was a knock on her door. She had just had a shower, her hair was dripping and she was wrapped only in a towel. She opened the door to find Tom Vallely on the threshold.

'Oh!'

'Is it a bad time?'

'It's all right.'

She stared at him awkwardly. Behind him, she could hear comments.

'Cor, look who's visiting our Jane.'

'Go, Jane, go!'

'Don't keep him waiting, Jane.'

'Look, you'd better come in,' she said hastily, stepping back for him to pass.

He pulled a bottle of vodka out of one capacious pocket of his oversized tweed coat, then a bottle of Coca-Cola out of the other.

'I come bearing gifts.'

Jane, who never drank spirits, couldn't help smiling back. He was charming, natural, friendly – irresistible in every way.

'And...'

Bending slightly, he beat out a drum roll on the small desk beneath the window.

'—Ta-da!'

Like a magician, he produced a wad of notes.

'What's that?'

He held the money aloft and squinted up at it. 'Is this a dagger I see before me? Methinks not. It is the stuff of dreams, sweet Titania, or at least, the money I owe you.'

He placed it on the desk and looked around. 'Got any glasses?'

Jane was dumbfounded.

'Glasses? Erm ... cupboard,' she gulped, pulling the towel more tightly round herself.

'Great. You'd better get dressed or you'll catch your death. I won't look.'

He swung away and started pouring drinks. Jane stared at him, astonished, then grabbed her clothes and dressed rapidly.

'I'll need to dry my hair.'

'Let me.'

To her great astonishment, Tom picked up the hairdryer and plugged it in, then pressed her shoulders gently until she sank dizzily onto her bed. He brushed her hair as he dried it, his touch gentle but firm. It was the sexiest thing that had ever happened to her.

He stood back and admired his handiwork.

'Beautiful. Take a look.'

She looked. She saw Jane Porter, skinny, plain, her normal, slightly anxious expression emphasised by her desire to please him.

'You've done a good job,' she said shyly. In truth, her hair looked the same as usual – long, straight, in need of a good cut.

'Don't you agree?'

'What with?'

'That you're beautiful.'

She looked at him, puzzled. She could name a hundred other girls who were much more beautiful. 'Me?'

He traced his finger round her face.

'Lovely. You don't plaster make-up all over your skin and your hair's so natural. You look good enough to eat.'

Jane's heart began to race. She had never considered herself in Tom Vallely's league, but now here he was, touching her face softly, intimately. She held her breath and willed the moment to last forever.

He dropped his finger and stood, offering her a glass of vodka and coke.

'To natural beauty,' he raised his glass towards her, 'and to one generous, lovely girl.'

He drained the glass in one gulp.

They never did go out that evening. Tom, sorting through her CD collection, started with Beethoven, moved on to Debussy, then to pop. When it was nearly eleven, he pulled a CD out of another deep pocket, pressed play, and Marvin Gaye's 'Sexual Healing' blasted out, the lyrics a sultry invitation to sex.

He was looking at her. He was smiling softly. His eyebrows were raised questioningly. She lifted her hand and pushed aside his hair, trembling.

And then she was in his arms and the kissing was urgent and as absolutely necessary as breathing.

They'd lain in bed all night and until late the next morning. When she'd woken at last, to find the sun coming through the thin curtains, she'd turned expecting to find that Tom had gone, maybe even discover that she'd dreamed the whole thing.

But there he was by her side, a miracle. She studied the smooth muscles of his arm, curled above the covers, the dark hairs thick on his chest, and caught her breath.

'Hello, witch.'

He had woken and was looking up at her, sleepily.

'Hello, spinner of magic spells,' she replied, smiling shyly.

He hooked his arm round her neck and pulled her down towards him. Her hair fell over his shoulders and he caught at it, smoothing it between his fingers before taking her face between his hands and kissing her.

She really did believe that something magical had happened.

'Home, Benji. Home b-boy.'

Damn the stutter. It had started again. She couldn't believe it. And now it was starting to rain. If she didn't get home in the next ten minutes, she'd be soaked.

Magical. Yes. The sorcerer had cast a spell over her and it had lasted for years before the scales had fallen from her eyes.

And then, dear God, the pain had been excruciating.

But that was another story, one that she had buried – until Tom's reappearance yesterday had exposed the flimsiness of the fabric she had woven to cover everything.

One word from Tom and the world she had constructed would rip apart.

She had to hold strong.

No-one must never know what had happened.

Chapter Eight

'I adore this painting, Marta. You've got a lovely house. Your pictures ... the colour scheme ... it's pretty.'

'Thank you. We like it.'

'You and Jake.'

'Of course, me and Jake. Talking of Jake, Tom, can I ask you a favour?'

'Sure.'

'Yesterday – it's my fault, I know – but, well, you woke him up with the radio and of course I'd forgotten to tell you you were coming so he got a bit of a shock, but anyway, would you mind keeping the noise down a bit? During the day when he's sleeping, I mean?'

'Darling! Of course. *Mea culpa*.' He thumped his chest. 'How thoughtless of me.'

'No, it's all right, it was my fault.'

'Sweetie, I'll be an angel. You won't even know I'm here.'

'Don't be silly, we love having you here.'

'Enough to feed me?'

'Are you hungry?'

'Ravenous, darling. Just finished the show and I never like eating before it. Got to keep sharp. That edge of hunger adds a certain *je ne sais quoi*, I always think.'

Marta smiled. 'I'm sure you're right. I was just going to forage in the fridge, I think there's some lamb left.'

'Su-perb.' Tom followed Marta through to the kitchen and settled himself at the scrubbed pine table. 'Jakey out?'

'Jake's working tonight.'

'He's *so* admirable. Pulling pints. Such a thankless job, I

49

always think.'

'He enjoys it,' Marta said defensively. 'He meets lots of interesting people. Anyway, it's only temporary.'

'Of course. He's job hunting. What's his line again?'

'Marketing. He used to work for one of the big banks before—'

'Tell me about it, darling.'

'I suppose actors are used to the kind of life where jobs come and go. But you must get lots of parts, Tom, don't you?'

'Bits here, bits there. What I need are more weighty parts and a better mix of theatre and television.'

'I thought you liked theatre?'

'Love it, darling, simply adore it. There's nothing like connecting with a live audience, know what I mean? It's an actor's life blood. Got any wine, by the way?'

'Oh sorry.' She pulled a bottle out of the fridge, found two glasses and placed everything in front of him.

'Thanks. But theatre doesn't pay. Truly, that's the long and the short of it. And living out of suitcases all the time, well—' he shrugged, '—you can imagine how tedious it gets. Bottoms up, darling.'

'Is television harder to get, then?'

'Not harder, not exactly.' He frowned. 'Maybe I should change my agent. Angela Cutler. She just doesn't seem to have the right contacts. I mean, I get ten theatre auditions to every one in film or television. And I think some people,' he lowered his voice conspiratorially, 'you know—'

Marta didn't know. 'What?'

'Well, offer favours. To the casting director. Or the producer.'

Marta laughed. 'You mean those old stories about the casting couch? I thought that kind of stuff went out with the silent movies.'

'How sweet. Sadly, not. And I'm too principled to stoop to that kind of thing.'

'Of course. So you'd like more television roles?'

'I'd kill for them, sweetie. Simply kill for them.'

Marta scraped the remains of the lamb casserole into a saucepan and started stirring. When they sat down to eat a few minutes later, she said thoughtfully, 'I know someone. A script writer.'

'Oh yeah?'

'My old English teacher, as a matter of fact. Ann Playfair. She taught all three of us, Jane and Carrie and me. She was brilliant, the kind of teacher who inspires you. I think we all had a bit of a crush on her.'

'What kind of stuff does she do? This is still fantastic, by the way,' he said, waving a forkful of lamb towards her before it found its way to his mouth.

'She writes one-off dramas. Soaps, too. She writes for *Emergency Admissions*.'

Tom choked and coughed. '*Emergency Admissions*? You're kidding!'

'She's been with the show for years. Do you watch it?'

'Do I watch it? Darling, who doesn't?'

'I could call her if you like. Just to get some advice. See if there's anything on the horizon.'

'You're adorable, did anyone ever tell you that?'

Marta smiled broadly. 'And other names. But I do like to help, if I can. Would it help?'

'Who knows? But nothing ventured, as they say.' He grinned again. 'A part in *EA*, now that would be an income.' He dropped his fork on his plate and held out his hand towards her, curled it round hers softly, then lifted it to his lips and kissed it with a show of gallantry. 'I'd be forever in your debt. A call from you. A personal recommendation, even to the script writer, I mean, it all helps, you've no idea.'

Marta retrieved her hand. 'Then I'll do it. As soon as I get time.'

She caught the kiss Tom blew her playfully. Having Tom here was fun.

Tom, strolling up the road from the newspaper shop the next morning, saw Jake Davidson close the front door of the cottage, stride down the path and turn towards the bus stop.

The pastry in the brown paper bag was still warm. There was plenty of money in the pot in the hall, enough to get both the paper and a Danish. So thoughtful of his hosts to provide pocket money. And now he'd have the place to himself to brew a cup of roasted coffee and settle down with the *Mail* and some good gossip.

His mobile rang when he'd barely sipped the first cup. 'Tom here.'

'Tom?' It was Angela, his agent, sounding apologetic.

'Hello Angela darling. Any news about *Look Back in Anger*?'

He knew there was news and he knew by the sound of her voice it was bad. Bloody Angela, she was so hopeless.

'Sorry Tom. You didn't get it.'

Damn. Stupid, bloody West End, he never had managed to break into the big time. She was putting him up for the wrong parts, that was the problem. He should never have read for Cliff, he should've been auditioning for the lead, Jimmy Porter, that was much more his style. She couldn't get anything right. 'Fuck.'

'I know, I know. Sorry.'

'Who got it?'

She named a well-known actor.

'The ginger fucking fruitcake? Sod it, Angela, you'll have to do better than this. I do need to live, you know.'

'Sure, Tom, but—'

'Don't give me your buts.' Tom's anger fizzled, then sputtered out. 'Anything else in the pipeline?'

There was a sigh and the rustle of paper. 'Not at the moment, Tom, no. I'll keep looking. How's Edinburgh going?'

'You know how it is up here. A thousand bloody shows on the Fringe every sodding day. There's no chance of getting a decent audience.'

'How many last night?'

'Five.'

'Oh.'

'Yeah, five. There are more of us in the cast, for fuck's sake. I've got a good mind to jack it in and come back to London.'

'You can't do that, Tom. Anyway, it's only a few more days. What have the crits been like?'

'All right. Moderate to good. Listen, do you know anyone on *Emergency Admissions*?'

'Don't think so. Why?'

'Might have a line in there. I'll keep you posted.'

'Great.'

'And Angela—'

'Tom?'

'Get off your backside and get me some fucking work.'

'I'm doing my best, Tom.'

'Maybe your best isn't good enough.'

'Well, if you feel like that—' She sounded hurt.

'No, no,' he said hastily. He couldn't do without Angela Cutler, not yet anyway. 'You know I love you really. Just do it, huh?'

'Do you really? I sometimes wonder.'

'You know I do, sweetheart. You're the best.'

There was a small sigh, before she said, 'Bye Tom.'

Fuck her. Fuck them all. Women. They needed so much bloody maintenance.

Now he had indigestion. He'd been banking on the part in *Look Back in Anger*. Even Cliff would have done, a few months in the West End would have been good news. He shoved the pastry away from him, topped up his coffee and downed it quickly. Maybe he'd have a quick look around while Jake was out. He could use the computer, do his emails.

The master bedroom was spotless – Marta kept a neat household. He pulled open a drawer in the long dressing table beneath the window. Women's stuff. Nail polish, cosmetic brushes, hairbrushes, lipstick. The next drawer held knickers, tights, socks. Tom felt through them expertly. Women often concealed small, valuable items in their lingerie drawer.

His fingers tightened round a polythene bag that felt lumpy and hard. Jewellery. Costume stuff mostly, silver chains with silly little pendants, hoop earrings of the kind Marta favoured, baubles. A couple of rather better items – a fire opal set in gold, on a gold chain, and a pair of earrings that looked as though they might be sapphire and pearl. A brooch in the shape of a bow, a clumsy thing, old fashioned and heavy, but the stones looked real and the setting just might be gold.

Tom weighed it in his hand, studied it, then shoved it in his pocket, rolled the polythene bag back up as he found it and replaced it carefully under the knickers. It didn't look like the kind of thing Marta Davidson would wear much. With any luck, she wouldn't even notice it was missing until he was long gone. He'd drop into the pawn shop with it tomorrow.

Tom found Jake's computer in the small room next door. He booted it up, signed in to his email, dealt with the dozen or so that required a response, then logged onto his favourite site.

A scarlet sheet floated into the screen, then settled into graceful folds.

Bed Buddies welcomes...

His breathing quickened. Screwing Angela Cutler was a duty – she had to be kept happy – but with Bed Buddies he could get great sex with absolutely no commitment and at no cost. Ideal. And perhaps he'd find a new buddy while he was here in Edinburgh, that'd just be the icing on the cake.

'Hairy Mary.' She sounded a laugh.

'Annie get your gun.' Hmmm.

'Super Ficial.' Maybe not.

'D.A. Delight.' Fucking hell. Now that was a name he hadn't seen in a long time. D.A. Delight.

Tom smiled radiantly at the screen and tapped in a message. Now he could really have some fun.

Chapter Nine

'So he's like, *what*? And I was so embarrassed, Suzy, I just can't tell you,' Emily Harvie said into her mobile. She was lying on her bed, staring at the poster of her idol, Stephen Isserlis, wrapped around a cello and smiling at the camera like it was a woman he was about to seduce.

'Forget it, Ems. You've sown the seed in his brain, haven't you? And you can take it one step further at my party.'

'Yeah, your party.' Emily perked up at the thought of her friend Suzy's party. 'I've got to get some new clothes. My mum's so mean though, I don't know how I'll do it.'

'Do the old "all my friends are getting a new dress" routine. Never fails.'

'You don't know my mum. Still, I'll work on her.'

'You need to look really wicked to get Robbie's attention.'

'Robbie,' Emily sighed dreamily. 'Do you really think I've got a chance, Suze?'

'Course you have, you're sweet looking and clever, too, and he likes clever girls.'

'He's so much older. I don't think he thinks I'm cool.'

'That's why the new dress is important.'

'Yeah, I know.' The sound of a snigger outside her bedroom door triggered an alarm in Emily's head. 'Listen, Suzy, gotta go. See you in the morning.'

'See you, Ems. Bye.'

While she was saying these last words, Emily was crossing the floor of her bedroom and now she flung open the door to find Ross darting across the landing towards his own room.

'Stop, you sneaky little brat! Come here.'

Ross turned and stuck his tongue out, his round face cheeky. 'Emily fancies Robbie,' he chanted. 'Emily fancies Robbie.'

'Shut *up*!'

Ross turned and faced her, crossing his arms across his chest. Already his figure was filling out and his shoulders were becoming broader and squarer. He was shaping up to have his father's stocky frame. 'Robbie Jamieson's really into drugs,' he said knowingly.

'He so is not!'

'Is.'

'He's not. Anyway, how would you know?'

'His brother Sandy's in my class, remember? He tells me stuff.'

'I don't believe you. Robbie's really cool.'

'I'll tell Mum you're going to get off with him.'

'You will not! Why would you do that?'

'Keep my big sister safe,' he smirked.

Emily strode across the landing and grabbed her brother by the T-shirt. 'You dare and I'll kill you,' she said threateningly.

'Oh, I'm really scared.'

It had been some years since Emily could dominate Ross physically. She let go of the T-shirt with a small thrust and studied him. 'Okay,' she said. 'What do you want?'

Ross pretended to think. 'Let me see—'

'*Ross.*'

'Okay, okay. You know I'm off to school camp soon? I want to borrow your iPod.'

'But you're away a whole week!'

'Yup.'

'That's too much.'

'I'll just go and tell her now, shall I?' He moved towards the top of the stairs.

'All right, all right,' Emily said hastily. 'You're a smelly toad though.'

'And you're a smelly armpit,' Ross giggled and ducked into his room as Emily's hand flashed out at him.

She could hear him laughing inside his room. Having little brothers was such a pain.

Casting aside her irritation, she set her mind instead on the challenge ahead: getting finance for a new, Robbie-catching outfit. She skipped down the stairs and into the kitchen.

'Hi.'

Her mother looked round from the stove, where she was staring vacantly at a saucepan of spaghetti that was bubbling and spluttering and dribbling over the rim and down in spurts onto the worn white enamel.

'It's boiling over, Mum.'

'Mmm?'

'The saucepan.'

As her mother continued to stare at her, the pot gave a extra-vehement hiss and a small fountain of bubbles shot in the air and cascaded downwards. Emily stepped across the kitchen and pulled the saucepan off the heat.

'Mu-um,' she said reproachfully. 'Spaghetti. Water. Boiling over?'

'Oh.' Jane's gaze began to focus and she looked first at Emily and then at the saucepan. 'Oh sorry. I hadn't noticed.'

What on earth was wrong with her? She'd been acting really strangely in the last few days. She'd forgotten to buy Emily's favourite cereal bars for her lunch box, there were no clean knickers this morning because apparently the washing hadn't been done and now she didn't even seem able to cook supper without burning it. Emily's mood, itself stretched to breaking point by Ross's pathetic but all too successful attempts at blackmail and her own anxiety about the challenges that lay ahead, veered to irritation rather than sympathy. Still, she needed to choose her words carefully.

'Can I help, Mum? I mean, you seem a bit tired.'

'Help? Oh, would you Emily? Thanks.' Jane dragged a hand over her forehead in a fruitless attempt to prevent her hair falling into her eyes. 'Can you stir the sauce?'

Emily lifted a tomato-smeared wooden spoon from the work top and stirred as her mother appeared to pull herself together and swing into action, laying out cutlery and place mats for supper.

She waited a few minutes.

'Mum?'

'Mmm? What?'

'You know you said I could play the Forster if I passed my Grade Six?'

'We haven't had the results yet.'

'But if I do—'

'I'll think about it, Emily.'

Her mother spat the words out as if they were something nasty. Her face was all screwed up. Not good. Bother. Maybe she should've started with the dress. Emily turned away, hunched her shoulders and stirred crossly. Mum had been putting her off and putting her off about the cello. What was wrong with her anyway? Her teacher said that all cellos needed to be played to keep sweet and that was even truer of the best cellos than cheap ones – and anyway, Mum hadn't played the thing for years.

She turned the problem over in her mind, watching the lumps in the Bolognese sauce and wondering vaguely if she should try to break them up. Perhaps her mother was feeling bad about not letting her play the Forster, so maybe she could capitalise on this by asking for a new dress. What was the best plan? To argue more about the cello, or move straight on to the request for a new outfit? On this occasion, the need to impress Robbie won over her music.

'You know I'm going to Suzy's party in a couple of weeks?'

'Mmm.'

'And you remember it's my birthday soon?'

'I'm not l-likely to forget that, Emily.'

Promising.

'I really need a new dress.' She glanced at her mother, whose face was a blank canvas. 'And some shoes?'

'Dad and I have already bought your present. And I'm not sure about going to Suzy's party, Em'

Emily threw the spoon into the pot, turned her back on the stove, crossed her arms and stuck out her lower lip. 'Honestly, Mum! I'm not a baby. I can look after myself. Everyone's going. And I'll be the only person there looking like a complete twat.'

'Emily!'

She'd gone too far. Her mother hated bad language.

'Sorry. But still—'

Jane sighed. 'I'll think about it, Emily. I'll see what your father says. Have you d-done your homework?'

'Mostly.'

'Well, why don't you go and finish it, then you can watch that television programme after supper.'

Emily sighed again, this time more heavily.

'G-go.'

It was hard to make bare feet sound indignant on cushion flooring, but she slapped her soles down as hard as she could anyway. Benji, curled up in his bed in the far corner of the kitchen, half-heartedly raised one ear and peered at her with sleepy curiosity, out of one eye.

Jane watched her daughter flounce across the kitchen and out of the door. If she hadn't been feeling so agitated about – well, about everything at the moment – she would find it quite funny. But since the other night, since the moment when Marta's front door opened and Tom Vallely appeared, her sense of humour had vanished.

She pulled out a chair and slumped down. The good times had been thrilling, a ride on a wave that seemed to have no crest and would never break. From the day he'd appeared at her door they'd become a possibly the most unlikely couple in the whole of Guildhall, and yet inseparable.

That first room they'd rented together ... she'd thought she'd died and gone to heaven. They'd stood, stunned, in the middle of the huge bedroom, staring at each other, gawping at the high ceiling. The bed was huge, a massive ship of a bed, an ocean liner of a bed.

'*How* much did you say she's charging?' she'd whispered.

'It's affordable. Just. I may have to pimp your body on the streets of Soho to pay for it, but you can put up with a little prosti—'

'*Tom*!' She'd swung a pillow at him, laughing. He'd retaliated, seizing her wrist and wrestling her to the bed, where they'd made love like it was the first time.

It had just been a room in a shared house, but it had been their kingdom and Jane had felt like a queen.

Just before her final examinations she was offered a place with the London Philharmonic, and Tom, even before he'd graduated, landed a sizeable part in a film. His performance attracted the attention of other producers and for a spell he was regarded as one of the biggest new talents around.

Had it started then? Was that when, unnoticed by her, the wave had started to curl at the top, its momentum fading? He'd been the toast of the town and starlets and wannabees were drawn to him like bees to exotic flowers. She had never believed she was pretty enough, funny enough, glamorous enough for Tom and she'd been surprised but profoundly thankful that their relationship had held fast. They had more money and they moved to a comfortable flat in unfashionable Battersea, but with a fine view of the river. Her future seemed secure while Tom's career, though patchy, had more ups than downs. She floated through the months on a cloud of euphoria.

And then, the wave broke, as waves do, and her world collapsed.

She'd been touring up in Leeds, doing a Christmas extravaganza of popular classics. She had hidden a small store of carefully wrapped and thoughtfully chosen Christmas gifts for Tom in the bottom of the wardrobe in the light-filled riverside bedroom in Battersea, behind a pile of shoes. On Christmas Eve, when she was due to get back, all she'd have to do was arrange them under the tree. The next day, Tom's parents were coming over to share lunch with them.

She called Tom before the last concert, excited at the approach of Christmas and the idea of being home again very soon.

'Hello, Wiz.'

The nickname has grown from that first wonderful night they spent together. Weaver of magic spells. Wizard.

'Hey, Witchy.'

Tom wasn't working. In January, he was due to start in a new production in the West End. For the last couple of weeks he'd been in rehearsal and learning his lines – the boring bit. That hadn't changed since college.

'Learnt them yet?' she asked.

'What? Oh, the lines. Yeah.'

He sounded odd. The achievement of memorising usually made him euphoric. 'Are you okay, Tom?'

'Yeah. You?'

They were playing the concert that night in Santa hats – ridiculous, but fun. Everyone was in a festive mood and it was catching.

'Yes. Dying to get home, sweetheart, to be with you. Have you got the food sorted?'

She'd left Tom a shopping list, knowing that she wouldn't be home in time herself.

'Shopping?' Tom sounded vague. 'Oh sure, yes. Shopping.'

He didn't sound too sure. Jane pressed him.

'The turkey? You remembered to drop by the butcher's? The queue wasn't too long? I ordered a big one, with your folks coming and everything.'

61

'Turkey? Yeah.'

'And the sausage-meat stuffing?'

'Mmm. Listen Jane, I've got to go. Hope it goes well tonight.'

'Are you sure you're okay, Tom?' she asked, but he'd already rung off. She was perplexed and disappointed. There'd been none of the usual silly farewells, 'Bye Witch' or any of the dozen other ridiculous phrases they had adopted into their personal language and privately found so hilarious.

It was Christmas Eve when she turned her key in the lock and opened the door in excited anticipation.

'Hello?'

The flat was dark and empty – Tom must be out doing some last-minute shopping. She propped her cello carefully in its corner in the hallway and flicked on the light in the kitchen. The place felt chilly. She had been dreaming about a cup of tea for at least the last two hours. Crossing the room, she spotted an envelope propped against the kettle.

JANE..

It was Tom's bold writing, dashing, confident, stylish, the J a flourish, the word underlined by an curving line that ended in two dots, his trademark. JANE..

She dropped the envelope as though it was on fire. It fell lightly to the floor and lay JANE.. side down.

She backed away from it. Walked around it. Retreated to the other side of the kitchen and looked at it as though it might explode if she went any closer. Why did she have such a bad feeling about this? Ridiculous. It would just announce he'd gone to a party, or out for some last-minute gift shopping.

She should call him.

Two or three times she did dial his mobile, but it was off.

The bad feeling persisted and grew stronger. He should be here. It was Christmas Eve. She had been away for ten days.

He liked cooking, while she was hopeless at it. Usually, if he wasn't working, he'd make a nice meal, have the table set and a bottle of wine open.

No matter how often she tried, Tom's phone remained stubbornly off. At last she dashed at the envelope, swooped down to pick it up and tore it open frantically, as though energy and determination might ward off whatever lurked inside.

Hey Witch, I didn't know how to tell you this, so I've taken the coward's way out. The truth is I have met someone else. I don't know how else to say it and, you know me, I like everything straight, so there, that's it, time to move on. Thanks for everything. Tom..

She spent Christmas Day alone. There was no food. The cupboard yielded little more than tinned spaghetti, which she hated, and porridge oats, ditto. After twenty hours without food, she finally made a pot of porridge and forced down a small bowlful, leavened by the addition of some tinned evaporated milk.

She didn't talk to anyone except, briefly, her parents. She forced a smile into her voice and told them Tom had gone out for a walk. Her mother adored Tom.

Anger took the place of desolation. How dare he! How dare he break up with her like this, after all they had shared together?

She thumped her fist into a pillow then, dissatisfied, slammed it into the kitchen wall, again and again, until her knuckles bled.

Jane was shaking. How could memories make you shake? She'd put it all behind her, years ago. She jumped up to drain the pasta. It had overcooked and looked horribly gloopy.

Damn Tom Vallely! She *would* not let him get to her.

Ian barrelled into the kitchen full of angry energy.

'Mu-um. Em and Ross are fighting and Ross won't let me in to my room.'

'Oh, Dumpling.'

She scooped him into her arms and buried her face in his soft brown hair, inhaling the scent of him as if it might magically bestow sanity.

'We're just about to have supper. Never mind about them.'

She hugged his sturdy young body like a talisman and prayed.

Tom was back, unchanged in all his dangerous charm. Worse – he brought with him the undreamed of possibility that the cover up she had so successfully maintained for all these years might unravel. And then what would happen to the life she had constructed?

Chapter Ten

Portobello was blanketed by damp fog. Jake called it haar.

'Sea mist to you,' he said to Tom.

He was wearing joggers and a T-shirt and looked rumpled and tired, his skinny body oddly childlike. Tom, already dressed in pressed navy chinos and a striped Duchamp shirt, was drinking coffee and reading yesterday's paper, which had been abandoned on the kitchen table.

'Get it a lot, do you?'

Jake seemed reluctant to admit any defect in his home city. 'More than I'd like.'

'Are you off to get the brew? That's what they call the dole here, isn't it?'

'Not in Edinburgh, no,' Jake said shortly, refilling the kettle. 'And I'm not claiming it.'

'Really?' Tom was genuinely surprised. 'Why ever not?'

'Because, it may have escaped your notice, I am actually working. Where's the coffee?'

Tom waved at a crumpled packet by the sink.

'Oh sorry, I finished it. You'll need to get some more.'

'Shit. Couldn't you have left a spoonful?'

'Hey, mate.' Tom held his hands in front of him in a protective gesture. 'Not my fault if there's not enough.'

He saw Jake's lips tighten and backtracked quickly. He was going to be at least another week and experience had taught him that charm was an effective tool. He turned the defensive hands into placatory ones and said, 'I'll buy another packet when I'm out, okay? My contribution.'

He needed to get to the pawn shop first, though, so he caught a bus into Edinburgh, where the haar was still hanging miserably over the streets. He put his fedora back on his head and stepped off the bus in Princes Street into the dampness. He had donned a soft leather jacket, a present from Angela after a particularly intense weekend of screwing, and he turned up the collar, enjoying the feel of the skin under his fingers. It was a good jacket – though by God, he'd earned it.

The girl in the pawn shop was a dumpy brunette with a surprisingly sweet face. Two attractive dimples appeared as she smiled hello.

'You're looking delightful on this depressing day. Love the blouse.' He gestured at the vulgar floral top she was wearing and added a touch of lust to his gaze. Easy meat.

She blushed and giggled. 'Have you come to pawn or redeem?'

'I've brought something in today.' He opened his jacket and felt inside the inner pocket. The heavy brooch he'd found in Marta's drawer was resting there safely.

'It was my grandmother's. I'll be back for it in a week or two. After pay day.'

'Sure.' The girl looked at it curiously. 'That's pretty. I've never seen anything quite like that.' She took out an eyeglass and studied it closely in the light of a lamp. 'Gold. Hallmarked. The stones look real. I'll have to call Mr MacFarlane.'

'Fine.' Tom feigned indifference and busied himself by looking in the display cabinets. He'd done this so often that really he should be more relaxed, because he'd never yet been challenged. Even so, he could feel his heart rate rising as the manager examined the brooch.

'Your grandmother's, you say?'

'Yeah, mate, that's right. Hard to believe, I know, but my grandmother was in service. Many years ago, of course, she's been dead now for twenty years or more, bless her. The brooch was a gift from one of the grand ladies she worked for, before the first war, of course.'

'Not stolen then?'

'Stolen, mate?' Tom looked hurt. 'Why d'you say that?'

'Seems odd. A man like you, carrying round a brooch like this.'

'Tell you the truth,' Tom leant on the counter confidingly, 'I'm an actor. Up here for the Festival. You know what it's like – money's always tight. I need a bit to tide me over till the end of the run. Pay day. Always carry the brooch with me. Can't tell you how many times it's seen the inside of a pawn shop. Always come and reclaim it as soon as the old pay packet hits the bank.'

'Hmm. I don't like lending outside of the city, certainly not on something like this. It's a bit risky.' He laid the brooch on the counter. 'It's a fine piece. Old. Scottish.' He squinted at Tom. 'The hallmark dates it to the late eighteenth century.'

'Yeah.' Scottish. His brain was racing. 'My dear grandma, she was Scottish.'

'Hmm. Have we done business before?'

'Last week. My signet ring.'

'I thought I remembered you.'

The manager made his decision. He reached for a pad of papers and named a valuation figure. It was much higher than Tom had anticipated. Was there a risk? Might the absence of the brooch be noticed and traced to him? Maybe he'd have to come and redeem it, slip it back in Marta's drawer. Usually he only took small things, the kind of stuff that wouldn't be noticed – perhaps taking this brooch had been a mistake?

'I can't give you a fraction of that, of course, especially not with you not being local. The risk's too high.' He made a considerably lower offer. 'That okay? How long for?'

Gradually, Tom's heart began to slow.

'Seems fair. A week should be fine.'

Surely Marta wouldn't miss it quickly. He'd be able to redeem it as soon as his run finished.

At last the formalities were completed.

'Your ticket, sir. Fine piece, if I may say so.'

'Thanks.'

Tom took the documentation, folded it carefully and placed it neatly between the pages of his pocket notebook. He smiled at the girl, simpering in her silly blouse, and left the shop with an idea – he would go and visit Janie. Why not?

The dampness was lifting at last and some warmth was creeping into the day. Removing his jacket, Tom hooked it onto a finger and trailed it over his shoulder. He would walk.

'Mrs Porter. And looking not a day older, I swear.'

A dog was playing round the elderly woman's feet, a yappy, shaggy creature.

'Benji! Hush!'

Evelyn Porter bent to scold the dog. Tom could see the pink of her scalp through the thinness of her hair, but lying cost him nothing. He took off his fedora and smiled.

'Tom? Tom Vallely?'

Her eyes had aged too. A pale ring lurked round the iris, but her expression had brightened considerably.

'How wonderful. But how—?'

He stooped to take her arms firmly in his hands and turned his head to air kiss lavishly beside each of her furrowed cheeks.

'Didn't Jane tell you I was here? I'm desolated.'

'She's met you?'

'Last week. We had dinner at Marta Davidson's. Am I to be invited in or must I stand forever in the garden?'

'I'm so sorry, Tom. Of course, do come in. I was just surprised – Jane, look who's here to see you. What are you doing in Edinburgh? What have you been doing all this time? I'm sure Jane – here she is – Jane, dear, it's Tom.'

'Hello, Janie.'

'I'm astonished that you've got the n-n-nerve to come here.'

'Just wanted to see you, Janie. You won't deny me that, will you? Hey? Just a quiet chat? Last week there were so many people around.'

'Of course you want a wee talk together,' Mrs Porter was muttering to Jane. 'I'm just away now, in any case.'

'No!' Jane's voice was vehement.

'You haven't seen him for such a long time, dearie. I'd love to stay and catch up with all your news, Tom, but I've got a hair appointment in twenty minutes.'

'T-Tom. Go.'

She was holding firm. Maybe she had changed, then.

'I've walked all the way from Princes Street, Jane. Surely you'll offer me a cup of tea, after all these years? Witchy?'

He could see the hesitation – the merest fraction of a beat, but it was enough. He laughed softly.

'I don't take sugar any more. But I did bring you some biscuits.'

He tossed the fedora onto the coat rack and felt in the pocket of the jacket. Coming through Morningside he'd passed a deli and spotted the Leibniz dark chocolate biscuits that had been Jane's passion.

'There, Jane, isn't that lovely. He's remembered. Now Tom dear, I must go, but I'll see you before you disappear, now, won't I? I want to hear all your news.'

'Of course, Mrs Porter. I'll come round again, just say the word.'

'Bye Jane. I'll collect Ian from school.'

Jane still hadn't moved.

'Where's your kettle?'

As he moved towards her, she jumped aside.

'Hey. What's this? Witchy?' He stopped a few inches in front of her and looked at her searchingly. 'No need to be afraid, Janie dearest. Life's moved on, hasn't it?'

69

Tom could feel tremors. She was like a rabbit, trapped and fearful. What fun. There it was again, the old feeling of power. Even the stirring of desire.

No. That would be unwise.

'There.'

He kissed her forehead and stepped into the kitchen.

'Nice. Bit shambolic, perhaps. Not like your friend Marta's house. Now there's a woman who likes to be organised, don't you agree? Kettle? Oh yes, here it is. Mugs? You'll have tea too, I hope?'

'What do you want, T-Tom?'

He swung round and looked at her.

'Want? Just to see you, Janie, that's all. Talk about the old times. Here. Shall we sit down?'

She sank onto a chair obediently. Already she was a servant to his will, no longer mistress of her own home.

Old patterns replaying themselves. Learned behaviour. Remembered ways. He'd always loved the way she bent so pathetically to his will.

'So. Tell me. What's new in your life, Janie? Or no, I think I can tell you that. Let me see. The husband. Solid man you have there, Witchy. A bit unimaginative, I reckon, not the creative type, more of a plodder, hardly sex on legs but loyal, I would guess. Am I right? Quite unlike me, in fact, in almost every respect.'

He laughed, a real laugh, from the stomach.

'Not a bad thing, I suppose, bearing in mind my track record.'

Jane sat like a stick, straight but brittle, ready to splinter at the slightest pressure.

'Three children. Are these the dear mites?'

He picked up an old school photograph from the dresser. 'I would have thought they would be a little older, or did you decide to wait a bit? After your little mistake.'

Little mistake.

That first week – Christmas week – she didn't eat, sleep, or talk to anybody, she just walked round the streets, through the parks, tramping the soles off her shoes until she could feel every rut, every crack on the pavement, every pebble, on the paths. Then it was back to work. Music was her balm. Music would help her heal.

One day when she was out at a rehearsal, he sneaked back and packed all his things. He even took some of her favourite CDs and she no longer had the energy to be angry. She struggled across town to rehearsals, bowed her way mechanically through concerts, found a way to survive.

Then it got worse – much worse.

She was numb. She wasn't eating much. She began to suffer heartburn. She felt wretched, exhausted and querulous. She plodded doggedly into rehearsals and prayed that her lack of form didn't show.

One day, standing on the Tube clutching her cello, she was staring vacantly at a beautiful young woman with the blackest of skin and the sweetest face and thinking vaguely how nice it would be to be able to paint, when the light in the train receded to a pinprick. For a moment, all she could see was a large gold cross glistening on the soft contours between the girl's breasts. And then that, too, went dark and the last thing Jane was aware of was a dull thump.

Later, she realised the noise must have been her body hitting the floor of the carriage. She resurfaced at some point to a circle of curious faces peering down at her and a sensation akin to seasickness. She closed her eyes, turned her face to one side, and felt the roughness of tweed on her cheek. Someone had rolled up a coat and placed it under her head.

'You alright, my darling? Clear a space, folks, give the girl some air.'

Her angel was brisk and kind and turned out to be a nurse at St Thomas's Hospital. She was large and very black and spoke with a strong Welsh accent.

'You feel better, my lovely? Did you have breakfast this morning?'

She chattered inconsequentially and steadily until Jane grew calmer and the crowds lost interest.

'My cello!' Anxiety flooded through her and the sweat stood cold on her forehead.

'Here. It's safe.'

Someone thrust the case into her hands and she grabbed at it with relief.

'You go to your doctor, now, promise?'

'I promise. And thank you. Thank you so much.'

'You're welcome, my darling. Take care now.'

A few days later, and only because she had promised, Jane walked into her local surgery convinced that she would be prescribed a placebo and instructed to go away and eat sensibly.

The doctor's words make no sense.

'You're pregnant, Mrs Porter.'

There was a nick on his throat, an early morning shaving error, onto which he had stuck a blob of cotton wool. It wiggled grotesquely up and down as he spoke.

'Miss.'

'Miss Porter.' His smile disappeared and the cotton wool froze as he scanned her notes.

It hit her later, as she walked out of his consulting room and onto a damp pavement.

Pregnant.

With Tom's child.

They had never discussed children, it hadn't been on the radar, it was too early, their livelihoods were too precarious, but now – *pregnant*?

She itched to tell him. The baby was a blessing from heaven. Her beautiful man would come back to her and all would be well.

She was in the flat at midday, which almost never happened. She'd been violently sick in the morning and was still feeling wretched.

The lock scraped. Someone was opening the front door. Tom! It was four days, seven hours and sixteen minutes since she'd left the doctor's surgery, and she had been rubbing her lamp and making her wish a thousand and one times.

Her genie appeared.

'Hello, Tom.'

'Jane!'

'You've come back.'

'Just for the last of my things. I didn't think you'd be here.'

'But I am.'

'So I see.'

She turned, filled the kettle; replayed her tidings in her head, selected words.

'Tea?'

'No. Thanks. I'm just here to—'

She dumped the kettle on the counter and swung round to face him.

'We're going to have a baby, Tom.'

She said it in exactly the right way. Not, 'I'm pregnant'. No coy euphemisms. A child. *Their* child.

'I'm sorry?'

'Don't be sorry. A baby. You're going to be a father.'

She didn't see the violence coming. He moved across the space between them in an instant, caught her wrists in his hands, was holding them hard, twisting them, burning the skin viciously so that she cried out.

'No. Don't kid yourself, Jane. Get rid of it.'

'Tom! You're hurting me!' She yelped with pain and shock. She had never seen Tom like this, his face twisted and dark with fury. 'What are you talking about? I can't—'

73

He shoved her roughly against the table. The edge cuts across her buttocks painfully. 'Is it mine?'

'What do you mean?'

'All those weeks away. Leeds. Manchester. Birmingham. Taunton. West-of-back-of beyond. Wherever. All those *fiddlers*,' he said the word sneeringly, 'the drummers, the brass. Fine strapping men those brass players. Don't tell me you never slept with them.'

'Tom! I never – would never – how could you—?'

'I'm told getting rid of these things is easy. Tell you what, I'll be generous. I'll even pay for it. There should be some cash in our account, unless you've been on a spending spree.'

'I won't! I can't! I would never do that.'

His face darkened and for a minute she thought he was going to strike her. Then he shrugged.

'Suit yourself. Just don't come running to me for cash when the kid needs school clothes – or anything else, for that matter. And don't expect me to acknowledge the little bastard either, because I never will.'

He tossed the keys on the kitchen table.

'Here. I won't need these again. I'm taking the last of my stuff. And by the way,' he stopped in the doorway and spun round, 'I'm getting married.'

His smile was more wounding than any accusation.

'Wish me happiness.'

Jane sank onto a chair, her legs weak. Married? Who to? What was he talking about? How could he accuse her of infidelity? Had he been unfaithful? All those times she was away, had *he* been sleeping with someone else?

Married?

'After your little mistake...'

Dear God – how had she ever thought the past was buried? She raised a hand to her mouth to stifle a sob. It wasn't dead, it never had been, it had only been hibernating.

'Bye, Witchy.'

Tom half turned, and registered the brown eyes, wide and scared. Great stuff, really great.

He stepped onto the path. Behind him, the door clicked shut.

On the coatstand in Jane's hall, a brown fedora hung limply.

Chapter Eleven

Carrie logged on to Bed Buddies after work. She was sitting cross-legged on the white rug in her living room, her laptop perched perilously across the angle between her calves and her thighs, Lily Allen crooning on the sound system. She scanned her message board.

<The Big Man wltm D.A. Delight asap>

<High Five yeah? When?>

Nothing from Jury Service. Shame – she quite fancied a romp with the dear man tonight. She abandoned her message board and searched the Edinburgh area lists.

<Star Turn would like Festival Fun. London based, in north for a few days only. Serious offers only please. vbg.>

Star Turn? She had spotted his posts before. He always sounded entertaining – a little spicy, a little full of himself perhaps, but deliciously wicked. Once before, when she was in London on business, she'd been on the point of sending him an invitation, but something urgent had cropped up at work and her attention had been diverted. She clicked a link and went into a secure chat area.

< Star Turn, this is D.A. Delight, responding to your offer. I can be as serious as you like. Or maybe we could just have a

few laughs? Free tonight, just say the word. And the word is ... justice.

The reply came at once.

<Justice? Or just desserts? If the latter, mine's a Bailey's ice cream, preferably licked off your stomach, tee hee.>

It wasn't the wittiest of chat-up lines, but it would do. The usual precautions were necessary, that went without saying. The arrangement was to meet for drinks in the bar at the Salamander Hotel. Over a couple of gins she would be able to assess whether or not she wanted to proceed upstairs. If she didn't like the look of the man, she would simply say goodbye. It had happened a few times and it was no big deal. Carrie was very discriminating and took no risks. When she met her regulars, she often had dinner first – though sometimes she preferred room service. Room service with Jury Service. That was funny.

The Salamander Hotel in Leith, Edinburgh's dockland district, was a bit of an oddity. Tucked away in a side street, it missed out on custom by being off the beaten track. The area was hardly Edinburgh's most salubrious but the hotel itself, originally the home of some *nouveau riche* dock manager in Victorian times, was hidden behind a large wall and had a pretty garden. Some years ago, Carrie remembered, the building had been derelict, the tiles on its roof slipping, the windows cracked and dismal. Green fungus had lurked round leaky downpipes, and the paint on doors and window frames had been peeling. The potential of the place had been spotted by an enterprising young couple, Tim and Stella Morrison, who had used all their savings to renovate the building and turn it into a small hotel.

Carrie liked the Salamander because it was discreet. The car park was hidden behind the high wall, the area was not much visited by the smart set of Edinburgh city, more by foreign tourists unaware of the environs and by businessmen on the move, looking for value for money and comfort. Tim and Stella didn't ask questions. Over the past couple of years – she'd been one of their first guests – Carrie had stayed at the Salamander maybe once a month, sometimes more often.

She seldom stayed the whole night. She settled her bill in advance and left hours before breakfast, knowing that the Morrisons would be too polite to comment. Not that she was ashamed of her lifestyle, but she knew that not everyone would approve. The 'not everyone' included her bosses at Ascher Frew, and with the partnership review coming up soon, it wouldn't do to blot her copybook.

She turned into the Salamander's car park and slid into a narrow space next to the wall, under the spreading branches of an old chestnut tree. She turned off the ignition and sat for a few moments, relishing the quiet.

Work was manic. She had been putting in extra hours – and heaven knows, that meant extra on extra – and there had been little time for play. Tonight was pure self-indulgence. She deserved it. Whatever happened, she would leave early, hopefully reinvigorated and ready for whatever Ascher Frew could throw at her.

The bar was a small one, but it had nooks and crannies. A bay window, a recess half hidden by bookcases, an old inglenook fireplace, big enough to house a small table and two bench seats. There was privacy.

'Hi Stella.'

'Hello Carrie. The usual?'

Stella Morrison was a tiny woman, plain looking but with an energy that translated into attractiveness. A well-tended dark bob framed her small face, dark eyes gleamed brightly as she held her head to one side inquiringly.

'Please.'

Small arms reached for a glass, poured Tanqueray into a measure, splashed in tonic water from a bottle – never draft – added ice and a slice. Carrie slid onto a tall stool at the corner of the bar and surveyed the place carefully. In the window, two businessmen were intent on some spreadsheets, forgotten pints glinting in front of them as they talked. A young couple sat in the inglenook, holding hands across the small table and looking intently into each other's eyes. Honeymooners? Dirty weekenders? No, definitely not the latter, they looked far too pure.

Carrie sipped her gin and smiled to herself. She couldn't picture sanctified sex. Would it be exciting? Racy? Wicked? Deliciously exploratory? How could it be? She imagined sorry fumblings under winceyette nightgowns, coyness and, ultimately, boredom.

'Hi.'

The voice came from behind her, deep, rich – and amused.

She whipped round. Tom Vallely! Bloody flaming hell! Of all the bad luck, for Tom to be here, of all people, just as she was waiting for Star Turn. Carrie felt her cheeks ignite. She put her hands up to shield them from him.

'Tom? Hi.'

She tried to sound calm, but this scenario had thrown her.

'Can I join you?'

'No! Sorry, I mean, no, it's not a good time. I'm waiting for a friend.'

'I'll wait with you.'

'No, you can't—' She checked herself. Disaster! 'I'd prefer if – why don't we meet some other time?'

'Another time? I can't really, no. I'm only here for a few more days.' He beckoned to Stella. 'Pint please. Thanks. Who are you waiting for?'

'A friend. A colleague. A business colleague. Private business. Things. Not really suitable—' She was stuttering like a schoolgirl. Surely she could handle this?

'That's all right. I can leave when she comes. Or is it a he?' The wretched man was beaming. He was *enjoying* her discomfiture. She had to get control.

'She's a he. I mean, I'm waiting for a man, not that it's any business of yours. Listen, you have your pint, I can wait in the snug next door. My meeting really is private.'

Tom took a long pull on his pint. She watched, transfixed, as his head went back and the muscles in his throat contracted and relaxed. God, he was still beautiful. Always had been.

But now she was older. Mature. She knew how to handle a man like Tom Vallely. If she could handle Jury Service she could handle anyone. She slapped her gin down on the bar and stood up purposefully. Beside her gin, a half-empty pint glass appeared. She watched the hand as it placed it on the granite surface, the hairs on the wrist dark and smooth.

Leave. Now.

The hand moved. It was round her wrist.

Tom was standing close to her, so close that she could actually feel the heat of his body, like a furnace, a calling card from the devil.

She reacted automatically, pulling her arm away, trying to release her wrist from his grip.

He lowered his head towards her, his hair falling across his brow with picturesque grace. His eyes were like a hawk's, as grey as the sky before snow, mesmeric. His lips were moving, he was whispering something. At the bar, the businessmen, abandoning their spreadsheets, were ordering more beer. Tom's words hung by her ear, floating on the cloud of her disbelief.

'I think, D.A. Delight, that it's me you're waiting for.'

The coolness of his eyes was as enticing as an icy lake on a hot summer's day and just as dangerous.

'Sorry?'

'I've been looking forward to this. Really looking forward to it.'

'I don't know what—'

'Oh come now. You didn't guess I was Star Turn? You're slipping, Carrie darling, you really are. I thought you were cleverer than that.'

He released her wrist and she sat down abruptly on the stool, her mouth open, her eyes wide with shock.

'How did you—?'

'Guess? Darling.' His voice was dry, amused. 'It didn't take a genius. As I recall, you always were fascinated with the American legal system.'

D.A. District Attorney. It was true. She had always wished she could have trained in the States, ever since she'd watched Gregory Peck in *To Kill a Mockingbird*.

'You remembered that?'

A long finger slid down her cheek. She met his gaze reluctantly.

'I remember everything, Carrie.'

He released her face, dropped his hand fleetingly to the soft curve of her breast, brushed his fingers across it. It was designed to look accidental, if noticed, but the intent was quite different and the touch did its work. The blaze that had earlier lit her cheeks licked through her body and ran along her nerves like a flame along touchpaper.

'We can't.' She was trembling now. 'We mustn't.'

'No? Why ever not?'

His mouth was still pliant, deliciously curved, deeply sensual. She looked at it, riveted, fighting her instincts as valiantly as she could.

'Janie ... dangerous ...'

He laughed. 'Janie? But Carrie darling, that was over many years ago.'

'If she finds out—'

'Why would she find out? It's a story long ended.'

'Tom. I—'

82

He leaned closer again.

'You're not frightened of *falling in love* are you, Carrie darling?'

'Certainly not.'

She spoke the words loudly, defiantly. Further along the bar, the businessmen turned their heads in her direction. She cleared her throat and said more softly, 'With you?' She tried a laugh and was more or less successful. 'Don't flatter yourself, Tom Vallely.'

'Then what are you so afraid of?'

He laid his hand on her thigh. She felt the touch like a brand on her skin.

'Bed Buddies. That's what you're into, darling, isn't it? "Safe sex without commitment". That's what you like. You've always liked sex, Carrie, don't forget I know that. I'm no threat to you. I'll be gone in a few days. No pressure. You need never see me again. But for tonight—'

Carrie was melting, her insides had turned into an unfamiliar kind of mush. She no longer had any control over this. None. She made one last attempt to think. He was right – he would be gone soon. What harm could it do? Just this once, just tonight. Below the level of the bar, masked from public gaze, his hand slid between her thighs, moved upwards and despite herself, the audacity of it thrilled her.

'All right.' She caught his hand and stopped him. 'Just once. And don't you dare say "For old time's sake".'

'So corny. No, not for old time's sake. But because you're still a very ... very...' he moved closer, inched his hand up her thigh and breathed heavily, '... attractive ...' his tongue flickered lightly in her ear, '...woman.'

She had to stop this, now. Again she stood up. This time she lifted her handbag from the bar and said quietly, 'All right. Once. I'll get the room. I'll call you in ten minutes, give you the number. See you there. Got it?'

He didn't even nod; he just gazed at her, a mocking satisfaction in his eyes. She hated him. Hated herself. And knew it would be very, very good.

Tom saw that she was still dressed when she opened the bedroom door. Why was she still dressed? He'd have her knickers off her as soon as spit.

'Just this once, Tom, and only because you're going back to London.'

She was a gorgeous bitch. 'Why only once? I'm not with Serena anymore.'

'Why am I not surprised?'

'So what's the problem?'

'The *problem*, Tom, the *problem* is I don't really like you very much. I don't like your morals, or rather your lack of them. I don't like the way you treat women—'

'Morals, Carrie?' he said mockingly. 'What about you?'

Carrie, normally so speedy with her retorts, hesitated for a fraction of a second, just long enough for him to silence any further objections with a kiss.

The bonfire reignited and the heat consumed them both.

The woman was just as voracious as she'd ever been, never mind the passing of the years. Christ. The reluctance he'd sensed in the bar switched into a ferocious sexual energy as soon as he touched her. Thirty seconds more and he was inside her knickers. The spark between them needed little to ignite it, never had. That first night, back in Richmond had been crude, lewd and unforgettably sensational. Seventeen years later – slightly to his surprise – nothing had changed. Her waist was maybe an inch thicker, her breasts a few tasty ounces heavier, that was all.

He left, reluctantly but at her steadfast insistence, a few hours later.

'I'll be in touch.'

'No.'

'I will.'

'I won't answer.'

'Oh Carrie, darling, I think you will.'

He leant towards her naked body, lowering his head to kiss her thigh, but she kicked him, firmly, and rolled away and out of bed on the other side.

'What part of "go" don't you understand, Tom?'

He laughed, dressed, flicked the main light on maliciously as he left, so that she'd have to get up to put it off.

All the way along the plushly carpeted corridor and down the stairs he had the fun of picturing her walking across the room, magnificently naked, her firm breasts bouncing gently as she moved.

Chapter Twelve

They hadn't made love, Marta realised, since Tom's arrival. The presence of the man in the cottage was beginning to seem like a shadow – insubstantial, constantly moving and changing shape, barely there yet impossible to shake off.

She hadn't thought it would be like this. She'd liked Tom. Not warmed to him exactly – he was too theatrical for her taste, she could not tell where genuineness ended and acting began – but she had enjoyed his company.

As the days went on, her feelings about him changed. Little things began to irritate her. Rising for work one morning, she found that the olive oil had been placed on the right of the hob. She moved it back to left, where it belonged. The tea caddy had been shifted and was hidden behind a jar of marmalade.

It was hardly his fault – why should he notice where she liked to keep things or, indeed, care? But then again, an inner voice nagged, someone who respected the space they were borrowing would notice.

She finished wiping down the worktop and glanced up at the dresser. The teapot was on the wrong shelf and the mugs were arranged badly – she liked the large ones on the hooks to the right. She moved them deftly to their proper places. The bread had been left out of the bread bin and had dried up. She hit the pedal of the trash with her foot and tossed the remainder of the loaf into it.

Was it just the odd misplaced kitchen utensil that was feeding her sense of unease? Things had changed since Tom had appeared back in their lives. Jane was unaccountably nervy – she'd started stuttering again, and Carrie had become elusive. Marta had the feeling that her friend was deliberately avoiding her.

The telephone rang shrilly, and she grabbed it quickly before it could disturb Jake.

'Marta?'

'Hi Jane.'

'Can you do lunch today?'

Marta reviewed her day quickly. Busy, but nothing, so far as she could remember, in the diary. 'Think so.'

'Clarinda's? One o'clock?'

'Okay. Something special?'

'I need to t-talk. About Emily.'

'Nothing wrong, is there?'

'No. Yes. Just ... you know.'

'Sure Jane. See you at one.'

When she left the cottage, it was peaceful. Early sunlight, gleaming on the roof, lent a golden glow to the slate and the whitewashed walls shone with hopeful brightness. Shadows from the apple tree played across the window where Jake lay sleeping. She clicked the gate shut, holding the top of it for a moment in her hand, feeling the smoothness of the glossy paint on her palm.

She was mistaken – there was nothing to make her apprehensive. Tom Vallely would leave them in a day or two, Jake's efforts to find a job would be rewarded, she would resume her regular nights out with Carrie and Jane. Life would return to normal.

Clarinda's Tearoom, half way down Canongate, was busy. Marta spied Jane sitting in a corner, valiantly defending an extra chair.

'Hi!' Jane waved as Marta threaded her way through the crowded space.

'Hi. You're looking great.'

A tight smile flashed across Jane's face. 'Really? I can't think why.'

'Intense' was the best word to describe Jane Harvie. In all the years Marta had known her, there had been a fluttery anxiety about all she said and did. Will people like me? Can I get the grades I need? What if I don't get in to college? She'd always been a worrier – and she'd always been over-protective of her children.

Squeezing in next to Jane, Marta was confident that whatever was wrong, it was almost certainly no cause for real alarm.

'So,' she said, conscious that she had a hundred and one things to do back at the office. 'Tell me about Emily.'

She was right. It was a teenage thing and Jane was just a mother fretting. To Marta it was obvious – Emily was flapping her wings, itching to fly, and Jane was being over-protective, that was all.

'She was so rude, Marta. I couldn't believe it.' Jane finished off another tale of some tantrum of Emily's.

'She's frustrated. She doesn't want to be a baby anymore.'

'That's no excuse for rudeness.'

'No, but think back – don't tell me you were never like that.'

But even as she said it, Marta realised Jane had almost certainly never been rude to her parents. She had gone through adolescence nervously, negotiating a careful path in the slipstream created by Marta and Carrie. Handling an adventurous teenager was always bound to be a challenge. Heaven help her when Ross's testosterone booted up.

'I'm worried for her, Marta.'

'I know.' She reached for Jane's hand and held it lightly between her own. 'What can I do?'

Jane glanced sideways up at Marta and smiled her crooked smile. 'It's her birthday soon. Did you remember?'

'Of course. I'm her godmother.'

'I thought maybe you could take her out for a treat? Maybe have a little t-talk with her.'

'I'd love to. If she's not too self-conscious about going out with an old fogey like me.'

'She thinks the world of you. She's always going on about your glamorous lifestyle.'

Marta laughed. 'Just because I'm in tourism and get to some rather nice places doesn't make it glamorous. It's a load of hard work.'

'I know that, Marta, but she doesn't. Will you call her?'

'Sure.' Marta glanced at her watch. 'I must head back to work. Sorry, but it's really busy. How much is my share?'

'I'll pay. Let me. P-please. You're doing me a favour.'

At Emily's request, they went shopping. Marta bought few clothes, but when she did, she chose timeless, high-quality garments. Emily, child of her time, craved the latest fashions, regarded everything as disposable and wasn't prepared to spend more than the minimum. In fairness, Marta thought as she stood patiently among racks of garish, skimpy dresses while Emily trawled the rails, her goddaughter didn't have much money to spend. That was why, after Emily had chosen what appeared to Marta to be not much more than a T-shirt that just covered her bum, she said, 'I'll give you some shoes to go with it. My birthday present.'

'You are *sweet*.' Emily hugged her impulsively.

'Thanks. You make it easy. I could do with a coffee. Are you ready for a drink?'

'There's a place along here that does great smoothies. Can we go there?'

Over their drinks, Marta launched a sideways conversation.

'So, apart from your cello, what do you like to do? You and your friends.'

'Oh, you know, we like, hang out.'

'Hang out? What does that mean?'

'Just meet and talk. Have fun.'

'With boys? Have you got a boyfriend, Em?'

Did she detect a blush? It was hot in the café. Emily's hair fell across her face, hiding her expression. 'No, not really. My friend Suzy's, like, dating one of the guys from the school down the road but—' Her voice tailed off.

'Perhaps best to leave it till you find someone special.'

The hair was pushed aside and Emily looked up, her expression curious. 'When did you start dating? You and Carrie and ... my mum?'

Marta smiled. 'Everyone's different, Emily. You might not think it now, because she's never married, but Carrie had an eye for the boys when she was young. I was more cautious. I was in my last year at school before I had my first proper boyfriend. Your mum – well, that's her story, isn't it? Why don't you ask her?'

The hair fell back again, shadowing Emily's face.

'Emily?'

'She doesn't understand.' Emily's voice was sulky.

'About...?'

'You know. Boys and stuff.'

'I'm sure she does. She just cares about you.'

'She just wants to stop me enjoying myself.'

'All mothers want to protect their children.'

'I'm *sixteen* next week.'

'I know you feel grown up, Emily, but being sixteen is really just when life's adventures start. Honestly.' Emily was fidgeting. 'Do you feel ready to date someone seriously?'

'Maybe.'

The exuberance of earlier in the day had dissipated and huffiness had replaced it and Marta's heart went out to the slight girl seated in front of her. She could see uncertainty, awkwardness, a child poised on the brink of adulthood but not yet equipped to handle it. She was so like Jane. This shyness was all Jane.

'Suzy says—'

'Em?' Marta reached out and took hold of the slim hand. 'Don't do anything you're not ready for. Don't let Suzy, or anyone else, pressure you into doing something you don't want to do. You're in charge. Listen to your heart but act with your head. Okay?'

Silence. Then a small nod. 'Cool.'

Marta felt satisfied. Emily might be moody, a little awkward, boomeranging between unwarranted confidence and self-doubt, but she was essentially a nice girl. Jane was clearly fussing unnecessarily.

Spurred by her assessment, she said impulsively, 'I meant to ask, is there anything you really want? I'm very happy to go and find another little present.'

She was thinking of an iTunes voucher, or a book, so Emily's answer was unexpected.

'I'd really, really love to get my hair dyed.'

'Oh? Are you allowed? At school, I mean?'

'Yeah, sure. Everyone does it.'

'And what about your parents? What will they say? Maybe I'd better check with your mum.'

'There's no need. They'll be cool.'

'Are you sure?'

'Certain sure.'

'Okay then,' Marta agreed reluctantly. 'So long as it's something subtle.'

'Ooh thanks, Marta.'

They tried three hairdressers, but it was a Saturday afternoon and they were all booked out.

'Maybe we'd be best to make an appointment at your usual salon,' Marta said.

'But I'd really love to get it done today,' said Emily.

They walked right along George Street without any luck.

'There's a place, there!' Emily said, pointing down a side street.

'We'll make this the last one then, okay?' Marta was having second thoughts about the whole idea – but when Emily repeated her plea for an appointment yet again, the receptionist smiled.

'You're in luck! We've just this minute had a cancellation.'

'Great!' Emily turned to Marta. 'Why don't you go and do some shopping of your own? There's no point in hanging around here just, like, watching.'

'Really? I'm not keen on just leaving you.'

'It'll take an hour and a half minimum,' said the receptionist, scratching out a name in her appointments' book. 'She'll be fine with us if you want to leave her. Most mums do.'

Marta weighed the options rapidly. Emily was going to be sixteen in a few days, she was certainly old enough to be left in a hairdresser's – and it was ages since she'd had any free time in town to browse the shops.

'Emily? Would that be all right with you? I'll be back before you know it.'

'Of course!' Emily's face was shining with excitement.

'Good. See you soon then. Nothing too drastic. Promise?'

'Promise.'

Marta was back in under the hour and a half. She looked round the salon, but couldn't spot Emily anywhere. There was a middle-aged woman whose hair was completely hidden by dozens of folded tinfoil packets, and another whose gray locks had been crisply cut close to her scalp. In the far corner, a younger woman was getting a blow dry. Her hair was peroxide blonde. Six inches at the ends had been dyed a vivid purple.

The things, Marta thought, the young think are smart these days.

'It's great, isn't it?'

Emily's voice floated across the room. From somewhere near the corner.

What the...?

'*Emily*?' Marta gasped, the horror of the transformation sinking in. She strode across the salon. 'You promised not to do anything drastic!'

Emily shrugged. 'There was this girl just leaving and she'd gone for this kind of look. It was so cool. A proper statement. And Kylie said she could do mine like that, didn't you, Kylie?'

The stylist avoided Marta's horrified gaze. 'It'll wash out in a few weeks,' she said, switching off the dryer and smoothing down the multi-coloured locks with a final flourish of the brush. 'There, all finished now.'

She picked up a mirror and showed Emily the back of her head.

'Wicked,' Emily said.

What on earth, Marta thought, was she going to say to Jane?

Chapter Thirteen

With the Festival in full swing, Tartan Ribbon Tours was at its busiest. There were currently twenty-three groups in Scotland: six out on tour in the west, south, east, far north-west and the Islands, the rest in Edinburgh itself. Most were American, though there were a number from various parts of Europe and two from Japan. Some of the Edinburgh-based groups were self-supporting – they had tickets pre-booked for their events, they were staying on a half-board basis, they had been thoroughly briefed about places to see and visit. All Marta had to do was to sort out the occasional problem that landed on her desk or, to be more accurate, that fell to her if she happened to be the unlucky member of staff who picked up the telephone when a complaint came in.

A few days after her shopping trip with Emily, Marta's generally sunny nature was pushed to its limits by a dozen minor but time-consuming and irritating mishaps: a whole bunch of lost theatre tickets; a visitor with a domestic problem back home who needed a flight change urgently; someone who had forgotten to bring vital medication and had no prescription; a lost wallet. So when the telephone rang in the late afternoon, she was more than reluctant to pick it up.

'Can you take it, Marta?' The request came from her boss and so couldn't be ignored.

Marta glanced her colleague Andy, whose desk faced hers. 'Bad luck,' he mouthed, then grinned and returned to his work.

Pulling a wry face, she lifted the receiver. 'Good afternoon, Tartan Ribbon Tours, how may I help you?'

'Ah, good day to you ma'am, I was wondering if you could put together a special vacation? I guess this might not be your kinda thing, but someone gave me your name. He said you guys were real good at making people feel special.'

The voice was Texan, rich and sonorous, drawling and slow.

Marta smiled. 'That was generous,' she said in her most helpful voice. 'We'll certainly do our best. How can we help?'

'The name's Drew McGraw. I'm an entrepreneur.' He said it in the American way, *en-tra-pren-oor*. 'I run a business helping scientists turn their research into dollars. Making ideas turn into reality.'

'Sounds interesting.' She was truly alert now, the phone tucked onto her shoulder, her pen poised above her notebook, her mind already clicking into gear.

'Oh it is, believe me. Fact is – and please, ma'am, this is confidential—'

'Of course.'

'—I would like to open an office in Scotland, maybe Edinburgh, maybe Dundee. What I need is a vacation where I can come and do my own little bit of private research if you get my drift, then join up with some colleagues to do Scotland. See the scenery, bit of shooting and fishing, a little fine dining.'

'That sounds fantastic. We can certainly help you with that.'

'Yeah, a little fun, huh? But with a purpose,' he chuckled.

Marta was getting a clear picture of the man. He was big, bear-like, but a softie. Nice, but when it came to business, uncompromising. A soft paw, but with strength enough to kill if he chose to. She was warming to Drew McGraw.

'My guests may have partners too, so something to entertain the ladies while the guys are blasting dear little birdies out of the skies.'

Again he laughed comfortably, the sound making Marta smile too, despite the gruesome vision he had conjured up.

'I need to persuade these guys to invest. Get my drift?'

'I'm beginning to.'

'So it will need to be real smart, money is not a concern, but service and comfort are. Are you up for that?'

'Mr McGraw, the only thing I cannot guarantee for you in Scotland is the weather.'

'I will make my own intercessions for that, ma'am. I was thinking early October? It's not much notice. Party of eight. I will come a day or two in advance.'

'No problem. It may be cold for fishing, though.'

She could almost see him shrug, visualised huge shoulders.

'Sure. I guess they'll know that. Think Tartan Ribbon Tours can come up with the goods?'

'Sure I can. I mean, yes, certainly.'

They talked through details. Marta put down the phone and sat smiling.

Andy's voice broke into her thoughts. 'Not another complaint then?'

'Not exactly, no. A new client, with a bit of luck.'

Marta had always been eager to help others. Carrie and Jane used to tease her about it.

'Honest to God, Marta, do you *have* to fill your pockets full of rubbish?' Carrie would protest if they went for a walk. Marta hated to see rubbish discarded carelessly in beautiful places. She picked up carrier bags and cans, sweet wrappers, bottles, paper, cardboard boxes and, once, even a broken picnic hamper that someone hadn't bothered to take home to throw away.

'I can't bear to see it lying around – it spoils things for others.'

'Let someone else do it,' Carrie would say, impatiently.

Marta was always undeterred. 'If everyone said that, it would still be here.'

Just after they left school, they all went on holiday together, Carrie thrilled to be driving her mother's convertible. Somewhere along the road to Kyle of Lochalsh they came across a lamb, clearly distressed and looking for its mother. 'Stop!' Marta demanded. Carrie stopped.

'We've got to help it.'

'Wrong,' Jane said, 'We've got a ferry to catch.'

'And it's the last one to Skye tonight,' Carrie pointed out.

'But it's lost. It's got out of some field somewhere and it could be knocked down.'

'Yum,' Carrie said, heartlessly.

'Mint sauce,' Jane grinned. It was the wrong response. Marta, fired with righteous indignation, dug her heels in, spent the next half hour wandering along the road in both directions until she found a loudly baa-ing sheep, reunited mother and lamb, before finally climbing back into the car.

They missed the ferry and had to spend a night in a cramped and none too clean bed and breakfast on the wrong side of the water, much to the disgust of Carrie and Jane. It was an incident they liked to remind her about whenever she tried to do a good turn.

'Baa,' Carrie would say. Jane rendered it as 'Me-eh.' Either way, it was a coded message designed to deter her.

Now, however, ignoring the animal noises in her head, Marta felt justified in launching into good-deed mode, because something was telling her loud and clear that getting Tom Vallely out of the house was not only necessary but urgent.

'Ann Playfair, hello.'

The voice was deep, for a woman, and had a husky, nicotine edge. Years ago, at school, Marta had been in awe of Miss Playfair, the English teacher with a background in theatre and a voice that could carry the length of Princes Street. By the sixth year, however, she, Carrie and Jane had been accepted into the teacher's inner circle – not favourites ('I don't do favourites') – but an exclusive group who gave their spare time to help her run the drama group. When she'd left the school for a career in scriptwriting, they'd kept in touch.

'Hello Miss Playfair, it's Marta Davidson.' She still found it hard to use Miss Playfair's first name.

'Marta! How lovely to hear from you. Are you in Glasgow?'

'No, sorry. Not today.'

'I thought maybe you were up for a drink.'

God, a glass of wine would slip down well right now. 'I would be, but sorry, I'm still chained to my desk here in the east.'

'Pity. What can I do for you then, Marta?'

'Are you still one of the scriptwriters on *Emergency Admissions* by any chance?'

'I do write the odd episode for them. Why?'

Marta explained about Tom. 'He's pretty well known. Fantastic looking. Wanting something a bit more regular and better paid than the theatre work he's been doing recently and when I mentioned—'

'Yes, yes. I know. Say the word "scriptwriter" and suddenly a key new role could appear.'

Marta laughed, embarrassed. 'Something like that. Sorry.'

'Don't be. It's human nature. Well, the nature of all actors, at any rate. Tom Vallely – remind me. What's he been in?'

Marta ran through some of Tom's credits.

'Got him now. Well, as it happens, I do know they're about to audition for a new role and your Tom sounds like he could be in the zone. Get his agent to call the producer, the timing might be lucky.'

'Brilliant. Tom will be ecstatic.'

'It's just an audition, Marta.'

'Of course. Even so. Thanks so much.'

'Let's have that drink sometime, eh?'

'Soon. I'd love to.'

'Life treating you well?'

Marta thought about Jake, his redundancy, her continual failure to conceive, the tensions that were beginning to run noticeably between them.

'Yes, fine,' she said. 'Everything's fine.'

As she walked up the hill to the cottage, Marta found herself humming. The conversation with Drew McGraw had lifted her spirits after a difficult day, she had managed to establish a pleasant relationship with Emily Harvie and she had taken a positive first step in helping Tom achieve his ambition. Plus, the sun was still shining. What was not to be happy about?

She found that out as soon as she opened the front door. A thump. A curse. An ill-tempered Jake.

He was on the floor, peering under the sofa.

'Hi.' She addressed his backside. 'Lost something?'

'Yeah.' Jake abandoned his search, wriggled round and jumped to his feet. 'My Coldplay CD. Seen it?'

'Haven't played it in ages. Isn't it on the rack?'

'Nope.'

'Sure?' She started to cross the room.

'Course I'm sure,' he said irritably, 'I've looked through everything.'

'Well, could you have put it somewhere else? The bedroom?'

'I've looked everywhere. It's gone.'

'I'm sure it'll turn up Jake.'

'How long's Sir Kenneth staying, Marta?' The question seemed at a tangent. 'Because I've really had enough.'

'Has something happened?'

'Maybe. I dunno. I want him out, anyway. He's outstayed his welcome.'

Marta sighed. 'I'm working on it, Jake. Okay? Aren't you on duty tonight?'

'I'm on my way.'

Jake's tense shoulders revealed his mood. Marta opened her arms because she couldn't bear to let him go in a cloud of irritability. 'Hugs?'

He held her close, but carefully, as though she were made of glass. The hug felt uncomfortable and left her feeling edgy and unsatisfied.

'Kiss me when you get in? Even if I'm asleep?'

'Sure.' He strode into the hall and opened the front door. 'Oh, by the way,' he said, swivelling back towards her, 'Jane called. She sounded furious.'

'Furious? Did she say why?' The hair. It must be the hair.

'I don't know,' Jake said shortly. 'Why don't you call back? Find out yourself.'

Marta had phoned Jane as soon as she'd put Emily on the bus home, but there'd been no-one in. She'd left a message – nothing specific, she wanted to tell Jane about what had happened directly. But Jane hadn't telephoned back.

She picked up the phone and dialled. 'Hi, Jane?'

'I t-trusted you Marta.' Jane's voice was full of rage, barely suppressed. 'When I saw Emily I was so furious I couldn't bring myself to even speak to you. I trusted you to look after my daughter and you let me down. How *could* you?'

'Listen, Jane,' Marta said smoothly, 'I'm really sorry the way it turned out. Emily promised she'd just get a few highlights. I never expected her to go for anything like that. But it's not the end of the world. The stylist said it'd wash out soon.'

'Wash out? *Wash out*? It's bleached, Marta. It's p-permanent. What were you *thinking*?'

'She'd given me her promise. I just went and did a bit of shopping and when I came back—'

'You left her alone? To get her hair dyed?'

'I just... I didn't expect—'

'Didn't I tell you she was being bolshie? Wasn't that what it was all supposed to be about? You were meant to find reassure me, not... She came home with a dress that makes her look like a tart and her hair platinum and p-purple. *Honestly*, Marta! You have no right to make that kind of decision about my daughter!'

'It was just a little treat. She loved the day.' Marta, feeling her failure deeply, grew defensive in the face of Jane's assault.

'I bet she did. We can stop her wearing the dress, but her *hair*, Marta! It looks hideous! And the school's already torn us off a strip.'

'Really? She told me the school would be fine with dyed hair. I asked her expressly. She told me there was no problem either with the school or with you and Neal.'

'Are you saying my daughter lied to you?'

Marta felt caught. Whatever she said now was bound to be wrong. 'I don't believe I misunderstood her,' she started, carefully.

Jane exploded. 'How *dare* you let this happen? As if you know what's best for my daughter? You've never even had a baby. What do you know about b-bringing up a child? And while we're talking—' her stutter was becoming ever more pronounced, '—what were you thinking of, Marta? Bringing T-Tom Vallely back into my life? He's an evil man. *Evil*. I hate him. And I can't forgive you—'

Marta's eyes became blurred with tears.

What do you know about bringing up a child?

A constriction in her throat threatened her breathing. She dropped the telephone back onto its cradle, cutting Jane off in full flow.

What do you know about bringing up a child?

The words burrowed into her skin. She hugged her stomach and doubled over, feeling the cruelty of Jane's jibe like the punch of a fist into the emptiness of her womb. How could her *best friend* deploy the weapon that she knew would hurt her most?

'Hi! Hello, darling.'

Marta shot upright as Tom dropped his sweater on the back of a chair, his smile warm and easy.

'Everything all right? Seen my hat, by the way? I must have left it somewhere.'

'Hat?' She was still stupid with shock.

'My brown fedora. You haven't seen it anywhere?'

She shook her head. 'No, sorry.'

'Damn. I've had it for ages. I really liked it. Fancy a drink?'

'Maybe it'll turn up.'

He had turned, without asking permission, to the cupboard where Jake stored the spirits. She watched, blinking back tears.

At least there was some good news. 'By the way, Tom —'

'Yeah?' He had poured a generous two fingers of whisky into a tumbler. 'Drink this stuff, do you?'

'No. Listen, I spoke to my friend today, the one I told you about.' She reached for a tissue and gave her nose a good blow.

'Friend?'

'The scriptwriter.'

'Oh yeah?' The concentration on swirling, sniffing and sipping stopped and smokey eyes focused intensely on her. 'And?'

'And it's good news. There could be a part coming up.'

The golden spirits, still swirling gently in the glass, slowed and stilled. 'A ... part?'

'You're to ask your agent to get in touch,' Marta went on, disconcerted by the intensity of his gaze, 'Miss Playfair thinks you might have the right look.'

He dumped the glass down unceremoniously on the top of the drinks' cupboard. The whisky slopped slightly over the rim and dribbled down onto the polished wood.

'Marta darling, I've said it before and I'll say it again, you are an angel,' he said, a smile of extraordinary sweetness splitting his face.

Evil? Surely Jane was wrong about him – Tom craved work, that was all, and the lack of it undermined him.

On the cupboard, Tom's whisky sat, forgotten. Some days later, Marta found a sad ring leached into the wood by the dampness and the alcohol. It took a great deal of effort to polish out.

Chapter Fourteen

Carrie Edwards was a challenge. That was partly what attracted Tom, because few women resisted him for long, or matched him in sexual appetite. Since reaching maturity (which he reckoned was when he'd walked out of his relationship with Jane and taken charge of his life), Carrie had been the only woman he'd really wanted to spend time with. She was no beauty, not a patch on the kind of arm candy he liked to be seen around town with, but she had spirit and a dry wit, and besides, he liked a challenge.

Hell, though, the woman could be impossible. She'd always been the one in control, turning him down and agreeing to meet him whenever pleased her. He hated that.

He'd miscalculated, too. He hadn't figured for a minute that she'd refuse to see him again after he married Serena. He could still remember how angry he'd been the day he'd spotted her on the platform at Covent Garden tube station, looking frustrated as a train pulled away. She must just have missed it. He could see her nose wrinkle and made out a crisp 'Pah' of annoyance as he approached, unnoticed.

'Well, look who it is,' he'd said, sidling up behind her and throwing an arm casually around her shoulders.

'Hello, Tom.' She had not been welcoming.

'You could sound more pleased to see me.'

'Really? You think?'

'What's biting you, Carrie? Late for a meeting?'

'Yep. And I could do without bumping into the biggest liar in London.'

'Me?' His surprise had been genuine. 'What are you talking about?'

'Come on, Tom.'

'What? Come on, what?'

'You told me it was over with Jane.'

'It was. I just had to find the right moment to get out.'

'It took a while, didn't it?'

'What's eating you, Carrie? It's done, isn't it?'

She stared at him. Another train was approaching, he could feel the blast of compressed air sweeping towards them as it emerged from the tunnel into the station. Carrie stepped forward, poised to board.

'Is this about Serena? Serena's just a career move. You know that, Carrie.' He'd focused all his charm on her as she turned to glare at him again. 'So when can we meet? Eh, sexy?'

The train had stopped, passengers were disgorging and he'd had to struggle to stay close to her.

'Bugger that, Tom.' They were on the train now and her words rang into the carriage. Heads turned.

He'd bent towards her and said in a low voice, 'I don't want things to change between us, Carrie.'

Silence. Another withering glance, then, 'Poor Serena,' she'd said. Her eyes, normally so bright and amused, had been full of a pity that had incensed him.

'I'll treat her right.'

'What, by sleeping with me?'

'What's wrong with that? She'll never know.'

People were looking away, but he'd sensed them straining to listen. They'd reached Holborn. The doors opened and Carrie jumped out. The last he'd seen of her had been an averted profile and a nose held high.

Fuck her, he'd thought. Then – *if only I could*.

That thought had stayed with him a long time.

He was in Marta's spare bedroom when his agent called.

'Hey, Angela,' Tom smiled at his reflection in the mirror.

'It's fixed. Friday at noon.'

'Okay.'

'Is that it? Okay? Aren't you pleased?'

She sounded whiney, desperate for bloody praise. Tom smothered a sigh and turned on his most appreciative voice. Best keep her sweet, for now at least. 'Thrilled, darling, absolutely thrilled.'

'Tom—' The hesitation was almost palpable.

'What?'

'You won't mess this one up, will you? Get there late, forget your audition piece...' Her voice tailed away nervously.

'What do you think I am, Angela? Some kind of amateur?'

'No, darling, but I was wondering if I should perhaps come up? Be with you?'

Fuck that. Tom had plans for Friday night and Angela Cutler didn't figure in them.

'No,' he said firmly. 'I don't need that.'

'I just thought ... maybe I could ... help relax you?'

Christ. Maybe he should get a male agent, it would be a load less demanding. On the other hand ... Tom thought about the male agents he knew and took barely half a second to decide to stick with Angela. At least he could control her.

'Not necessary, darling. I promise. I'll be great.'

'If you're sure.'

'Sweetheart, listen, if I get this part I'll be back in London before you can blink. And I'll give you a night to remember, I promise you.'

'Really?'

'Scout's honour.' Stupid expression. Tom, never having been a Boy Scout, had no idea what it meant, but Angela seemed to appreciate it.

'I'll hold you to that. Come to think of it, I'd hold you to anything.'

He laughed indulgently.

'Call me after.'

'I will.'

Call me after. Maybe he would. Call her after a celebratory night with D.A. Delight, the delectable Caroline Edwards. Carrie Delight. He hadn't contacted her for a week, but now the time was not only right, it was necessary – he needed someone to pay for his room in Glasgow.

Jake had gone to work. Marta was out. Tom walked into Jake's study, booted up the computer and logged on to the bed-buddies.net site.

<Hello D.A>

He thought she might not reply, or that he might have to wait till she got home from work – Carrie wouldn't be so stupid as to use her work computer for this site. But the answer popped up right away.

<Fuck off.>

He laughed out loud.

<Plan to. Friday?>
<Said I wouldn't see you again.>
<Sweet Delight. Glasgow? Then I'm off south.>
<No.>
<Last time ever.>
<Nope.>
<Okay then.>

There was a pause. He had backed off deliberately, to throw her, but it was a calculated risk. After three minutes, Tom stared out of the window and watched a magpie pecking at something on the lawn, its black and white plumage resplendent in the sun. Nothing. Had he miscalculated? Four minutes passed. The magpie had hopped out of sight. One for sorrow. Damn.

Ping. He twisted back to the computer.

<Last time?>

Result!

<Promise.>
<Last time then.>
<Great. You know Glasgow – where? Can you book with your card? Mine's just gone out of date – new one will be down south.>
<Same old Tom, huh?>
<Where then?>

It had worked. An audition for a television part, a free hotel room for the night and some fantastic sex thrown in. What could be better? Tom smoothed back his hair and winked at himself in the mirror behind Jake's computer. Star Turn had come up trumps again.

Humming softly, he opened Jake's desk drawer to find a pen and paper to jot down details of the hotel. He rummaged inside and dislodged a notebook. Beneath it, partially hidden by a pile of bills and bank statements, was a bundle of bank notes.

Handy. Thanks mate, many thanks indeed.

He left half a dozen notes, folded the rest and stuffed them in his pocket. With any luck Jake would forget how much he'd put in the drawer, stupid sod.

Chapter Fifteen

Carrie eased her car through the evening traffic on the motorway, her mood darkening with every mile. She should never have agreed to this. In the days since she'd exchanged emails with Tom, she'd been on the point of calling off at least a dozen times, but each time lust had countermanded common sense. She had turned down three invitations from Bed Buddy regulars – and for what? A romp with an old flame – never a good idea, because there was always the risk that old emotions might be smouldering rather than cold.

Look after Tom for me.

Jane's words. The words that had sparked the whole affair. And no matter how much Carrie had rationalised things, she'd felt guilty from the beginning. What sort of friend had she been? A criminally poor one, whichever way you looked at it.

In front of her, the traffic ground to a halt again. Carrie hit the brakes and stopped so suddenly that her body swayed forwards, then back, hitting the seat with some force. Damnation. She should concentrate more or she'd never even get to the hotel. If she did decide to go – even at this late stage she could easily pull off at the next exit from the motorway, turn around and head for home.

Sight, touch, sound, smell, taste.

She knew in her heart she wouldn't cancel. She was weak willed and self-indulgent and she despised herself – but this would be the last time, the very last. It was too dangerous. Tom was gorgeous, but totally untrustworthy. If he said something to Jane, all her careful efforts to sustain their friendship would count for nothing.

The traffic eased. Three times before her turn off she was offered choices. Left here, instead of right? Down the first road, not the second? Round the roundabout and head back to Edinburgh? Yet ten minutes later, she was easing her car into a space in the car park under the hotel – because this was going to be the last time.

Truly.

There was an edge to illicit sex that was a sure-fire turn-on.

'Tom, we shouldn't – this is a big mistake—' her words were stopped by Tom's lips and tongue, hot on her own, working feverishly on and in her mouth as his hands tugged at her clothes.

It was hopeless. Talking was impossible. From the second she opened the door to Tom's knock, their bodies were drawn together with a force she couldn't resist.

'Stop,' Carrie moaned as he bit on her breast. He had tugged open her blouse and pushed her bra up roughly so that she was exposed, but the roughness of it only added to her state of deep arousal. His hands were everywhere, pulling, stroking, rubbing, he was walking her towards the bed even as they were entwined. She heard the door to the corridor click shut as they fell together onto the mattress, and then sensation overtook thought completely, as he pulled her knickers down forcefully and entered her.

'Aaah...' It wasn't a cry of pain, but of ecstasy. They climaxed together in an explosion of lust. Carrie lay under him, panting, a sheen of sweat on her face, her thighs wet with their mingled body fluids.

Tom lifted his head and grinned down at her. 'You little minx, Carrie, you just can't keep your hands off me, can you?'

'You cheeky bastard!' Despite herself, the impudence of it amused her and she laughed.

He rolled off, picked up her knickers and used them to dry himself. 'Well, what shall we do now? We've got all night.'

'We could talk.'

'Talk? Now there's a novel idea.'

She regarded her soiled underwear with a sudden surge of distaste. What was she doing here? Just dragging an unnecessary and absolutely unwanted complication back into her life.

She eased herself away from Tom, leant over to rescue her Max Mara shift dress and slipped it over her head.

'Take it off.'

She stood up and turned to look down at him. 'No, Tom. This was a mistake. I'd like you to leave. Now.'

'Leave? No chance. I'm enjoying myself.'

She couldn't help noticing that his lean body was still in magnificent shape, despite the fact that he was forty now.

'And don't tell me you're not because, darling Carrie, your orgasm spoke for you, I believe.'

'I mean it Tom. I'm sorry I came here. It's time for this to stop. Jane—'

There was a sudden movement and a whirl of arms and then the room was spinning and next thing Carrie knew was that she was on the floor and there were flashing lights in front of her eyes and a scalding pain in her head.

'What the—?'

He was standing above her, his hair across his eyes, the muscles in his body tense.

He'd hit her! Her hand shaking, Carrie lifted it to her head and felt a trickle of blood down her temple. It was throbbing. She could feel the pain pulsing in rhythm with her heart.

Not good.

Talk.

Nicely.

Get him to move. Calm him.

Through the haze, voices of logic and reason counselled her.

'I seem to be bleeding. Will you help me, Tom?'

It took all her bravery to raise her hand to him, but some deep-seated instinct was dictating to her, telling her not to oppose him. It might have been counter-intuitive but it paid off. She saw him hesitate, then the tension eased and he held out his hand to help her up.

'Thanks. I'll just wash this. Are you all right? I'm not sure what happened.'

She was lying, talking smoothly, placidly, making her voice even, lowering the tone, using every trick she knew to try to relax him. She needed to defuse his sense of power, because she guessed that domination was a turn-on for him, as it was for most bullies.

She took a tentative step towards the bathroom, terrified that he would stop her, try to follow her, attack her again.

'I must have fallen. Thanks.' A wobbly smile. 'I need a towel. Wait there. I'll just be a moment.'

The carpet under her feet was rough. Through the pain she felt the texture change to smooth coldness as she entered the bathroom. It took all her willpower not to shut herself in, bolt the door, protect herself from the man's wildness – but there'd be no point. Her mobile phone was in her handbag in the bedroom, she could hardly stay there until the maid came in the morning. She would simply have to deal with the situation.

Think, Carrie.

She had always known that when she used Bed Buddies there could be a danger of something like this happening – she had just never thought that it might be someone she knew who would do it.

Stay calm. Keep talking.

'So, Tom,' she called as she ran the water, stared at her white face in the mirror and examined the cut. Her hands were shaking and she was scared, but thinking fast. How to get out? What was the next move? What caused the violence? The rational intelligence that had always been her gift kicked in through the fear.

Jane. She'd mentioned Jane. Had that been it – or the fact that she'd told him it had to end?

'So, Tom, you haven't told me why you're in Glasgow?'

She took the white flannel, soaked it in cool water, dabbed it against her head. This would look nasty in the morning, but it wasn't fatal and it wouldn't need stitches.

'I had an audition.'

Carrie jumped. He was right next to her, staring at her, the grey of his eyes steely. Christ, this was scary.

'Yeah? Did it go well?'

Could he see her shaking? She tried to still her hands.

'Here. Let me help.'

He was beside her, taking the flannel. Jesus. She closed her eyes and sent up a prayer.

'It was for a part in a soap.'

His touch was surprisingly tender.

'It went well. I thought we could celebrate.'

'Fine. That's good. Great. What was the soap?'

'Thing called *Emergency Admissions*. Heard of it?'

'*EA*? Of course. I'm addicted,' she lied. She had watched the hospital drama a few times, but though it was well written and the core characters believable, it wasn't really her kind of thing. 'Wow, it would be brilliant if you got the part. What are your chances, do you think?' The bleeding had abated, though her head was still thumping.

'If they have any sense they'll offer it to me. Hey, Carrie, come to bed. Lie down. Come.' His voice was gentle, but every sinew in her body screamed at her to resist and she tensed, clutching the basin. 'No more talk about leaving, hey? You and me, Carrie, we're good together.' The tone was back to normal, rich and deep, though what once sounded to her ears like sexual allure was now repulsive. 'I didn't mean to hurt you, Carr. You upset me.'

Carrie forced herself to relinquish the steadying feel of the porcelain. 'I know,' she said softly, 'I know, Tom. Sorry.'

How could she get out of there? She couldn't get back into bed with him, she really couldn't.

'I don't like to think about Janie. I don't like to think about how upset she would be if she knew about what you'd done to her. Sleeping with me while I was still living with her. That wasn't a very loyal thing to do, was it, Carrie?'

The red haze in front of Carrie's eyes deepened and intensified. She heard his words with disbelief.

'Not really something a friend would do. Hey?'

'No. You're right.'

'Because if you don't behave yourself, my D.A. Delight, I might just have to tell our Janie about just how much you valued her friendship back then. How the way you seduced me destroyed my relationship with her. She knows about Bed Buddies, I take it?'

This time there was nothing Carrie could do to stop the trembling.

No. Christ no. Please.

'She doesn't? No, I suppose dear Janie, who has neatly protected herself behind her sanctimonious husband, her dear, sweet old mother and her nicely brought up little children, might be a little bit shocked about that. Maybe she should know. Hey? What do you think? Maybe she should have a little glimpse into how her *very dear* friend chooses to spend her nights off?'

He had her wrist in his hand. He was leading her towards the bed.

Think, Carrie, think.

She shook her head. 'I think maybe that's best between us, Tom.'

'What? I didn't hear?'

'Best between us.' She tried to keep it level, firm but warm. She even tried a smile.

'You may be right.' He appeared to consider this. 'Yes, perhaps you may be right. Little secrets can be fun, can't they? But I'd like to hear your views, Caroline darling, on my performance.'

'Performance? The audition? I—'

116

'Not that.' He pulled her closer, so that her face was up against his naked chest and she could smell the sweat on him. How had she ever thought he was desirable? *Breathe. In. Out. In. Out. Control. You can do this.*

'In bed, my little Bed Buddy.'

'Magnificent.'

'A stallion in full splendour.'

'Exactly.'

'You've never known a better lover.'

'I was just going to tell you that. You're great. You know you are.'

She was trapped. Flatter him and he'd want to repeat the experience. Criticise him and he'd get violent. Panic invaded her every sense. *He's going to make me do it again.* Her head was whirling, with possibilities, with anxiety, trying to weigh the options, take a view on a course of action.

It's just sex, Carrie. Just do it. Don't provoke him. He's dangerous. Something in her had always known that, tonight had proved it. Best to play along with it, grit her teeth, do what he wanted.

She took a deep breath, closed her eyes and tried to ignore the pounding of her head.

Just. Do. What. He. Wants.

Afterwards, he slept. She lay next to him, stiff and fearful, every minute like an hour, every hour a day. By three o'clock, she could bear it no longer. He seemed to be in a deep sleep. She got up, dressed hurriedly, went into the bathroom and, using the tiny flashlight on her key ring, scrawled him a note.

'Dear Tom. Sorry, had to go – I know it's Saturday but I have an early meeting at the office. Thanks for everything. Room is paid for. C.'

She thought for a minute before signing off, but couldn't bear to put 'Love, Carrie'. That was a lie too far. She put a vague squiggle under the initial, something that might be a kiss or merely a flourish, and propped it on the tap. She opened the bathroom door a crack and listened fearfully. His breathing was still steady. She sped through the door to the corridor before he could wake. Even if he tried to follow her now, surely she could get away.

The hotel was silent, its transient occupants slumbering, each in the square box designed to accommodate this most basic of human needs.

He wouldn't come now, she was safe. For the moment.

Chapter Sixteen

At three o'clock, in Edinburgh – or at least, in its seaside suburb of Portobello – a young girl was running along the pavement, her shoes in her hand, her long hair streaming out behind her, a look of sheer panic on her face. At one street corner, a drunk lurched towards her, well-meant concern masked by a face contorted by an effort at concentration.

'Y'all right, hen? Y'all right by yoursel'? Oot sae late.'

The girl twisted away from the figure frantically, sped on. He turned, loose-limbed and shambling, steadied himself against a wall and muttered, 'S'no right. Should be in her bed, the wee lassie.'

A hundred yards further and a police car slowed down, watched her progress, then lowered a window. The girl, glancing frenziedly over her shoulder, clicked open a gate, ran along the path and pushed at the bell. Once. Twice. A third time. The police car hovered, watchfully, by the kerb. A light came on in an upper window of the small white cottage, then the front door opened. The girl turned, waved a vague hand at the patrol car, as if to say, 'I'm fine,' then disappeared into the cottage. The car moved away. There were other problems to deal with, more challenging demands on time and expertise. This situation, at least, appeared under control.

'Emily?' Marta, hazy with sleep, assessed the pale apparition and groped for alertness. 'What are you doing here? What's the time? Are you on your own? Has something happened?'

The girl was shuddering, her breath coming in sobs. Mascara had run down her face, leaving dark streaks and the absurd platinum and purple hair was tangled. Marta's gaze travelled downwards – her feet were completely bare. Concern bit through sleepiness. Now she was fully awake.

'Come in for heaven's sake, come into the kitchen.'

She took Emily's hand and led her towards the darkness of an open doorway and the reassuring hum of the refrigerator. She flicked on the light as the noise gurgled and died. Marta liked the hum of the machinery in her home. She liked the dishwasher doing its work, rinsing, cleaning, drying. She loved the washing machine, filling, emptying, spinning. The tumble dryer was best of all because it tossed its contents lazily to and fro, to and fro, before delivering soft, warm, comforting clothes, ready to be neatly folded and stowed in drawers. Her appliances spoke to her. This is our home too, they reminded her, we like to keep it nice for you. Even now, even through her concern for Emily, they carried on doing their work of calming and soothing.

'Sit down.' She helped Emily gently onto a chair.

Didn't the child have a coat, for heaven's sake? Even a wrap of some sort? She should never be out on her own, late at night, dressed like this. She surveyed the garments as Emily's thin shoulders continued to heave. Surely that was the dress Emily had bought on their outing a couple of weeks ago?

'It's all right, Em. You're safe.'

Another small sob, another shudder.

Marta leant forward and folded her into her embrace, felt the tension in the slight body as the girl's head thudded onto her shoulder.

'It's all right. Hey. Shh. It's all right.'

What in heaven's name had happened? When the heaving stopped, she disentangled herself carefully, took Emily's arms firmly between her hands and said, 'Tell me.'

At last Emily looked at her. Her lower lip was wobbling, but she managed to speak with no more than a tremor.

'Suzy was having a party, at her house. It's in Portobello, not too far from here.'

She flicked a multi-coloured strand of hair out of her eyes, wiped a shaky hand across them and fumbled in her bag for a hankie. She blew her nose noisily and settled back in her chair, the tissue still crumpled damply in her fist.

'It was only meant to be a small one, you know? Like her best mates, some of the guys from school and the orchestra—'

'So what happened?'

'She put the invitation out on Facebook.'

Marta groaned. 'Let me guess. There were gatecrashers?'

'Yeah. Like, hundreds.'

'Where were Suzy's parents? Did they know she was having this party?'

'Yeah. Honest. They're at her mum's sister's in Stirling. She's had parties before. There's never been a problem.'

She was eying Marta with a spark of defiance now. Whatever had scared her, the effect was wearing off.

'I believe you, Emily. Maybe she hadn't put it on Facebook before?'

'Maybe.'

Marta eyed the child worriedly. What should she do? Call Jane and Neal, ask them to fetch her? Put her in the car and drive her home herself?

'Can I stay here tonight, Marta? Please?'

'Oh, I don't know—' Tom had gone to Glasgow, the spare room was empty and it would save a lot of trouble... 'Well, all right, I suppose so. I'll just go and call your mum, so she doesn't worry.'

'You needn't bother, I've texted her already,' Emily said quickly, her eyes flickering to her handbag where, Marta supposed, her mobile was nestling.

'Really? When?'

'On the way here.'

121

'Honestly?' Marta pressed, filled with doubt. Her goddaughter had not been exactly honest the last time Marta had asked her about her parents' views.

'Cross my heart and hope to die. She said great, it would save Dad coming out to get me.'

'If you're sure.'

'Yeah.'

'Okay then, come along. Let's get you into bed as soon as possible. Need a drink of water?'

'Yes please.' She followed Marta upstairs, carrying the glass carefully. She seemed to have recovered, Marta thought, watching her climb the last few steps. The water wasn't even rippling.

At nine o'clock the telephone rang. Jake, who must have come in some time after Emily's late night appearance, rolled over sluggishly and lifted the receiver.

'Hello? Jake here.'

Marta, ascending the dark tunnel from somnolence into conscious thought, could hear only a muffled high-pitched yammering down the receiver.

'No, she's not here, Jane. Sorry.'

She was instantly alert. 'Is it about Emily? She is here, Jake,' she said, raising her voice to cut through the conversation.

'What? Sorry, Marta interrupted, I didn't hear ... no, I don't think so, no. *What*?'

'Emily *is* here.'

'Christ, well what do I know? I only live here.'

Clearly peeved, he handed her the phone, then pulled the duvet back up over his head and rolled away.

'Jane? Hi, it's Marta. Listen, Emily's here, she's still sleeping. She said she'd texted you.'

Jane's voice exploded down the line. 'She's *there*! Christ, Marta, why the hell didn't you let me know? I've been going frantic here. When I phoned Suzy's m-mum to find out when to pick her up, I got this long story about how the whole house had been trashed, they'd got a call from Suzy in the middle of the night, in tears. They had to come back from Stirling to deal with it. Hundreds of yobs, apparently, the whole p-place is a complete wreck and she didn't know where Emily was, she thought she'd come back here because she just d-d-disappeared. What in heaven's name is she doing with you? What happened? Is she all right? And why didn't you phone me? Didn't you stop to think for one m-minute that I would be going off my head with worry—'

'Jane, stop. Calm down, will you?' What was wrong with Jane these days? 'She told me she'd texted you. Okay?'

'Are you saying she was lying?'

'Oh for heaven's sake. No Jane, I am not saying she was lying. Have you checked your phone?'

'Of course I've checked my phone. I've been checking it every two minutes since I found she wasn't at the P-Pattersons.'

'Well, maybe her text didn't get through. Sometimes they don't.'

'You should have phoned me yourself, M-Marta.'

'What, at three in the morning?'

'Was that when she came round to you? P-please, Jesus, tell me she wasn't running around the streets at that hour, on her own?'

'Relax, Jane, will you? She's fine. She's safe. She's here. Now, what would you like to me to do? Bring her round?'

'No thanks, M-Marta.' The voice had switched from raging to icy. 'I can't really trust you with my child. One of us will come for her.'

'Fine.'

Marta jabbed at the off button. She had a sudden image of the very first time she'd seen Emily Harvie. Still a baby – pink and tiny, her nose peeping out over a pure white blanket, her eyes closed, the lashes already long and dark, her lips puckering exquisitely in an involuntary search for sustenance. And Jane, laughing and proud, holding the tiny bundle out to her.

'Hold her,' she was saying, 'Hold my baby.'

Marta had taken the precious package gingerly, marvelling at the miracle that was a new life.

She'd had no idea then just how elusive that miracle would prove for her and Jake.

Trust. Friendship. Loyalty. What had happened to all of that? What had happened to Jane, for heaven's sake? Ever since that dinner with Tom she'd been edgy and irritable – no, more than irritable, downright angry.

'Is there any chance at all of being told about what is going on in my own house?'

Jake's voice had a sarcastic edge that wasn't like him at all. Marta kissed his forehead and ruffled her hand through his tousled morning hair.

Everything is falling apart, she thought. My friend is furious with me and my husband is peevish and unhappy. I have a just-turned-sixteen-year-old child in the next room, who has quite possibly been telling me lies, and I seem absolutely unable to conceive a child of my own.

She explained, patiently. 'Emily rang the bell around three. She was upset. Suzy's party had been gatecrashed and there were about a hundred yobs trashing the place. She was frightened. I calmed her down and offered to run her home, but she asked if she could stay.'

'And you said yes? And didn't bother to let Jane know? Didn't you stop for a minute to think that her parents might worry about her?'

'Jake, of course I did. Didn't you hear me? Emily told me she had already texted her mum.'

'For heaven's sake, Marta, she's a teenager. She's running rings around you and you're letting her do things her own parents won't.'

'That's not fair. I would have called Jane if I'd thought for one minute that Emily was lying. Anyway, it's just as well someone listens to the poor kid. Jane and Neal are far too controlling. If Emily is trying to break out, it's hardly surprising.'

'It's not up to you to tell them how to bring up their child.'

'Whose side are you on, Jake? I have never tried to tell them how to bring up their child. I have simply spent a bit of time with Emily and if she chooses to come here when she's in trouble, instead of going home, well actually, I am quite proud of that.'

Jake sat up and swung his legs out of bed. 'I'm going for a shower.'

Marta watched as he strode naked across the room, muscle, bone and sinew moving smoothly under the taut, pale skin. He had lost weight recently, surely? She glanced at the clock. Nine thirty. He can't have come in till four, he should still be sleeping – no wonder he was irritable.

She pulled on a white cotton robe and went reluctantly to rouse Emily. The girl was curled up, her face peaceful and young, her dyed hair a reproach. Looking at her now, Marta understood why Jane had been so upset. There was nothing about the style that suited Emily, it simply made her look trashy.

Marta's heart ached as she watched her friend's child breathing softly. She didn't want to fall out with Jane. She was only trying to help. Misunderstandings and arguments made her miserable, they always had. Whatever was eating away at Jane, she had to get to the bottom of it.

Maybe she'd get Carrie's take on it. And where *was* Carrie anyway? She hadn't heard from her in an age.

'Emily.'

She stooped, touched the girl on the shoulder.

'Em,' she said, slightly louder, when there was no response. 'You'll need to wake up, sweetheart.'

Marta wasn't ready for a conversation with Jane – wrong time, wrong place, wrong circumstances – so she was relieved that it was Neal who came for the child.

Neal, in contrast to Jane's earlier histrionics, was calm, polite and non-confrontational. He even thanked Marta for giving his daughter shelter. 'It was really kind of you, I'm sorry you were woken up so late. Emily must have been really relieved you were here. Emily?'

'Yeah. Thanks.'

Emily looked wan. Her face was pale and there were shadows under her eyes, where the delicate skin looked drawn. She'd refused breakfast, she'd barely spoken since she'd appeared and she hadn't looked directly at Marta at all. The skimpy dress was draped precariously over her thin shoulders and looked, in the cool light of morning, even more inappropriate than it had last night.

'Would you like to borrow a cardi, Emily, or a T-shirt? It's a bit chilly this morning.'

She shook her head. 'I'm all right.'

'Thank you,' Neal prompted.

'Thanks.'

'Right, Emily, we'd better get back to your mother. Thanks again, Marta. Bye for now.'

'Bye, Neal. Tell Jane I'll give her a call.'

'Will do.'

She watched as the car eased away and disappeared down the road.

Jake said, 'Well. Does that mean we have the house to ourselves for an hour or two? For the first time in – how long? Two weeks?'

Marta closed the front door and stared at a chip in the cream paintwork thinking, *we must touch that up*, while her mind was processing more urgent thoughts – *don't let him do this, don't let him descend into sarcasm.*

'Yes. How shall we celebrate? It's probably too early in the day for Bollinger, so shall I make coffee?'

Jake followed her into the kitchen. 'Did you take some cash out of the drawer in my study, by the way?'

'Cash? No, why would I do that?'

'I didn't suppose you had, but there's some missing.'

'Really? How much?'

'About two hundred pounds.'

She whirled round, the kettle in her hand, her mouth open in shock. '*Two hundred pounds*? Jesus, Jake, I didn't know you had two hundred pounds, let alone cash like that lying around in the house.'

'I'd been saving my tips.'

'Why not put them in the bank?'

Marta had always adored Jake's hazel eyes, they'd been the first thing she'd noticed about him when they'd met. They were intelligent eyes, thoughtful but full of humour. The intelligence was still there, but there was little sign of humour, only a kind of weary defeat. She put down the kettle and took a step towards him, meaning to hold him, but he stepped away from her.

'Because I needed to have some money of my own, Marta.'

'You can spend the money in our joint account.'

'It's your money. Money you have earned.'

'And you. You put your wages in too.'

'They're nothing like what you're putting in.'

'That doesn't matter. You're doing what you can and we're managing.'

She tried to move closer again, but again he retreated.

'I hate this, Marta.'

'What? Hate what?'

'Living off your earnings.'

His body was all angles and joints and sharp edges, jagged and defensive.

'I felt as though that money was mine, really mine, so I could use it without having to dip into your money. It was important to me, Marta. And it's gone.'

How had she not realised how much Jake's independence meant to him?

'Are you sure it was as much as that? Could you have used some and forgotten?'

'Two hundred pounds? No.'

'Well ... where do you think it might have gone?'

'That friend of yours. His Luvviness. He's always snooping around.'

'Tom? Surely not. He wouldn't look in your drawers.'

Jake fiddled with an apple from the fruit bowl, lifted it, examined the skin, polished it, replaced it.

'There's a chance of some work in London, with a firm that did some work for me when I was at the bank. They need maternity cover for a few months.'

'*London*! Oh Jake.' Something in Marta twisted. 'Surely something will turn up here before too long. Let's look online again. Or you could call round the agencies on Monday, push them.'

Jake sucked in his breath. An orange caught his eye and he reached for it. He rested his fingertips on the bright skin, but didn't pick it up.

'Don't tell me what to do, Marta. You're always trying to organise me and I'm getting ... I said I'd think about London.'

Marta stared at him, stung. 'I didn't ... I only ... Jake, if I took the initiative it was only because I'm good at finding leads and networking.'

She bit on her lip to stop it trembling.

Jake sighed heavily, then reached out and put his arms round her, resting his cheek on her hair.

It'll be fine, she tried to persuade herself, leaning in to the warmth of his body, feeling the rough knit of his sweater against the soft skin of her face. We'll work it out. So long as he loves me, it'll be fine.

Chapter Seventeen

'Cool it, will you, Mum?'

'Cool it? When you've been missing half the night and we've been worried sick?'

'I'm home safe, aren't I? I was fine at Marta's.'

'What happened?'

Emily shuffled from one foot to the other. 'I didn't know Suze had posted the party on Facebook.'

'Why didn't you call us when it happened? Why run off to Marta's?'

Emily recalled exactly what she'd been doing when the first terrifying battering of the front door ricocheted round the house. She'd been about to launch on her very first snog with Robbie. She could feel the heat of his breath on her face, see his dark eyes narrowing as they focused on her. *On her*!

Her skin tingled with the memory of it and her heart began to race. Damn, her face was going scarlet! She spun round to hide her tell-tale cheeks from her mother. Run some water, rinse a mug, take a drink, anything to allow a few seconds to cool down, recover. She turned back, half hiding behind the mug.

'It was fine, Mum. Honest it was. Marta was near and I knew she wouldn't mind. I didn't want to have to wait around with all those NEDs there, I just wanted to get away.'

'Oh, Em.'

The pathos in her mother's voice cut through Emily's discomfiture. 'I'm all right, Mum. You worry too much.'

'You're only just sixteen, precious.'

Sympathy could only stretch so far. 'It's old enough to take responsibility for myself.'

'It's a tough world out there, Em. There's a million risks. D-drugs. B-booze.'

Her stuttering was getting impossible, Emily thought, torn between concern and irritation.

'B-boys. You don't know—'

'Mum, I *do* know. We get all that stuff at school. I don't do drugs, that's just stupid. And *you* drink alcohol. It's only when you go crazy that you have to worry about it and I don't even like the taste that much. I can look after myself. With boys, I mean. You know.' She looked away, embarrassed. 'You can trust me.'

'Sweetheart, you haven't exactly proved that, have you? I think it's best if we ground you, at least till after your concert.'

'That's not till Christmas!'

'That's enough time to think about your behaviour.'

'*Mu-um*!'

'D-don't argue, Emily. You've put your father and me through more in the last few hours than I can bear again. Just think about that.'

Emily glimpsed the brightness of tears in her mother's eyes as she walked out of the kitchen. Her own feelings were too complicated to analyse properly. Defiant, angry, indignant and perhaps ... perhaps just a tiny bit ashamed? But why? She hadn't really done anything wrong. If Suzy hadn't been so stupid as to put the details on Facebook, she'd have had a magic night with Robbie and no harm would have been done.

All recollection of fear was replaced by crossness at the sheer thoughtlessness of those NEDs. She found her mobile.

'Hi, Suze? Yeah, it's me. How's it going?'

'Dad's freaked out – the house is well trashed. You should see it—'

Suzy launched into a description of the chaos. Alcohol spilled everywhere, vomit on the new front-room carpet, syringes in the kitchen, the bathroom and behind the sofa. God knows what the mess was on one of the living-room chairs and the garden had been wrecked.

'Mum's in a right state about that. You know how she is about her garden.'

'Yeah. So what's happening?'

'Nothing much. Dad's stalking round with a clipboard, making notes for the insurance. Mum's just dabbing her eyes with a boxful of hankies and wailing, "My precious begonias".'

Emily giggled. 'Is she really mad?'

'A bit. She'll calm down. They're like, "so long as you weren't hurt, darling, it's just things, nobody's died." I've got them around to thinking it was all their fault anyway. They shouldn't have gone away for the night. What about you? What happened when you left here? I lost the plot about then.'

'I went to Marta Davidson's, you know? Mum's friend. She lives not too far from you.'

'Cool. So you stayed there?'

'Yeah. Just got back. Haven't heard from Robbie yet though.'

'Where did he go?'

Emily's shoulders hunched. 'Not sure.'

'Didn't he take you to Marta's?'

'No, he legged it with some of the other guys.'

'What a jerk.'

'Suzy! He's so not a jerk.'

'Why'd he run off then?'

'You know,' Emily said feebly. 'Anyway, I'm going to call him now.'

'Don't.'

'Why not?'

'Well, for a start, boys don't like girls who do the running. Let him call you.'

'Okay,' Emily said dubiously, remembering Robbie's broad shoulders and the slenderness of his hips in his low-slung jeans.

131

'Trust me, Em. I know about these things.'

Suzy, a veteran of half-a-dozen relationships, did know, reflected Emily. Smart, sassy, fearless, she drew boys to her like a scented flower attracted bees. She ended the call with the usual kisses and promises to phone again soon, set down her phone, and waited.

She didn't have to hold her breath too long. When her mobile launched into the Hayden cello concerto – her favourite – she managed to snatch it from the dresser just as Ross's hand shot out to pick it up.

'Get off, Ross, it's mine.'

'Just trying to be helpful.'

'Yeah, right,' Emily said sarcastically then, seeing the name Robbie flashing on the screen, inhaled sharply and sped out of the kitchen. 'Back in a minute.'

'Supper's ready, Emily,' her father called after her.

'Yeah, just coming.' She pressed the green button as she ran and tried to sound nonchalant. 'Hi.'

'Ems? You okay?'

'Yeah, sure. You?'

'Cool. I was worried about you. I didn't see you in that mob. What happened?'

A clear vision flashed in front of Emily, of Andy, Robbie's friend, scurrying to the window in the upstairs bedroom where they'd all been sprawled, looking out and saying in a shrill, scared voice, 'Oh my God, oh my God, they've got baseball bats,' as another bang reverberated round the room.

There'd been a chorus of 'Shit!' and 'Let's get out of her, fast!' and a mad rush for the door, during which she'd been knocked over and left doubled up on the floor, the imprint of a foot clear on her hand. But he hadn't meant to leave her. Robbie wouldn't have done that. He must've thought she'd been with him, that they'd meet up outside and head off safely together.

'I don't know. When I got out, I couldn't see you,' she said, her voice small.

'I looked for you everywhere, babes. Didn't know what had happened.'

'I got knocked over. It took me a few minutes to get out. I made it just before the front door came down.'

'You okay though? What did you do?'

'I went to a friend of my mum's. I stayed the night there. You?'

'Oh, we headed back into town, ended up in some club.'

Emily was shocked. He sounded so casual about it. He'd run off and left her – and then gone off clubbing as though nothing had happened!

'Oh,' she said, her voice little more than a whisper.

'I'd've called but my battery'd gone flat.'

'Emily! Supper's on the table!' Her father's voice was sounding stern.

'That your dad?' Robbie asked.

'Yeah. I've got to go.'

'Thought we might hang out on Thursday. After orchestra?'

With a bump and a jolt, her heart restarted. He still wanted to see her! He really liked her! Then she remembered her mother's curfew. Bother.

'Okay,' she said, a smile creeping back into her voice. She'd work something out.

'Emily!' Cross now.

'Coming!' She turned back to her phone. 'Cool,' she said. 'See you.'

'See you, babes.'

She sauntered back into the kitchen. Macaroni cheese, the way her mum made it, with a crispy cheese and cornflake topping. Yum.

'I'm ravenous,' she said appreciatively, and was surprised to find that it was true.

Chapter Eighteen

It was eleven o'clock on Saturday morning and Carrie Edwards, although aspiring to one of the two partner's offices on the third floor of Ascher Frew that were currently standing empty, was still sitting at her corner desk in the open-plan office on the second. It had the merit, at least, of being near the window – she had won that much seniority. Frustratingly, though, she was now the most senior lawyer in the firm who still did not have a partnership.

She willed herself to concentrate on the stack of closely typed papers in front of her and prayed that this was something that would be put right very soon. It was all very well having a smart, single, professional lifestyle but her ambition demanded status.

Words jumped and jiggled in front of her eyes, their sense and order scrambling. '*Put the remaining assets into ... assets put the ... ensure that the estate taxable bulk of does not ... fund trust set up for the marriage offspring of the first ... asset prudent for the purposes of management ...*'

Damn Tom Vallely. Carrie put a hand to her forehead, where she could feel the barely congealed line of the gash from her fall. Perhaps she should have gone to hospital? She took a small mirror out of her handbag and examined the damage. Her eye was swollen and turning a dark shade of blackcurrant. She could only half open it, but the cut wasn't gaping. It looked tender, but not serious. With luck, there wouldn't be any scarring. There were still two weeks to go till her partnership review and it would have healed by then. No doubt there'd be some ribbing on Monday, but she'd just have to put up with that. She had forty-eight hours to get her story sharpened up. Fall ... pavement

... no she had not been drunk, she'd merely been wearing an over-ambitious pair of Christian Louboutin gladiator heels. Enough. Back to Sir Edward Chalmers and his complex estate-management plans.

On her desk, beneath the pile of papers, the office phone warbled. Not Tom, surely? She hesitated, reached out her hand then retracted it once more, undecided. It might be one of the partners, checking on some point for this job. Steeling herself, she picked up the receiver.

'Carrie Edwards.'

'Carrie? It's Marta.'

'Oh.' Relief flooded through her like valium, bringing her heart rate down by several beats. Marta. Just Marta. 'What do you want?'

'Uh, well – a "hello" would be nice.'

'Hi, Marta. Sorry. You caught me on the hop.'

'What are you doing in that place anyway? It's Saturday.'

'I've got an urgent job on. And a partnership review coming up. Got to be seen to be eager.'

'Time for a coffee?'

'Not really, no. Sorry.'

'Oh.'

She could hear the disappointment in Marta's voice.

'Why are you asking?'

'I really need to talk'

'Is something wrong?'

'Nothing. And everything. Please Carrie. Just half an hour. I'll come to the café on the corner. I'm sure you could handle a short break.'

Carrie hesitated. She really wasn't achieving much and a coffee would do her no harm. On the other hand, how was she going to explain her bruising?

'Okay Marta, a quick one. What time?'

'Ten minutes? I'm in town.'

'See you there.

136

Everyone was looking at her – at least, that was how Carrie felt as she swayed into the café. Heads turned, people stared and Marta, rising from the corner table where she had already established herself, said with concern, 'Jesus, Carrie, what happened?'

No-one was looking really. Carrie slid into the empty chair next to Marta and tried to think rationally. Okay, so heads had perhaps turned for a second, but who cared about her face, for heaven's sake? Be calm.

'I knew I should never have bought those new sandals. You know, the Roman slave sandals with the five-inch heels?'

Marta laughed. 'Did you fall?'

Carrie nodded. Pain flashed through her skull and she lifted her hand automatically towards the site of ignition, then put it on her lap and forced herself to be still. She tried a smile and when that worked turned it into a laugh.

'It's funny now,' she lied, 'but it was painful at the time. I got out of the car and simply fell up the pavement.'

'You were *driving* in them?'

'Well, yes.'

'You didn't twist your ankle?'

'No, just banged my head. I'm going to get some comments on Monday.'

'You certainly are. Were you on your own?'

Over the years, Carrie had developed a skilful and harmless line of deviousness where Marta and Jane were concerned. Rather than suffer their endless efforts to match her up with some unsuitable male or other – Marta was particularly bad about this – she had cultivated a number of platonic escorts. Sometimes she really did go out with them – they were particularly useful for theatre outings or dinner engagements – but quite often she simply made up stories around them.

'No, no,' she said blithely, 'I was with Jim Anderson. We were going to the cinema. *Were* going,' she added, looking wry.

'I ended up with a pack of cold peas on my head and a night in.'

'Poor you.' Marta was all sympathy. 'Are you really okay?'

'I am. Can we talk about something else, please? Like what's bothering you? And what about that coffee you promised me?'

'It's Jane,' Marta said, sliding without further persuasion into her own agenda as soon as Carrie's coffee was on the table. 'She's mad at me. And I'm beginning to think she's gone a bit ... well, you know ... she seems to have reverted ... Remember the old stutter? When she first came to our school? She was so shy, so unsure of herself. We got rid of it – at least, I don't remember hearing it for years and years now – but it's back.'

'Whoa, hold on there. One thing at a time. Why is Jane mad at you?'

Marta pushed back her hair and bent her head forward to take a sip of coffee. Carrie, studying her carefully, noticed tiny crow's feet at the corners of her friend's eyes and the beginnings of slight vertical lines above her mouth. We are getting older, she thought. Life around us is changing. Perhaps even our friendship is changing.

Impulsively she leant forward and kissed Marta on the cheek, an awkward gesture in the confines of the café.

Marta smiled. 'What was that for?'

'Just because.' At Marta's look of enquiry, she expanded, 'Because you're you. You're lovely. And you're my friend. Now tell all.'

'It's funny,' Marta mused, with an expression that suggested she found it anything but. 'Jane was just – well – Jane, until that night I had you all round for dinner. She's been really weird ever since. And Jake and I were doing all right until Tom came to stay, but now Jake's really snippy. I don't suppose it's Tom's fault,' she said, always reluctant to criticise, 'just, well, it's a bit difficult having someone in your house and he is staying longer than I expected him to.'

Unable to hide the trembling of her hands from Marta,

Carrie rested them on her knees, under the table. Tom Vallely was dangerous. In inviting him back into their lives, Marta had unwittingly unleashed a dark force. She made herself laugh.

'Little Miss Do-Good. That's what we always used to call you, isn't it? Baa-aa. You've got such a big heart, sweetie, but sometimes it reaches out without thinking of the consequences. Go see Jane. Talk to her. She's twitchy because Emily's experimenting with adulthood. As for Jake – Tom's away now, isn't he?'

'More or less. He'll have to come back to collect his stuff, but he's off south to see his agent.'

'So relax. Support Jake, but don't push him. Find your own space, the two of you. Everything will work out fine.'

'You think?' Marta said doubtfully.

Carrie surveyed her. Simple blouse, pale blue cashmere cardi, neatly pressed black jeans, soft calf-length brown leather boots – Marta always had her own beautiful, fresh style. She looked barely a day older than when she left school. She was loving, well-meaning and sweet – how could you not love Marta?

'Don't beat yourself up, my love.'

As she said the words, Carrie felt their irony. She lifted her fingers to the bruising on her forehead and touched the spot lightly.

Don't beat yourself up. There are others who will do that for you.

Chapter Nineteen

Tom spent the morning shopping in Glasgow. He had the best part of two hundred pounds in his pocket, ready cash. His credit card hit its limit when he had rung the tills for two shirts, a new alpaca sweater and a couple of pairs of chinos, so the notes came in handy for some new loafers and the Ellis Cashmore book on celebrity culture he'd been looking for. The expedition helped to improve his mood, which had not been sunny when he'd woken up to find Carrie had gone.

He needed Carrie to be in his power. Sexually, she couldn't resist him, that much was obvious – talk about a bitch on heat – but her overnight disappearance did not please him one bit.

'Coffee please, black and very strong.'

He made the effort to smile at the curvy waitress in the coffee shop in Sauchiehall Street and was rewarded with blushing admiration. If only it was a bit later and they had somewhere to go...

'What's your name, darling?'

'Catriona, but everyone calls me Cat.'

'Cat. Lovely. More like a sweet little kitten though.'

Outside, it had started to rain. They said that Glasgow was four times wetter than Edinburgh and Tom could believe it. In all his visits to the city, he couldn't ever remember it being completely dry. Still, the place did have some merits – the shopping was good, and the patter. And, of course, the crumpet.

'Thanks, Cat.'

He smiled again at the girl as she set down his coffee. He put his hand over hers for a moment and enjoyed the reappearance of the blush. Her backside, as she sashayed self-consciously back to the counter, was worth watching too.

For a few minutes he sat, allowing the world to move around him, drifting through time and place – Jane; Carrie; Serena. Others. Dozens of others, their faces shadowy, their names forgotten, the memory of their bodies vague. He reached into his pocket, slid out a notebook and flipped through it. Names, numbers, notes – reminders of some great nights and some shocking ones. Coded encounters, pseudonyms, real names too. Take AN Other, for example. Code name for Anya Merton. Tom smiled broadly. He had 'taken' her, just about every way it was possible. What a night that had been, and Anya such a big star, too. Sadly, her long-term partner had arrived from the States and she'd been unable to give a repeat performance.

He ran his finger down the page. Here was a name, Kate H. He shook his head fondly, his smile broadening. Kate H was a television presenter, the sweet-looking, wholesome girl on a breakfast show whose career had taken off largely because she was married to a ferociously ambitious director. The world would be very interested in what he had to say about Kate H. Very interested indeed.

His mobile rang, interrupting the train of his thoughts. Angela.

'Hi.' Tom knew he was sounding tetchy. The audition for *Emergency Admissions* had been just twenty-four hours ago and he had no expectation of a decision yet. His agent's call bordered on the tedious. 'What's cooking, darling?'

Angela sounded breathy. '*Tom.*'

'Yeah?' He opened a sachet of sugar and absently emptied it into his coffee.

'You'll never guess.'

'You're right, I won't.'

Angela could be very irritating. He was not going to play her game.

'Go on. Guess.'

'Just tell me, Angela darling,' Tom sighed, lifting his coffee for a sip with his free hand.

'You've got the part.'

Tom froze, the coffee an inch from his lips. 'Say again?'

'You've got the part. Mr Darling, the surgeon. In *Emergency Admissions*.'

The cup clattered so loudly on the saucer as Tom dropped it that heads turned. His smile this time was genuine. 'You're kidding me? Already?'

'They *loved* you, darling. Absolutely *loved* you. Left a message on my phone last night after the auditions finished, but I didn't pick it up till right now. Isn't it exciting? Gosh. This could be it, Tom. The biggest thing since *After Eden*. Shall I come up to Edinburgh? Go over everything? Celebrate?'

'Christ, no. I'll come down.'

'Really? When?'

He thought for a second. 'Today. I'm still in Glasgow. I'll head back to Edinburgh and pack up my things, get a train down. I'll see you Monday, first thing.'

'You could come round tonight. To my flat in town? Have just a teensy-weensy private celebration before we sign and seal the deal next week?' Her voice was tentative with overtones of wistfulness.

'Why not?'

'Really?'

'Yeah. I'll call when I get into town. You can congratulate me then.'

Tom snapped off his phone and sat, grinning inanely at the world from the dry shelter of the café. Why not celebrate by shagging Angela? It would make her happy and besides, screwing Carrie last night had done little more than give him an appetite.

When Tom arrived back at Marta's cottage in Portobello, no-one was at home. He began to shuffle his few belongings into his case. Socks, underpants, some papers and books, his *Glass Ornament* script, a sweater. Anything else? He bent to check under the bed, spotted a book half hidden among some discarded rubbish. It had been kicked almost out of reach. Irritated, he burrowed into the narrow space to reach it.

Unnoticed, his pocket notebook slid first one inch out of its resting place, then another, and as he made the final lunge for the errant book, it finally slid among the crumpled tissues and screwed up wrappers and lay there, hidden.

The doorbell rang. Shit. He'd hoped to get away unseen. He backed out of the narrow space and peered out of the window. A plumber's van was parked in the road outside the cottage. Not so bad, then. The bell pealed again, its note insistent. Tom picked up his case and wandered downstairs. He still had to find his fedora.

'Yeah?'

'Morrison, plumber.' The man standing there was short and rotund, with thinning curly hair and bad teeth.

'So?'

'Here to mend the washing machine. Mrs Davidson not in?'

'No.'

Tom stared at him. Marta had said something about a washing machine the day he'd bumped into her at the café, hadn't she? She'd given him the key intended for the plumber. He stepped aside, opened the door. No skin off his nose.

'Come on in then.'

The man headed to the kitchen, obviously familiar with the layout of the house. Tom left him to it and glanced around. This was where he had come in that first day. Funny, it seemed an age ago now. Marta had arranged that charming little dinner, designed to surprise all her guests. It had done that all right. He'd seen the shock on Jane's face in an instant and Carrie had been scarcely less able to hide her dismay. There had been a few minutes when he'd wondered whether coming to Edinburgh had been a good idea, but then it had all become such fun. Free fun at that. He hadn't had to pay a penny for a bed since he'd arrived at Marta's, hotels included. Not bad going.

He'd tossed his hat here that first day, onto the hall stand, but there was no fedora there now. Living room? Nope. Kitchen? Already the washing machine was in the middle of the floor.

'All right, mate?'

Getting a grunt in return, he scanned the kitchen. Nothing. In the bathroom he spotted Jake's iPod and pocketed it. Fedora? Not in Jake and Marta's bedroom or en suite, nor in the airing cupboard. When had he had it last? He stood, thinking. Downstairs there were noises of hammering and clattering.

Jane's house. Yup. That was it. Definitely. He'd arrived in the damp and left in the sunshine and had forgotten to put it back on. Unlike him but hey, he'd had other things on his mind.

One thirty already. He'd need to speed things up a little if he was to get a train south, but he was reluctant to leave his favourite hat in Edinburgh and besides, if Janie was at home there was always the chance of a little more fun. He put his key on the hallstand, raided the contents of the change pot one last time – with a net gain of four pounds eighty-three pence – and closed the door behind him. It had been a cool place to stay but he wouldn't be writing any thank-you letters.

'Tom!'

'Hello, Janie. On your own?'

Jane was looking even skinnier than he remembered.

'Neal's due home any minute.'

She was lying. He could always tell.

'Great. I'm not staying long anyway. I just came for my hat.' He could see it, behind Jane, precarious atop a bundle of coats and jackets and what looked like a bedraggled duck. 'And to say goodbye.'

She stepped aside hesitantly as he inched assertively forward. 'G-goodbye?'

'You heard, darling. G-g-goodbye.'

He imitated her stutter cruelly but with great accuracy. Bending, he took her wrist in one hand and hooked up her chin with the other.

'Now my darling girl, what is it you're so afraid of? You always were a little mouse.'

A stifled, inarticulate sob was the only reply.

'Jesus, Janie, what's to be scared about?'

He nudged her away from him and studied her.

'Hard to believe you've got three kids. You're such a little scrap of a thing yourself. What kind of a mother are you, Jane? What do your kids make of you, hey? Do they run rings round you?' He laughed. 'Bet they do. And yet you thought you could make a decent fist of mothering back in the day?'

Again the flicker of the eyes. His gaze intensified.

'I'm assuming you had the thing adopted?' he said with enough force in his voice to make her stagger back a step. 'I half thought you might be stupid enough to keep it. I had an insane fantasy that you might even try to bring it up yourself, but you wouldn't have had the guts for that, would you? What would that strait-laced man of yours have said about that? Huh?'

Again the shiftiness in the eyes, and a subtle change in her expression that gave him pause for thought. 'Or did you change your mind and have the termination?'

Jane's hand flew to her mouth and her eyes filled with tears.

'You did, didn't you? Well, well, well. Little Janie, who would have thought it? And Neal so firmly against abortion, he was telling us all.'

'You won't—'

It was barely a whimper. He lifted his hand to stroke her cheek and felt her move away from him, startled, like a wild thing.

'Won't what, Janie darling?' he said, softly. 'Won't tell your man?'

That was it. He could see it in the way she slid her eyes away from him and looked at the floor, trembling. She was terrified that her husband would find out the truth. He laughed lightly and shook his head slowly, tutting under his breath.

'He doesn't know, does he? Oh Janie, Janie, Janie. A secret, eh? And such a very big one.'

'There's no secret. Neal and I have no secrets.'

'Oh really? Is that right? You know, I think I'll check with Carrie. Best to be sure of one's facts, don't you think? Especially when it's my child we're talking about.'

'Carrie knows nothing!' Jane's voice was frantic. 'You mustn't ask Carrie. She doesn't know anything about it!'

Tom reached up for his hat, put his on his head at a jaunty angle.

'For friends,' he said easily, 'it seems to me that you girls are oddly lacking in the usual array of female confidences. You never told Carrie about the baby? Such a very big thing in your life, surely? And did Carrie ever tell you about our affair?'

He turned to go, then paused and looked back at Jane.

'No? Do you know, I thought perhaps she hadn't,' he said shaking his head as if in wonderment, his voice mocking. 'Friends, eh? Friends.'

He went out into the cool Edinburgh afternoon, smiling at his own joke. By the time he had reached the garden gate he was humming.

Oh, life was good. Thanks to Marta he had found a wonderful hornet's nest to stir and with a bit of luck it could prove to be a profitable one. And thanks to dear Marta he had landed a part that might well be life changing.

Angela was waiting, legs akimbo, in London, and in a matter of weeks he should be a household name, thanks to *Emergency Admissions*.

Yes, life was good.

Behind him Jane stood exactly as he had left her, both hands on her throat, her mouth wide open, her face drained of all colour.

Getting a last-minute flight was expensive – but what the hell, he could afford it now. Tom slid through the security checks at Edinburgh airport in a cloud of euphoria. He could hardly stop smiling.

'Your birthday, is it?' the burly woman pulling the trays through the x-ray machine asked. Her mouth was curled in an unlikely rictus that approximated a grin.

'No, but you can pat me down any time, darling,' Tom flirted, not allowing even her Rosa Klebb looks to deter him.

'I wish.'

He winked at her and collected his belongings. Belt, passport, wallet, small change, phone, noteb— Notebook? Where was his notebook? Tom felt feverishly in his pockets for his precious journal. He must have packed it. Lifting his case, he retreated to a corner of the security area and started to rake through it. Socks, pants, all that, but no notebook. It was absolutely not among any of his belongings, nor in any of his pockets.

He crushed everything back into his case and stalked into the departure lounge. He had to find the notebook. Apart from all his precious records, it had a stack of pawn tickets tucked inside it, each with his name and London address – traceable and incriminating.

Think, man.

Yes. He'd had it in the café in Glasgow, definitely.

Quickly he searched for the phone number, found it, dialled, schooled his voice to calmness. 'I was in your café this morning. Is that Cat, by any chance?'

'Aye, this is Cat.'

'I'm Tom. The guy in the corner? We had a chat.'

'Aye, I remember.'

Her accent was much broader than he remembered. He tried to tune his ear in and persisted.

'Cat, sweetheart, I believe I left my notebook in your lovely café. Do you have it there?'

'I dinnae think so. Haud on a wee minute.'

He waited. In the background he could hear voices, their conversation too distant for him to make out, then she was back on the line.

'Naw. Sorry. It's no' here.'

Shit. 'Are you absolutely sure? I was sitting by the window—'

'Ah ken where ye were sittin'. It's no here.'

He ended the call, all thoughts of charm fleeing. No point in wasting energy on her now.

What could have happened? He'd hopped on a train to Edinburgh, but he hadn't looked at the notebook on the train, he was sure of it. He'd gone to Marta's and packed, but definitely hadn't emptied his pockets. Then to Janie's, but again, there had been no occasion to look at his notebook.

What, then? It had been picked up by someone in the café, someone who had taken his seat before the place had been cleared possibly. That seemed the most likely.

The loss was catastrophic. He had to hope that whoever had found the book would put it in an envelope and post it to him. He had to pray for it. He might even be moved to send a reward.

Above him, the departures board flashed up his gate. Time to go.

There was nothing he could do about it now.

Chapter Twenty

Marta spotted Tom's keys as soon as she let herself in. They were sitting neatly on the hall table like a precious gift.

He's gone. The realisation brought a shaft of sunlight into her heart.

Beside the keys, an envelope. She ripped it open. A bill from Mr Morrison for the repair of the washing machine. Reasonable, thank heavens. Tom or Jake must have let him in.

'Jake? Hi! I'm home!'

Her answer was a crash and a muffled thud from upstairs.

'Jake?'

She took the stairs two at a time, her slim legs scissoring across the treads.

'What's happened? Are you all right?'

He was in Tom's room – the spare room, she corrected herself mentally, spare. Free. Empty. Vide. Frei. The start of a new era of peace and order, of togetherness and renewal.

But Jake was looking anything but renewed. He'd been raking his hair with his hands, a clear sign of stress, and he was flushed. The bedclothes were heaped in an untidy pile behind the door and the bed itself was skewed across the room.

'What are you doing?'

Now that she could see he was unhurt, irritation surfaced. He didn't have to strip the bed or tidy and clean the room, she would have done that. Marta liked cleaning, she found it therapeutic. What she did not like was disorder. She stepped into the room to straighten the bed.

'You should have left that to me.'

'Left what?' Jake asked shortly, dropping on his knees behind the bed so that all she could see was his rump. She pulled up short, unable to move the bed until he shifted.

'The bed. The tidying. Now that Tom's gone—'

'Gone.' Jake's head appeared above the mattress and he twisted back onto his feet. 'He's gone all right – and the bugger's taken my iPod with him.'

'Your iPod? Surely not.'

'It's disappeared, Marta. I left it in the bathroom this morning and unless you have "tidied" it somewhere in your inimitable way, it has disappeared. Conjured by His Luvviness's amazing and famous sleight of hand from the cold, hard surface of the bathroom ledge into some snug and barely visible pocket no doubt.'

'I can't believe Tom would do that, Jake. Are you quite sure—'

'I've looked everywhere.'

'Mr Morrison was here,' Marta said, clutching at an unlikely straw in the form of Archie Morrison's well-padded person.

Jake stopped moving restlessly and stared at her.

'Are you seriously suggesting Mr Morrison came up to the bathroom and pocketed my iPod?'

The friendly plumber had fixed the leaky taps, the faulty central heating, the badly lagged pipes and broken cisterns in Jake's parent's aging 1930s bungalow so often that Mrs Davidson Senior almost regarded him as one of the family.

Marta quailed.

'No,' she admitted, 'I don't think your playlist would be quite Mr Morrison's thing.'

Jake, his hands clutching a small pile of assorted packaging he had salvaged from under the bed, sat heavily on the mattress.

'I've been offered that contract in London.'

'Oh.' She swayed and leaned back against the doorpost for support. 'Oh, Jake.'

Her mouth was dry.

'You won't take it,' she managed at last. It came out not as a question but a statement.

Jake's nostrils flared, his eyes widened and he turned to her with barely suppressed violence. Marta jerked back with shock, and her elbow hit the door frame with a jarring crunch.

'Don't tell me what I will or won't do, Marta. I'm sick of it. Absolutely sick of it, do you hear me? For years you've told me what I should do – do you realise that? Go for this promotion, Jake, move to that office. Buy some new clothes, Jake – or worse still, you've gone and bought them for me as though I don't even have a mind or an opinion of my own. We'll spend Christmas here, New Year there. We'll go to Corfu for our holidays. We'll learn to ski. There's been no end to your decision-making, Marta.'

'I thought—'

'What? What did you think, exactly?'

'You didn't seem to mind. I thought you liked being organised. You've always been so absorbed in your own work, you seemed quite pleased that things just ... happened ... around you.'

He had got up from the bed and was staring out of the window. 'This cottage ... living in Edinburgh, for Christ's sake ... did I ever have any part in any of the big decisions of our lives?'

She took a tentative step towards him. 'Jake? What's the matter, darling? What's changed? If you're upset about Tom, he's gone now—'

'Tom! Tom!'

He swivelled round so swiftly that she squeaked like a frightened kitten.

He said, slowly and carefully, 'Bringing Tom Vallely here to stay was a perfect example of just what is wrong in our relationship, Marta. You spend your entire life helping people. Very laudable, I'm sure. Unfortunately, sometimes that has a serious impact on the people closest to you and you just don't think it through before you go jumping in feet first.'

'That's not true!'

'Think about it. Just when I needed your support most, all I got was an intruder in our lives. Making himself at home. Helping himself to our food, our drink, our money—'

'I didn't know that he would—'

'Know? I don't suppose you did, Marta. But you didn't stop to think either, did you? That day he arrived – you hadn't even bothered to call me, to let me know he was coming.'

Disbelief at the change in her husband was changing into dread. All this anger ... something was pouring out of him that had clearly been long suppressed, something that altered him, made him a different person.

Or perhaps it wasn't like that at all? Maybe the fault was hers, maybe she'd been blind to his needs and his feelings, selfish in a way she had never understood.

'Don't do this, Jake. I know it's only for a few months, but don't go. Please? I really need you.' When did I last tell him I loved him? She raked her memory and found no references. 'I love you. Don't you love me?'

'Love you?'

Jake ran his hand through his hair. She watched as it stood on end and longed to go to him, smooth it down, but didn't dare.

'I don't know any more, Marta. I can say that quite truthfully. Maybe it's not all your fault. It was easier for me to let you make the decisions. But things have changed. I lost my job.'

The earlier anger had dissipated and sad weariness had replaced it.

'I've tried so hard to hold everything together, gone along with your suggestions about agencies, applications, revamping my CV. I've tried really hard – and when that didn't work, I took the job in the bar.'

Marta held her breath.

'I've been on the edge, Marta, hanging on above a sheer drop. The last thing I could handle was competing for your attention ...'

His voice trailed away and the uncharacteristic flare of temper subsided.

How had things come to this? From a mislaid iPod to a full-scale row.

'Let's talk again later, Jake, you're too upset right now. Here, give me a hug.'

The fury might have burned itself out, but he clearly wasn't prepared to unbend.

'I found this lot under the bed,' he said, avoiding her arms and instead indicating the rubbish he'd found. He picked out one item and held it out to her. 'Looks like a notebook of some kind. You might want to post it back to him. I'm doing a double shift tonight. I'll sleep in here. Tomorrow I'll pack some stuff and move to my mate's until I go down to London.'

'Jake! You aren't serious? This doesn't have to happen. Stay. Surely we can talk at least?'

'I need space, Marta. I know it's a corny old line, but Christ, how I understand what it means. I've lost all my self-respect, I don't really know who I am anymore. I haven't worked in marketing for the best part of a year, I feel as though part of me has died and there's nothing left to offer. It's no good. You're trying to have the perfect life, in the perfect home, with the perfect family, but the problem is I'm not perfect. I'm really not.'

'I don't want you to be perfect! I just want you to be you.'

'Here.' He shoved the notebook into her hands. 'I'll see you tomorrow, before I go.'

Marta stood in the empty room and stared after his retreating figure. She dropped Tom Vallely's notebook on the chest of drawers. The man had caused enough trouble. Posting the thing back to him could wait.

Marta watched Jake leave for his shift. His slight figure was hunched over as he marched along the path with his head down and his chin tucked in to his chest. Behind him, the gate closed with a fierce clang and in seconds he was out of sight.

The evening stretched out interminably. The cottage, so familiar and cherished, no longer felt like a haven of tranquility. Marching restlessly from kitchen to bedroom, from bedroom to hall, from hall to shower room and back to bedroom, Marta bundled Tom's sheets into the washing machine and started the cycle. She tidied the kitchen and scrubbed it from top to bottom. The bathroom got special attention. By the time she had finished cleaning the bath and shower they gleamed with unnatural brightness. She tackled the en suite, using bleach on an old toothbrush to attack the greying grout and lifting the trap in the shower completely to remove the hair – hers mostly – that had accumulated there.

In the living room, she vacuumed the carpet and puffed up the cushions, straightened the sofa, wiped down the window. She dusted the clock that sat on the small mantelpiece. At one end stood a small Moorcroft vase, a gift from her parents on some special birthday. She had always loved its rich dark colours, the sweet mystery of its swirling leaves and flowers. She dusted it and replaced it gently. At the other end was a glass bird, heavy, rounded, stylised, its core dark red, a thick layer of clear glass defining its outer shape. The bird had come from Jake's family, from an aunt or a grandmother, she thought. Marta could no longer remember the story of its provenance, but it formed some part of his heritage. She picked it up carefully and rubbed the cloth over it. She had dusted the thing a thousand times but for some reason, today, its weight seemed to pull and drag. She hurried to replace it, caught the long tail on the edge of the marble mantelpiece, felt the impact before hastily setting it down. There. She stood back and surveyed it. No damage. Nothing had happened. It was fine.

Turning, she started to move towards the door. A brittle noise made her stop, her heart racing. She turned, stared – and saw the tail, neatly severed, lying on the marble.

She flung herself on the sofa and howled.

Chapter Twenty-one

'Finished the proposal for Sir Edward Chalmers' estate planning yet, Carrie? Meeting's starting in half an hour.'

Peter Shepherd, the senior partner to whom Carrie reported, came across to her desk. It was eight-thirty on Monday morning and she had already been at work for two hours. Forgetting her bruises, she turned and answered, 'Just five minutes, Peter, and I'll print everything out.'

'Christ, what happened to you?' Peter was startled.

Carrie's hand flew up to her face. 'Oh, I'd forgotten. It's nothing. I fell over my new heels on Friday night.'

She'd spent nearly an hour this morning trying to apply make-up over the bruises, before finally deciding that it looked even worse and cleaning it all off again.

'You women and your slavery to fashion,' Peter grumbled, his ruddy face breaking into a grin. A big, gentle man, he had been a great mentor and supporter. Soon he would be telling her the result of her partnership review, conducted in the privacy of a full partnership meeting, the decisions relayed thereafter to the hopeful few. With a little luck and a fair following wind, there would be champagne and congratulations all round.

'Hey, I'm in good company,' Carrie said, elaborating her lie. 'Naomi Campbell fell off her heels a bit more publicly on one occasion, if you remember. And at least I didn't break my ankle.'

Peter glanced down at the mustard Ferragamo pumps she had selected today and nodded approval. 'You won't fall over those, at least. Shame about the face though.'

157

'Didn't stop me from working all weekend,' Carrie smiled ingratiatingly at him. She needed to flag up her eagerness at every opportunity.

'Good, good,' Peter was walking away, his mind clearly already on some other matter. 'Good, good.'

The words floated across the room, which was now filling up as others arrived to embark on their week's duties. A colleague, his thick black hair apparently still wet from his morning shower, grinned at her as he hung up his coat. Peter was well known for his vague utterances.

Carrie, encouraged, bent her head to her work, battling the half-hour deadline. With just a few minutes to go, she heard the muffled sounds of her mobile, its ring tone forcing itself impudently out of the confines of her bag. Quickly, she pressed 'Print' and bent to retrieve her phone.

Tom.

Her heart, jump-started by the name on the screen, accelerated into overdrive. A few seconds later her brain kicked in, sent an instruction to her finger and she pressed 'Divert'. By the time she had retrieved her papers from the printer on the other side of the room, both a voice message and a text awaited her. No time to retrieve the voice mail. Quickly, she scanned the text.

<Hi bed buddy. Need your help. Do believe you owe me? Call me. Tom.>

Owe him? Owe him? Owe him what, for heaven's sake? The message defied logic. Distractedly, she pulled together her papers, her notebook, her diary and her thoughts and headed for the door. Whatever Tom Vallely wanted, Sir Edward Chalmers had first call on her time.

The appointment did not go well. After less than ten minutes it became clear that, despite all the hours she had put in over the weekend, Carrie had omitted to take into account a vital piece of information and the simple oversight had invalidated most of the rest of her work. Peter Shepherd, covering smoothly, took over as much as he could, but they abandoned the meeting after less than an hour, unable to progress matters in the way that had been expected.

'I'm so sorry, Peter, so sorry,' Carrie said, over and over again after Sir Edward Chalmers had graciously departed. 'I don't know how it could have happened. My head ... I had such a headache on Saturday. The fall ... I'm so sorry.'

'Not to worry,' Peter smiled, but without the usual spark of warmth. 'I'm sure you'll have it sorted by Wednesday. We won't be able to bill him for the work you did, of course.'

'Of course not,' Carrie mumbled, trying to keep up with Peter as he strode along the corridor. 'I'll get it done, I promise you.'

Incompetence was hardly her hallmark – and to lose the smallest iota of her reputation for proficiency at this point was unfortunate, to say the least. Peter's comments were not exactly a threat – he was not given to that kind of language – but they were less than complimentary. Worse, she would have to work extremely hard to rectify the error in the couple of days left to her before the partnership meeting.

Implied threats appeared to be the order of the day. Later, finding the time and the courage to listen to Tom's message, she heard what sounded remarkably like a second ultimatum.

'Hi Carrie darling. So sorry you had to leave early. It was a blast. Listen, sweetie, I need a favour. That audition? I got the part. Good news, huh? So I can be out of your hair, D.A. Delight. We shoot in Manchester, so I'll need to get a flat there. Problem is, I'm a bit strapped for cash right now, so—' The 'so' hung suspended in time, its menace unspoken, before he resumed. 'But give me a bell and we can discuss a way round my little problem. Hey?'

At lunchtime Carrie snatched a quick chance for some air. She pounded the pavement down Queen Street Gardens towards

Stockbridge and thought through the options. Tom wanted money – so what was new? What hold did he have over her to force her to pay up?

One, the affair they had had sixteen years ago, while he'd still been living with Jane. Spilling that little secret would do her friendship with Jane no good at all.

And two, her lifestyle choice: Bed Buddies. Tom knew that Jane inclined to the puritanical and Marta to the naive and that there was every likelihood that she would have chosen to keep her personal life strictly that: personal.

There was, three, an outside chance that he would threaten to reveal her secret to the partners at Ascher Frew. He was smart enough to know that any question mark against her character would jeopardise her chances of success in the firm.

As she passed the traffic lights on Howe Street, she forced herself to be analytical. There were three choices open to her.

Option A, she could refuse to do whatever it was he was going to ask her.

Option B, she could comply with his request. Or, Option C, she could temporise, try to outwit him while she thought of the alternatives.

Perhaps it depended on what his demand was. 'I need your help.' What shape or form might that help take? Money, most likely, but maybe Tom would demand to see her again. Feebly, Carrie felt her forehead. Enough trouble had been caused by that little blow to her head already, she couldn't afford to expose herself to any possible further physical violence. She would pay almost anything to avoid that.

By the time she had tramped down Howe Street and north to Raeburn Place, Carrie was sweating with apprehension.

Get it over with, Carrie. You have no choice. Do it. Do it now. You haven't much time.

When she got to the charming Victorian artisan houses known as The Colonies, in a traffic-free spot next to the Water of Leith, she pulled out her mobile. Before she could change her mind, she dialled Tom's number.

'Hello, Delight.' The sound of his voice was chilling. Carrie sat down on a low wall, her phone clamped to her ear.

'Hi, Tom.'

'So sorry you had to leave so sharp on Saturday morning.'

'Yeah, me too,' Carrie lied, feeling sick.

'We could have had loads more fun.'

'I know.'

'And now I have to move to Manchester.'

'Yes! Congratulations, Tom, on getting the part. You must be pleased.'

'The part? I knew it was in the bag as soon as the audition was over. Half way through, really. I could tell from the reaction.'

'Congratulations again.' The man's ego was as big as a mountain. 'Big career move, huh?'

'Well, I've done television before, of course, Lots. But I guess a regular part won't do me any harm for a while.'

'No. Great.'

'Thing is, Carrie darling, nice as it sounds, the pay cheque won't kick in for month or more, so a little loan to help with the deposit on the rent wouldn't go amiss.'

'Won't your agent advance you the cash?'

Tom snorted with laughter. 'Angela? Tight as a rat's arse with cash. No, darling, it'll have to be you, I think.'

'I'm a bit tight myself this month.'

This time the laughter was full-bellied. 'Come on, Carrie, don't give me that. Short of cash? You? A partner in a big law firm, with your luxury flat and your smart car and no family to spend the money on?'

'I'm not a partner, Tom.'

'But soon will be. Anyway, I'm not trying to fleece you, darling,' he sounded nonchalant, 'just borrow a few hundred quid.'

'Do I hear an "or" somewhere?'

'Or?' He sounded injured. 'Or? You think I'm trying to blackmail you? Darling Carrie, nothing could be further from the truth. Though come to think of it I don't suppose your dear friend Jane would be too impressed if she knew you'd two-timed her in London.'

So she'd been right.

'And I guess your boss there in that smart law firm in Edinburgh would be, shall we say, just a little surprised to learn of some of your extra-curricular activities.'

'How much do you need, Tom?'

'Very kind of you to offer, darling. A couple of grand would set me on my way and I wouldn't need to trouble you again.'

'A couple of grand?'

'Come on, Carrie, what's that to you?'

'I could lend you five hundred.'

'Oh I think not. I'll need more than that to get the kind of flat I'll need. It's not so much, now, is it?'

Carrie sighed. There was little point in bargaining. Tom Vallely was very lacking in negotiating skills. 'All right. Just this once.'

'So sweet.'

'Tell me where to send the money.'

'A bank transfer would do just nicely, Carrie.' He gave her the details. 'What a pleasure it has been meeting you again.'

'Charmed, I'm sure.'

'Bye for now.'

'Goodbye Tom. I'll see you on the telly.'

She made the transfer at the bank in Stockbridge. Might as well get it over with. Half way up the hill, her pace slower now, she was beginning to set the incident aside and get her mind back on track, when her phone rang again.

'Hi Jane, great to hear you,' she answered, seeing the caller identity.

'How could you, Carrie? Friends for ever we swore at school. D-don't you remember? Friends. Is that what friends do? Well, is it?'

'Sorry?' Carrie said, taken aback by the ferocity of the verbal onslaught. 'What are you talking about, Jane?'

'You know what I'm talking about. Tom.'

'Tom?'

Christ! She knows.

'I asked you to take care of him and you—' The stutter, magnifying by the word, seemed to lock Jane's tongue in a complete knot. '—b-b-b-b-betrayed me.'

'I didn't. Jane, he told me it was over between you. He was just waiting for the best moment to tell you.'

The laugh that came down the line verged on the hysterical. 'Don't give me that. I was living with him. How could it be over?'

'He told me—'

'He told you. Right. And you believed him. You didn't even think to ask me if we had a problem before you jumped into b-bed with him?'

I should have asked Jane, Carrie thought, of course I should. Jane was absolutely right – you simply don't sleep with your best friend's man.

The guilt Carrie had felt for all these years rushed towards her like a tsunami and threatened to engulf her. Every instinct told her to turn and flee to safe ground – but where was safe? No chance of running and little chance of turning back the wave either. Still, she tried.

'I'm sorry, Jane. Really. So, so sorry. I didn't mean to ... he told me ... I believed ... what can I say? How can I make this better?'

But Jane was crying now, great sobs that made talking almost impossible. Carrie picked out some words.

'... Never trust you ... Emily ... Marta's stealing my daughter ... I thought we were friends ...'

163

'Jane, listen—'

How could she get her to calm down?

'—I'll come round. Let's talk. We've got to talk, Jane.'

'Fuck you, Carrie. Just fuck you.'

The line went dead.

Carrie stared at her phone.

Jane never swore – and she'd already transferred the money to Tom.

Christ, what a day.

Marta texted her four times in the afternoon, but Carrie, consumed with guilt about Jane and incandescent that Tom had manipulated her into giving him a great deal of cash, could not bear to get back to her. What would she say? Better to lie low.

Two messages from Marta on Tuesday. By Wednesday nothing.

Couldn't be urgent.

The summons to the top floor came sooner than Carrie had anticipated.

'Carrie? I know it's short notice, but could you come up to the boardroom please?'

The polished voice of the well-groomed and super-efficient Pammie Wynne-Armstrong, Henry Frew's right-hand woman, took Carrie by surprise. It was just two days after the rescheduled meeting with Sir Edward Chalmers.

'What, now?' she asked inelegantly.

'Yes, please, if you can.'

'Right. Of course. I'll be there in five minutes.'

The partnership. That was all Carrie could think of as she strode purposefully to the loo to tidy up, thanking the heavens that she was wearing the Cavalli jacket and, by chance, a very fine gold necklace, her favourite. What had prompted her to select them this morning? Some deep, hidden sense of anticipation?

Or pure luck? She fingered the necklace as she examined her reflection. At least the bruise had faded to a dull yellow that, finally, she had been able to browbeat into submission with a good tinted foundation. She took a brush out of her handbag and tidied her hair. Looking good.

Two minutes later she was knocking on the door of the boardroom.

'Hello, come in.'

Pammie, who never had a sleek black hair out of place, opened the door for her and waved her to a vacant chair. Henry Frew, white-haired but remarkably vigorous looking, sat at the head of the table. Susan James, head of Human Resources, was on his right, Pammie was making her way back to her chair on his left, then there was Peter Shepherd, glancing up at her, then away, then down at his papers. She advanced a few steps, enjoying the feel of the deep, rich pile of the carpet under her feet. This was what it was all about. She could smell success.

'Caroline. Thank you for coming so promptly and sorry to tear you away from your work.'

Henry, the essence of good manners, half stood to acknowledge her arrival, gesturing at an empty chair near the door.

Carrie smiled, sat down, placed her hands on the table, and smiled.

'As you know, we have been in the process of considering the possibility of appointing a new partner – or partners – to the firm.'

Henry picked up his glasses from the table and popped them on. He was looking down at some papers, but now he looked up at her and smiled apologetically.

'There's no way to say this that you're not going to find disappointing, Caroline, but the partners have decided not to extend the offer of a partnership to you at this time. After some considerations, it was felt that...'

Decided not to extend the offer of a partnership...

Not to extend...

No partnership...

As the words sank in, Carrie had the greatest difficulty in keeping her face still. No partnership. It was all she could think of. The words bounced round her brain. No partnership.

'...fact is, we have not felt that you have brought enough new business in to the firm, and as you must understand, in these times, this is a key requirement...'

No partnership.

'...do not be discouraged. We will, of course, continually be reviewing your performance and...'

No partnership.

'... another time perhaps. Do you have any questions?'

He had stopped speaking and was looking at Carrie, one eyebrow raised.

She tried to reach through the red mist that had descended in her brain so that she could put words together.

'Questions? No. No not really. I'm disappointed, of course.'

'Indeed. As are we. But I must stress, Caroline, that this is not the end of the road. We think very highly of you, very highly indeed. Perhaps in a little time ... is that correct, Susan?'

'Absolutely.'

Susan James, flame-haired and pale skinned, leant forward earnestly and flannelled about targets and objectives and assessments. Carrie tuned her out. What did it matter? There was only one fact of any consequence – she had failed.

She couldn't wait to get out of there. The boardroom, which had looked so plush, so elegant, so much where she wanted to be, now seemed to mock her. It felt stifling, unbearably sneering.

She said, 'I'd better get on.'

God, that sounded pathetic! She should be upbeat, gracious, philosophical but ... the bastards! She deserved this promotion, she'd ground out the hours for years.

'Yes of course.' Henry looked at her. 'Are you all right? You look very hot.'

Hot! Her head was bursting! If she didn't get out of there right now it would surely explode. She wanted to scream and kick and inflict actual violence on someone, though even in this extremity she'd never be able to do that to old Henry.

But blast him all the same!

'Yes. Fine. Thank you for your time.'

She pushed back her chair and stood up. Producing a smile cost her more effort than she could ever remember having to make, but she achieved it.

It was only when she was half way down the stairs that she realised that what she longed to do more than anything was call Jane or Marta and share her crashing disappointment with them. But there was no way she could look Jane in the face now, not since Tom had catapulted back into their lives bringing all the remembered guilt and shame with him. She could call Marta, perhaps.

She pulled out her phone.

'Congratulations!'

It was Yvonne, the girl from reception, smiling like there was something to celebrate. My God! She must know she'd been summoned and she'd jumped to the wrong conclusion. Shit! Her failure would rip round the place like wildfire.

There was no point in lying.

'Congratulations nothing,' she said sourly, pushing past into the loo as Yvonne gasped audibly.

She stared at her reflection, expecting transformation. But she was still Carrie, still faintly bruised under the make-up, still with the same familiar, uneven features and short sandy hair.

She could do this. She could be bright and upbeat and deflect all sympathy.

She started to dial Marta's number again, then dropped her phone into her handbag with a pathetic grimace.

No.

She could not talk to Marta. She was hiding too many truths.

'Back in ten if there are any calls,' she called to Yvonne as she sped past the desk in reception.

'But where—'

Yvonne's startled words floated after her as she escaped down the steps.

Carrie prided herself on her independence. Being alone, she always maintained, didn't mean you were lonely. But right now she knew that she had never felt so alone in her life. Jane and Neal had each other and the children. Marta had her gentle, devoted Jake. She had no-one at home she could turn to. There would be no loving presence when she opened her door tonight. She had no inclination for physical contact via Bed Buddies. It wasn't sex she needed right now, it was the touch of someone who loved her. Human warmth.

She had failed in every way – at work, in friendship, in love.

As she strode along Queen Street, the clouds that had been gathering all morning chose to deliver their load to the streets of Edinburgh. A few small drops of rain turned in seconds into a shower and soon to a torrent. In less than a minute, Carrie was soaked. She gave up and walked back to the office, her head down, rivulets of water trickling down her back.

Chapter Twenty-two

Suzy Patterson loosened the strings on her violin, placed it in its case and scowled at Emily. Her spiky black hair and the excessive eye liner round her huge, dark slate eyes were the only manifestations of the Goth look she favoured that she could get away with in school. At home, Emily knew, she would add various bits of hardware to her face – a nose ring and a small but vicious-looking spike through her left eyebrow among them.

But despite her efforts to express individuality and show a streak of rebelliousness, Suzy was totally not adventurous, thought Emily, irritated by her friend's outspoken opinion that 'Robbie Jamieson's a serious dope head'.

'He is so not, Suzy,' she said crossly as she stowed her cello away and unwound her hair. The school had made her clamp it up during the day to hide the vivid purple ends. 'Just 'cos he smokes the odd joint – so what? Everyone does.'

'I don't. Taking drugs is a ridiculous thing to do. Why would you want to mess up your brain like that?'

'It's just a bit of fun.' Emily shrugged on her blazer. 'Weed's not drugs anyway.'

'It is.'

'Tisn't.'

'Tis. You can do better than Robbie, Em. He's basically not a nice person.'

'Oh, and Stevie is?' Emily growled, automatically launching into attack mode. Suzy's new boyfriend, Stevie Ryder, went to a rival school and was an ugly lump of a boy, whose nose had already suffered two breaks at rugby.

Suzy stared at her. 'You've changed, Em. What the hell's wrong with you? You can't think straight any more. Stop seeing Robbie before something goes really wrong, that's my advice. And there's no call to be nasty about Steve.' She picked up her violin and swung away. 'Tell you what, Steve respects me. Can you honestly say the same about Robbie?'

She stalked out of the cloakroom without looking back. Emily stared after her, chewing her lip to stop it from wobbling, part of her feeling ashamed at her unwarranted bitchiness, the other part defiant.

In the past few weeks she had done everything in her power to flout her mother's curfew as Robbie's interest in her grew. She'd invented extra orchestra practices that went on till eight. 'The concert's coming up, right, and we're doing this like, really difficult piece and no-one gets it.' She took a tiny part in the school panto and insisted they had to attend all the rehearsals, even though only the principals had to rehearse before November.

Ross, wise to her tricks, was exerting an undue hold over her, much to her annoyance.

'I'll tell Mum,' he threatened one day as he was heading home after football practice. Emily was already wearing the baggy sweat shirt and micro skirt she had changed into in the loos so that she could meet Robbie in town, her slim legs encased in thick black tights, the blonde part of her hair messily clipped back, long tendrils of purple escaping randomly to frame her face.

'Don't, Ross,' she pleaded.

'What's it worth?'

She had to think fast. 'I'll buy you a ticket for the Hearts-Hibs home derby if you if you keep quiet till then.'

Ross whistled. 'Promise? Cross your heart and hope to die?'

Cursing inwardly, Emily nodded.

'And one for my mate, Ed?'

'Don't push your luck, Ross.'

'Cos I think Mum and Dad would be very interested to know that—'

'Okay, okay,' she said hastily, totting up the cost in her head. It was worth it.

'Then you got it.' Ross, his freckled face splitting into a grin, hared off to join his friends, who were now almost out of sight down the road.

Emily stared after him. He'd be all right. Ross knew how to keep a secret – and she'd done the same for him on occasion. She swung the large holdall, designed to conceal her spare clothing, onto her shoulder. Robbie would be waiting.

He was there. The familiar feelings of diffidence as she crossed the threshold of the pub were replaced by elation as she saw him.

'Hi, Ems. Got your voddy in.'

'Hi.' Emily dropped onto the bench seat beside him and lifted her face for a kiss. She loved the thrill of sitting in a dark corner with him, drinking vodka and coke.

He slung his arm across her shoulders in a gesture of careless ownership.

So cool.

'Another?' Robbie asked an hour later, when they'd downed three drinks already. 'Or shall we go somewhere and snog?'

Emily hadn't eaten. She had squirrelled away a Mars bar and some crisps in her bag in case she couldn't forage in the fridge when she got home, but for now, the alcohol was making her feel lightheaded. She looked at Robbie's handsome, square-cut features and squirmed with pleasure. He wanted her. He wanted her!

'Let's snog.'

She squeezed his hand excitedly. What did Suzy know? Robbie was the real thing.

The lane behind the pub smelled of stale beer and festering rubbish, but Emily didn't care. As Robbie's mouth came down hard on hers and his hand crept up her sweatshirt, she gave herself up to self-gratification.

'Mmm, Em, you taste so sweet.' He broke off for long enough to murmur in her ear. 'Let's sneak back to my place, huh? My folks won't mind.'

It was tempting. She knew what Robbie was suggesting and she was totally up for it. It was well time she lost her virginity and she loved Robbie so much. But not tonight. Getting home without her lie being detected was going to be enough of a challenge without compounding it by another hour or two's absence.

'I love you, Robbie,' she whispered achingly. 'I love you so much. But not tonight, hey? I've like, got loads to do at home.'

'Back to Mummy, eh?' Robbie teased.

'No! I just got stuff—'

'Yeah, yeah. Just kidding.' His fingers circled her small breasts, pinched a nipple so that she moaned and found his mouth again.

'Soon, Robbie. I promise.'

'Saturday? There's a party at Greg's place. His folks'll be away and there's loads of bedrooms.'

This was it then. Decision time.

'You'll get protection?'

He grinned down at her. 'A condom? No worries.'

'Okay then. Yeah.'

His kiss was all the thanks she needed.

On the bus home, Emily began to worry about where she could slip back into her school uniform. Why did she have to go through all this shit? She was being forced into lying and surely that was wrong? Resentment replaced the glow from Robbie's attentions and she used it to cover the insecurities that lay deep in her heart. She hated Suzy for being so bitchy about Robbie. She hated her parents for grounding her.

She glanced sideways, out of the window. It was dark already and all she could see was her own reflection staring back at her,

172

pale and ghost-like. She unclipped her hair and twisted it back into the tight knot demanded by the school.

What a faff. She grimaced at her image in the glass. What the hell – Robbie loved her and that was all that mattered.

Shortly after midnight on Saturday night, Emily eased open the window in her bedroom and climbed out onto the flat roof of the small porch above the front door. It looked further down than she had remembered and she wasn't at all sure about how she would get back up again, but it surely couldn't be that difficult to scale a small drainpipe?

She dropped to the ground with a soft thump. At least there was grass on this side.

The house was in darkness. Everyone was asleep. Robbie, who had passed his driving test two months ago, was picking her up at the end of the road.

'I can get my dad's car, no worries,' he had assured her and true to his word, he was waiting for her round the corner.

'Okay?' he grinned as she climbed in.

Her heart lurched at the sight of him and she leaned across for a kiss.

'Wicked,' she said, and smiled. This was exciting. Robbie already tasted vaguely of booze but he couldn't have had very much or he wouldn't be driving.

When they arrived at Greg's place across town in Portobello, the music was blaring, the lights were low and the smell of grass was drifting through every room. Soon Emily began to feel a bit dizzy. The front room was too noisy to talk and she abandoned Robbie as he started to roll a joint and went in search of booze. The Victorian house seemed positively palatial compared with her own. This was so cool. In the quieter kitchen she came across Suzy and Steve, sitting at the table discussing – of all things – politics.

'Hey, Emily,' Suzy called, 'Wanna join us? Where's Robbie?'

'Through there.' Emily waved vaguely. Suzy had added a red streak to the usual black in her hair and was looking really fancy in a tight black leather mini and studded leather jacket. 'Just come for a drink.'

'There's some punch, here, let me get you some,' said Greg. A couple of years older than Robbie, he was celebrating the end of his gap year and the start of student life.

'Thanks, great.' Emily took the mug. The punch was rich and fruity. It tasted good and slipped down easily. She eavesdropped on the conversation for a bit longer, refilled her mug and wandered off.

Upstairs, she counted four bedrooms. She opened one door to find a couple writhing on the bed. 'Oops, sorry,' she said, closing closed the door again quickly.

'There you are, Ems.' Robbie was behind her. 'Wondered where you'd gone.'

Emily's head was beginning to spin. Was there one Robbie or two? What was in this punch, for heaven's sake? Still, it tasted fantastic, much better than voddy and coke.

'Hi,' she said and aimed for one of his heads. Her kiss landed near his ear instead of on his mouth and she started to giggle. 'Hi handsome. Wherever you are.'

'Hi gorgeous.' He caught her round the waist. 'I think you need to lie down.' He opened the nearest door, saw the couple inside, pulled her to another room and helped her to the bed. 'Here Ems. Come here, sweetheart.'

She lay down thankfully, but oddly, the spinning got worse. She couldn't shut her eyes, it was better when she looked at the ceiling. Robbie was kissing her, pulling at her clothes, she could feel his hand between her thighs, forcing her legs apart. 'No, Robbie, not yet.'

'Gorgeous,' he murmured hotly into her ear. 'You're so gorgeous, Ems.'

She struggled feebly as he pulled off her knickers.

'No, Robbie, stop.'

This wasn't right, she wasn't ready, it wasn't how she'd imagined it at all. She wanted something special, romantic, loving and this felt ... grubby.

'You promised, sweetheart, remember? You do love me, don't you?'

'Yeah, of course I love you—'

'Well then. Look,' he half sat up, felt in his pocket, came out with a packet. 'I promised you, didn't I? No worries, it's safe.'

He put on the condom with such practiced ease that even through her numbed senses Emily realised that he must have done this before. And then he was on her, forcing her legs apart with his body, rubbing her breasts with his hands, and she felt him penetrate her.

'Oww!'

It hurt. Why did it hurt? As he began to pump up and down, in and out, Emily felt no pleasure, only soreness. And still the room was going round and round. It wasn't meant to be like this, not like this at all.

'Gorgeous Emily.' Finally, Robbie slumped on top of her, spent.

So that was it. She was his. Robbie's girl properly. That must be good, mustn't it?

Later, they went back downstairs. Robbie kept his arm round her shoulders and whispered, 'You were great, Em, honest,' in her ear and she smiled at him and forced aside the feelings of dissatisfaction at what had just happened. Still, another drink would go down well. She filled her mug up with punch.

'Watch it Emily, people have been pouring stuff into that all night,' someone said – was it Suzy?

''S all right. 'Sfine,' said Emily, and gulped down half the mug. It tasted good. Blissful. Nothing wrong with this.

Robbie laughed and handed her his joint.

'Good stuff, Em,' he said.

And it was good stuff. The booze and the joint. Lovely stuff. Lovely Robbie. She was a woman now, not a girl. Great stuff.

Marta couldn't get used to Jake's absence. It had been three weeks since he had gone to London and her bed felt horribly empty. Her life felt empty. The only thing that was sustaining her at all was her work because, just when she needed them most, she had lost her friends. She had never made things up with Jane after the disastrous incident with Emily and as for Carrie – she had just gone off the radar. Marta had lost count of the number of times she had texted her, asking her to call. She hadn't answered, not once, so Marta had given up.

Her life had imploded. She couldn't remember ever feeling so miserable.

Four o'clock on Sunday morning and the darkness outside was as impenetrable as the darkness in her heart. She turned over, instinctively reaching out for Jake, and the dull misery as she remembered he wasn't there weighed her heart down like lead.

Four fifteen. She thought about turning on the light and trying to read.

Four thirty. She checked the clock again – surely it couldn't just be fifteen minutes later? It felt like hours.

The phone rang. Marta jumped with shock. Jake she thought. He can't sleep either, he misses me, he wants to come back.

'Hello?' she snatched up the receiver and spoke into it breathlessly.

'Is that Marta Davidson?' The voice was young and high-pitched.

'Yes. Who's this?' Puzzlement mingled with profound disappointment.

'Suzy Patterson.' There was panic in the voice. 'I'm so sorry to bother you, honest I am, but it's Emily. I don't know what to do. I found your number on her mobile and I know she trusts you.'

'Emily? What's wrong? Do you know what time it is?'

'I know, sorry, honest, but she's, like, unconscious. I can't get her to wake up.'

'Unconscious? What's happened? Where are you?'

Marta switched the light on and sat up, very wide awake.

'She's had a lot to drink. And maybe some drugs too, I dunno. We've been at this party—'

'Party? Where?' Marta's recollections of Emily's party-going were still all too vivid.

'We're not far from you. That's why I'm calling. Can you help? Please? I don't want to ring her Mum. Em's not meant to be out, but I know she likes you, see, and—'

'Suzy, listen.' Marta's voice was urgent. 'I'm going to call an ambulance. And her parents. And I'll come there at once myself. Now where are you?'

'Are you sure that—'

She interrupted sternly. 'If she's unconscious and you can't wake her, she needs help. It sounds serious. Give me your address.'

Suzy gave it. Marta dialled the emergency services and requested an ambulance, right away. Then, before should could change her mind, she did what she felt in her heart was right – she phoned Jane.

'Neal? Hi, it's Marta. Sorry to wake you, it's about Emily,' she said hastily when a drowsy Neal answered the phone.

'Emily? What about her? She's fast asleep here.'

'Oh.' Marta was dismayed. Had Suzy been lying? Had she called out the ambulance on false pretences? She could see all sorts of trouble looming. 'Are you sure? I mean, it sounds stupid, but can you just check?'

'Hold on.' Neal sounded resigned, but she could hear him murmuring something – to Jane, presumably – and the sound of a door opening. Then running feet, and Emily's name being shouted and then he was back and she could hear the panic in his voice as he called out, 'She's not there. Emily's not there!'

177

'What the hell's happening, Marta?' Jane had snatched the telephone and was shouting down the line. 'Where is she? What have you d-done to her?'

'Done? I've done nothing,' Marta strove to keep her voice level. It wasn't surprising Jane was upset, her daughter was missing. What was odd was that she clearly had no idea she was out. 'Listen.' She emphasised the word. 'She's at a party. I just got a call. She seems to have passed out. I will go there now, because I'm quite near, but I've asked for an ambulance. Okay?'

'Okay? No, it's not okay, it's—'

'Marta?' Neal's voice came back on the line, much calmer. Thank heavens he was taking control. 'Give me the details.' He listened while she relayed the address. 'Thank you.'

Marta couldn't remember ever dressing so fast. She was in her jeans and a sweater in an instant, snatching her keys and her phone and then she was in her car and off.

She beat the ambulance by fifteen minutes. The house she'd been directed to was no student dive, but a smart, large house, clearly the home of a well-to-do family. The smell of marijuana was powerful and there were still a number of people in evidence, sprawled in the front room, on the rug in the hall, slumped on the stairs. Music was playing, but quietly. Marta remembered Suzy Patterson when she came to the door, her kohl-ringed eyes black in her ashen face.

'Where is she?' Marta tried to sound calm and authoritative.

'Here. She's in here.' Suzy opened a door.

It was a dining room, or a music room, or maybe a study, or some kind of combination of all three. A baby grand dominated the far corner but there was plenty of room for a dining table too. In the large bay window, a desk faced out to the world. Emily lay on the rug, absolutely still. Someone had placed her in the recovery position, curled round, foetus-like, and covered her with a coat. 'We can't get her to wake. I've tried and tried.'

Suzy sounded scared, but she'd done all the right things. Marta said reassuringly, 'Don't worry. You've done well. Thanks. You're a real friend. What's she taken?'

Suzy shrugged. 'Dunno. She's drunk a lot. There was a kind of punch and people kept pouring stuff into it – whatever was around really. I told her to stop drinking but she's mad at me right now and she didn't want to listen. She had some weed, too.'

'Anything else? Were there pills? Ecstasy? Coke? Crystal meth? Any legal highs? Think, Suzy. If you know it will help the medics.'

'Dunno,' Suzy said again. 'Sorry. I don't do any of that stuff but her boyfriend Robbie's a real smackhead. I told her, but she wouldn't listen. She thought she was being grown up.'

At last the ambulance came. Marta had never been so relieved. Still no sign of Jane and Neal. Quickly, she dialled Jane's mobile, but it was switched off.

'Want to come with us?' one of the paramedics asked when Emily was strapped onto the stretcher in the back of the vehicle.

It seemed sensible. 'Okay.'

By the time Jane and Neal arrived at the hospital, Marta was sitting in A&E amid a couple of dozen drunken or drugged youths in various states of damage. There was a smell of vomit and more than one person was lying across a row of chairs, moaning. Emily had been identified for speedy assessment and was in a cubicle being examined by a doctor.

Jane, white with worry, was obviously in no mood for thanks.

'What the hell has been g-going on, Marta? How could you let this happen? She's a child, for heaven's sake. A child. What were you thinking?'

The injustice made Marta furious. 'Me? What was I thinking? What's it got to do with me? You're her parents. You're the ones with a duty of care. Why did you let her go out at that time of night if she's just a child?'

'How come you knew all about it then?' Jane said, her thin face gaunt.

Surely she's lost weight, Marta thought. She can't afford to get any thinner, she looks positively anorexic.

'Her friend phoned me. No doubt she'd have phoned you if you were a little bit more understanding.'

Neal, clearly anxious to avoid confrontation, sensibly asked a more pressing question. 'Where is she, Marta? Where's Emily?'

'In there.' Marta, feeling suddenly shaky, sat down abruptly.

Jane abandoned her inquisition and swept off with Neal. From behind the curtain, Marta could hear a low murmur of voices. She waited a few minutes, but no-one came out. I can't stand this, she thought, I've got to get out of here. She looked round the room. In the far corner someone was vomiting into a bowl. Everywhere people sat huddled and forlorn. A small group seated near the back wall looked as though they might get into a fight at any minute.

She stood up and headed for the door. It was almost six in the morning, she was on the wrong side of town and she had no transport. She still had no idea how Emily was. Jane was furious with her over something that was absolutely not her fault – and as she made her way into the slow, grey light of dawn to search for a taxi, it occurred to Marta that she still hadn't told her friend that Jake had left her.

Chapter Twenty-three

'Hi, Ms Davidson? This is Drew McGraw, Innovation Enterprises.'

Years of dealing with clients from all over the world had built an inner clock into Marta's system. It was afternoon in Scotland, but morning in the States.

'Mr McGraw, good morning. How are you?'

'I'm good, thank you, extremely good. Now, about my trip, it's all finalised?'

'Indeed yes, I emailed the details, I believe?'

Whatever else Marta might be, she was a true professional. The one thing that had been keeping her going since Jake's departure was her work – and among the many humdrum jobs she had to deal with, Drew McGraw's trip stood out like a sparkling jewel. Organising it had been fun. From the fine-dining experiences in Edinburgh and elsewhere to the shooting trip in the Highlands, she had planned the tour down to the last detail.

'Is everything the way you want it?'

'Well, no, not quite everything.'

Marta's heart sank. I've been so thorough, she thought – what could I have missed?

'I'm sorry,' she said. 'What would you like me to address?'

'It's the trip round the Highlands itself.'

'Yes?'

'I'd like you to accompany the tour.'

'Oh, I see.'

Such a request wasn't particularly unusual and Marta had spent a considerable part of the working like as a tour guide so the prospect didn't daunt her. It was just that Mr McGraw hadn't mentioned the request before.

'Is that possible? I mean, I'd like you, not some other employee of Tartan Ribbon Tours.'

Travel was no novelty to Marta. She had spent her life travelling – or at least much of her life before she'd met Jake and settled for an office job – and she knew it sounded a great deal more glamorous than it usually was. However, this tour would be different. Everything she had arranged was top quality and, with Jake away, a break in the Highlands might be just what she needed. Swiftly, she reviewed the travel plans in her head. Were there any points at which she might run into accommodation problems? It seemed straightforward. 'I'll need to confirm that, Mr McGraw. I will just have to contact each hotel, make sure they can accommodate me. And I'll need to check with my boss here that I can be spared. And of course, there would be an extra cost – time and expenses, I'm afraid.'

'Sure, sure, I understand that. But I can't afford for anything to go wrong with this trip, Ms Davidson, and I have been extremely pleased with your service to date. Would you like me to clear it with your boss myself? Whatever it takes—'

'No, no, thank you, I'm sure that will be fine. Let me get back to you. Is there anything else?' There were just five days until Drew McGraw arrived. His party was to follow a couple of days later. She would need to act quickly.

'I'm sure it will all be fine. You'll be in touch?'

'As soon as I can, I promise.'

Marta opened the last drawer in her bedroom with a sense of mounting desperation. Her brooch was missing. It was an antique, a gold brooch set with diamonds and emeralds. It had belonged to her great-grandmother and although it was not something she wore often, it had enormous sentimental value. Besides, it was exactly what was needed to spruce up her outfits for the McGraw tour. When had she last worn it? At a reception for one of Jake's clients in the National Museum, so it must have been a year ago, before Jake had been made redundant.

An hour later, she'd searched every nook and cranny, every drawer and cupboard in the house. The brooch was definitely not there. She sat down in the living room and thought carefully. The cleaner? Out of character. Who else had been in the house? Mr Morrison, of course. Jake's face flashed into her mind, and his quiet but shocking sarcasm. 'Are you seriously suggesting Mr Morrison came up to the bathroom and pocketed my iPod?'

Tom Vallely. The source of all their troubles – the small change from the pot in the hall, the cash from Jake's study, Jake's iPod.

Her brooch.

More than anything, Marta longed to hear what Jake thought. He'd phoned a couple of times since his departure – to let her know he had arrived safely in London and to give her some contact details. They hadn't argued. The politeness had been even more painful.

Marta looked at the mantelpiece. The glass ornament lay exactly as it had the day she'd broken it. She eyed it dispiritedly. I should try to mend it, she thought.

Somewhere in her head she could hear whispers. Tom's fruity voice describing the message of his play: Friendship is like a glass ornament, once it is broken it can rarely be put back together exactly the same way. Contradictory whispers – Carrie and Jane, thirteen years old and so intense: Friends. Friends forever. Jake, long ago, his voice tender: I will always love you, Marta.

Life could not go on in this way. She must not allow her friendships – or her marriage – to slip away. A new determination took hold deep in her heart. I'll fight for Jake, she thought. I'll win him back, whatever it takes. And I'll mend whatever it is that's broken in my friendship with Jane and with Carrie. It's too important to allow it to shatter like this. The ornament might lie broken, but relationships are not the same – the more effort you put into them, the more rewarding they become. Whatever our problems are, for each of us and between us, we've got to sort them out and face the future together.

She picked up the telephone and, before she could change her mind, she dialled Jake's mobile.

'Hello, Jake,' she said. 'It's me. I need your help.'

His voice was heartbreakingly familiar. He listened without comment as she explained about the missing brooch, before saying, 'I've no idea, Marta. You know what my guess would be.'

'I know. Tom. I think you're right. What can I do?'

In the seconds while Jake was thinking about her missing brooch, Marta realised that she couldn't care a fig about it. She couldn't care about anything expect Jake.

'Remember we found some stuff under the bed?' Jake said.

'Did we?' It was the day Marta wanted to forget, the day Jake had walked out and her world had fractured. What had they found? She had a hazy memory of Jake handing her something – a book? Some papers?

'You haven't sent them back to him?'

'No. I'd forgotten, to tell you the truth. I haven't even been into the spare room.'

'And he hasn't been in touch to ask if he left anything?'

'No. I haven't heard from him at all.'

'Strange. Or maybe not.'

'What about it, anyway?'

'Well, have you looked to see what they are? At the very least, you might find his address and number. You could call him and ask.'

Marta shivered. 'I couldn't do that. I never want to speak to him again.'

'Frankly, Marta, I don't blame you.'

'I'll take a look, though. Thanks Jake. How are you, anyway? How's the job?'

'It's fantastic,' he said enthusiastically. 'I'm loving it.'

'That's good.' She forced herself to say the words, while all the time her heart felt like wood. She wanted him to hate it, to be homesick, to realise how much he missed her.

'It's amazing, being back doing what I love at last. I'm feeling so much better. How are you?'

'I'm okay.'

This was hard. Fight for him, she had decided – but how to start? She didn't want to sound hopeless or desperate, but she had to let him know how much she loved him.

'I'm off to the Highlands. A tour.'

'Really? Are you looking forward to it?'

Jake knew her better than anyone in the world. He knew she'd rather be at home – but that was when he'd been there to share her home with.

'Surprisingly, I am, just a little. It's a top-end tour. And Drew McGraw sounds fun.'

For a crazy moment she wondered whether to play Drew up, to try to make Jake jealous, but the thought passed in an instant – jealousy wasn't in Jake's nature, it never had been, even during the long weeks and months she'd been travelling over their years together. She went for honesty instead.

'I miss you though, Jake. I miss you all the time.'

'Me too.'

Marta drew a deep breath, and held it. Small steps, Marta. Keep the door open. 'Can you get a weekend off? Maybe come home for a couple of days?'

She could almost feel his hesitation. 'Maybe,' he said. 'Sometime.'

'Okay.'

'Call me when you get back from the Highlands.'

'Will do. And Jake… thanks.'

They were talking like friends, not shouting or making accusations. Maybe it was a tiny chink of light at the end of a very long corridor, but it was enough for now. Talking to Jake restored a measure of calm that Marta hadn't felt since he'd left. She wasn't happy, but she neither did she feel as though someone had ripped out her heart and was dragging it behind a car travelling at a hundred miles an hour along a road full of potholes.

She picked up her mobile. Now that she'd started, she would call Carrie and Jane. Her hands went into automatic, seeking Jane's number on short dial – but then, for a moment, she was a child again, remembering.

An old secret code.

A tiny tin, shoved between the cracks in the wall behind the bike shed at the back of the playground, checked twice daily.

Covert assignations, the stuff of childhood friendships. Harmless fun, cloaking their private circle behind a veil of secrecy, making them feel special, different.

No need for tins now. Quickly she searched on the internet, then composed a text.

<FFE 2 CI 0930 Saturday>

Carrie and Jane would know what she meant. 'FFE' – Friends For Ever. It was what they used to call themselves at school. '2 CI' – To Cramond Island. And the time, carefully selected after checking the tide tables. It was a rallying call, a summons they could not refuse. Buoyed up by the prospect of renewal and healing, Marta smiled, clicked Send, and waited.

There was no response.

Chapter Twenty-four

Cramond Island lay just offshore from the village, joined to the land by a causeway that revealed itself twice a day. It was possible to walk across the beach alongside the breakwater that marked the way, but care had to be taken to check the tides for the return.

The causeway converged to a pinprick in the distance, where the green slopes of the small island fell down to a golden fringe of sand, and when Marta stepped out on it on Saturday at nine it was wet, but not slippery. The sun was full on her face and although there was little warmth in its rays, the light lifted her spirits and gave her hope.

To her right, a series of concrete pillars stood like ragged teeth, a war fortification against enemy shipping. She stood for a moment, caught up in memories.

'Jump me, Papa! Jump me!'

A searingly hot day. Her father, impossibly tall and as strong as any giant, laughing and lifting her from tooth to tooth until they tired of the game and she rode on his shoulders instead.

A picnic – a hard-boiled egg and juicy tomatoes, squidged into a morning roll so that they spilled out onto her chin as she bit into the bread. Her mother laughing, mopping her face. And her father's voice, weaving her a magical story of the island's long history, of stone-age man, of the Romans who had a fortification near here, of farmers and fisher folk and of a peaceful return to nature.

A lost day of innocence.

Half way across, Marta stopped for a moment. There was a coolness in the air that carried with it the faint mouldering smell that signalled the start of autumn. To underline the point, the trees along the shoreline were turning red and gold. A brisk breeze ripped at the weakest leaves, plucking them free, and they twisted and twirled and plummeted to earth. Marta's hair whipped around her face and into her eyes. She pulled a woollen hat from her pocket and tugged it down over her ears so that the whistle of the wind between the teeth of the pillars was dulled.

It was a mile across the causeway. On her left, the sands spread as far as she could see, not smooth and even but ridged and rippling, sand imitating sea. Water still filled the deepest undulations, catching the light, reflecting the blue and the cloud of the skies above. At the edge of the causeway, seaweed sprawled wetly, trying to claim the path for its own. Striding on, she felt the sand shift beneath her feet, making an easy walk into a work-out.

From sand to soil – she'd reached land.

Without pausing, Marta began to scale the hill. It didn't take long and her reward was a view without parallel, across the Forth estuary to Fife in the north and back across the ragged skyline of Edinburgh to the south. She shrugged off her small backpack, took out a light mat, and lowered herself to the ground. The tea she had had the foresight to brew would be more than welcome.

It spun like molten copper in a steady stream from flask to cup, steaming gently in the cool air. Across the expanse of wet sand and concrete path, she spied a small figure skipping onto the first few stones of the causeway. The gait, bouncing and energetic, was familiar. A minute later she was able to make out short, stylishly cropped hair, the exact colour of the sand.

Marta smiled. Carrie. She's come. She's answered my call.

She drank her tea and waited.

'Hi.'

'Hi.'

'Tea?'

'Thanks.'

A shared cup. More humble than the breaking of bread and the sipping of wine, but a ritual with meaning nonetheless.

Carrie said, 'You've come well prepared.'

'But I've only got one mat. Sorry.'

Carrie reached inside her jacket. 'No worries. I bought a newspaper.' She unbent and flattened it, then sat on it before the breeze could whip it away. They sat shoulder to shoulder, gazing across the white-crested waves as though the timeless beauty of the scene could act as a salve, and sipped the tea in turn.

'You called,' Carrie said at last.

'I called for Jane too.'

Carrie looked at her watch. 'I don't think she's coming. It's past ten.'

'No.'

Jane won't come, Marta thought. Repairing the rift with Jane will take more than the glue of a meeting on Cramond Island.

'What's up?'

How should she should answer? What's up? Only that my husband has left and my friends have deserted me and I've never felt more alone in my life.

'Why haven't you answered my messages?' she said, evading the question for now. 'You've been hiding from me.'

When Carrie said nothing, Marta twisted to look at her. The profile was so familiar, so very dear to her. The small, snub nose, the sandy lashes, the clipped hair – she'd seen them mature from a child's features into an adult's and she knew them almost as well as her own. The chin was neat, but its set was always determined. Carrie was the driving force of the trio, she always had been. Marta was the peacemaker and Jane—? Jane had been sweetly, gratefully needy, her gratitude the velvet ribbon that pulled them all together.

Used to Carrie's restless ambition and her fiery energy, something about the absolute stillness of her now scared Marta and in an instant she forgot her own ills.

'You tell me, Carrie. You tell me what's up.'

The wind whipped Carrie's hair into a frenzy as she turned her head slowly. But whatever Marta had expected to see – worry, regret, sadness? – she had certainly not anticipated the raw bitterness in Carrie's eyes.

'Not returning your calls? No. Frankly, Marta, I was too angry with you.'

'Angry?' Marta rocked back, shocked. 'With me? Why?'

'Because it's your fault. Typical Marta. The do-gooder. Never thinking it through first.'

'What? Thinking what through?'

'Asking Tom Vallely to stay. Inviting us all round. If you hadn't brought Tom into our lives, we'd all have gone on very nicely, thank you very much, and none of this would have happened.'

'What's Tom done to you? I don't understand.'

Tom, Tom, the piper's son, stole a pig and away did run. Tom the charmer. Tom the thief.

'Didn't it even occur to you that seeing him again might upset Jane?'

'But it's years and years since they split and it was all very amicable.'

'Amicable?' Carrie's laugh was sour. 'Amicable? What in the name made you think that?'

'Jane said ... she wrote to me ... I was in South Africa ... She told me they'd agreed to split, that it had run its course, that she was fine about it.'

Again the dry laugh.

Marta was bewildered. 'It wasn't? Why would she fib about that?'

'Oh Marta. You're such a sweetie, you always believe the best of people. Jane was heartbroken, she was just too proud to let you see the hurt, I guess. When did she write?'

'I don't know – yes I do, around Christmas, just when it happened I think.'

190

'Did you realise she disappeared after that?'

'I – no! ... disappeared?'

'For months.'

'I suppose I didn't hear from her for a while. But letters weren't always reliable.'

'She had a nervous breakdown, Marta. She went to ground completely.'

'Oh God. I didn't know.'

'She left the orchestra.'

'She left before she met Neal? I thought she left when they got married, when she was pregnant with Emily.'

'No. Neal, bless him, has been her saviour – but bringing Tom back into her life has dragged her to the edge again. Her stutter has returned, haven't you noticed?'

'Yes, of course I noticed, but I didn't realise—' Marta's voice tailed away. 'You were around, though, Carrie. You were in London at that time. Weren't you able to help her?'

'I was the *last* person who could have helped her.'

'Why? Her best friend? If she couldn't turn to you—'

Carrie was silent. She looked away from Marta, as though she was scanning the horizon for some distant object.

'Carrie?' Marta prompted.

Carrie turned back slowly.

'Jane didn't know,' she said at last, 'but I had an affair with Tom Vallely.'

'You did? When? After they split up?'

Carrie shook her head slowly. 'No. They were still living together.'

Marta gasped. '*What*? How could you, Carrie? How could you do that to Jane? How could you do it to *anyone,* let alone your best friend?'

'I'm not proud of myself, Marta, believe me. But Tom is a very persuasive man and a very good liar. He made me believe that he was just about to split from Jane, that he was simply waiting for the right moment to tell her. He also made me believe that he loved me.'

'And you fell for it? Honestly, Carrie, I thought you were smarter than that.'

'Apparently not.'

'Jesus. But Jane didn't know?'

'No. And my affair with Tom wasn't why they split up. Tom was two-timing both of us. The sneaky rat went off and married the ghastly Serena.'

'Okay,' Marta said slowly. 'So Tom hurt you too. And I invited him to dinner. But what's eating you, Carrie? It was a long time ago – you can't still be hurting, surely? Presumably Jane still doesn't know? And she's happily married with three children. I mean, I can see in retrospect that it was a bit insensitive, to say the least. But surely it's not worth spoiling our friendship for, after all this time?'

'Maybe it would have been, but for one thing.'

'What?'

'Tom Vallely. And I call him "thing" advisedly. He was a rat back then and he hasn't changed. He made me give him money to stop him from telling Jane my secret—'

'You mean he blackmailed you? You didn't pay, surely?'

'I paid – and more fool me, because he told Jane anyway.'

'*No!* What a scumbag.'

'Yup. So you can see why Jane hasn't turned up this morning.'

'What a mess. Oh Carrie, what a mess,' Marta said miserably. 'That stupid dinner. I thought I was being so clever, bringing us all together again. I thought it would be a nice surprise. You know I've always worried about you being on your own, Carrie. You used to be so ... you lost your virginity ages before Jane and I did.'

'Simon Small. Small by name, small by nature.' Carrie's smile was pale. It had been an old joke, something she'd invented after splitting up with her first boyfriend, to mitigate the pain of that first broken romance.

'That's why I've tried to find nice men for you. I mean, it would be great if you found someone special.'

'Jesus, Marta.' Carrie dropped her head not her hands and rubbed at her eyes. 'You don't get it, do you?'

'What? Don't get what?'

Carrie looked at Marta. Slim, tall, pretty, her skin only now beginning to show the early signs of aging. Marta had always been all the things that Carrie was not, physically and temperamentally. She was meticulously monogamous, for a start. What did she really think about her, now that she had confessed that affair with Tom? What would she think about her if she told her now about how she conducted her private life? On the other hand, maybe now was the best time, when she had already taken a downwards slide on Marta's moral compass. Carrie was rarely impulsive, but she made a quick choice.

'You know what, Marta?' she said, 'Secrets are corrosive. I've had enough of them. So I'm going to tell you another one.'

Far to the north Carrie could see storm clouds swirling across the peaks of the distant hills. She shivered. No doubt about it, autumn was here and winter was already sending out its early warning signals. She drew her knees up to her chin and picked her words carefully.

'I have lovers, Marta. But I keep my emotions out of it.'

Marta looked nonplussed.

'I suppose you could say that after that affair with Tom, I took a decision. I was ambitious, I wanted to concentrate on my work, not get distracted by men, certainly not get sucked into the whole husband and babies thing. Quite soon, I became obsessive about it. I liked being in control. I liked not committing. To be honest, I was convinced that this was the way to be. I would not get hurt – and I wouldn't hurt anyone else either.'

'I don't understand.'

'No. I don't suppose you do.'

The clouds looked as though they were getting nearer. Perhaps soon the rain would reach them. Carrie didn't dare look at Marta. She plunged on. No point in stopping now.

'At first I went the route of singles clubs and lonely-hearts columns. There were plenty of guys out there who weren't really looking for love, they were simply looking for sex and that suited me just fine. Then, a few years ago, when the internet really took off, I joined a dating site called Bed Buddies. It's for people like me who want sex without strings. That's all.'

'You mean, not looking for a permanent relationship, just sex?' Marta sounded scandalised.

'Yes. Exactly.'

'But that's immoral!'

'Why?'

'Well—' Marta floundered. 'Who joins this site? Men who don't have partners, presumably?'

'Not always, no. Men – and women – who have an unsatisfactory sex life in their permanent relationship. People who want a change or a bit of fun without jeopardising their marriage. People who are on the road and lonely. People like me who just want to have sex without commitment.'

'Carrie!'

'What?' Feeling fiercely defensive, she swivelled to look at Marta and her defensiveness made her sound angry. '*What*? It worked fine for years. Until Tom came back and saw me and sussed out I was on the site, that is.'

'Tom did?'

'He worked out my pseudonym and set up a date with me.'

'And you went?'

'I didn't know who it was till I saw him, right?'

'But then you went home.'

Carrie looked at the grass. A ray of sun was hitting the ground just three yards in front of them and the grass appeared to be quite extraordinarily green.

'Didn't you, Carrie?' Marta pressed.

'Sadly, Marta, Tom Vallely is just as magnetic as he was sixteen years ago, or hadn't you noticed?'

'You mean, you *slept* with him again? Oh Carrie, surely not?'

Carrie swung round and glared at Marta. 'And why the hell shouldn't I? At least this time I wasn't doing anyone any harm. Only myself,' she added bitterly.

'But if Jane knew – she'd feel betrayed all over again, wouldn't she?'

'Why? What's it to do with her?'

Marta was staring at her. 'I can't believe you're the friend I thought I knew, Carrie.'

'And I can't believe you're such a prig. I'm sorry I told you now.'

'Tom's not to be trusted. You, of all people, should know that. And you don't even *like* him, so why the hell would you sleep with him?'

'Why would you invite him into your house? Because he's charming – until you find he's not. Anyway, he was a damn good lay.'

The accused is a passionate man, m'lud, on this occasion he allowed his feelings to run ahead of him. Convenient to forget the violence when you are defending your actions.

Marta jumped to her feet and started stuffing her mat and her flask into her backpack, her movements jerky.

'We've been rotten friends, Carrie. Jane's cut me dead. She thinks I'm trying to steal Emily's affections or that I'm a malign influence, I don't know which. You're trying to blame me for bringing Tom back into your life when I didn't even know he'd been in it in the first place.'

She swung her backpack onto her shoulder and glared down at Carrie.

'And neither of you knows or cares that my husband has left me.'

Carrie watched, stunned, as Marta's long legs took the slope at a pace that would have challenged even the best fell runner.

Left her? Jake had left her? How could she not have known this? Marta was right – communications between the three of them had broken down completely. She hadn't even told Marta yet about the partnership.

Overwhelmed by unhappiness she realised, as she squatted at the top of the grassy knoll, that she had always found their friendship to be a form of security. Certainly, she hadn't realised just how much she'd valued it until now, when she most needed warmth, familiarity, support, *love*.

'Marta!' The wind whipped her words away. 'Marta! Stop!'

She scrambled to her feet as Marta's slight figure disappeared down the steep path towards the beach. She was frantic at the thought that they might part in anger. Her newspaper, caught by the wind, blew into the air and a dozen sheets of gossip, innuendo and bigoted judgement scattered to the skies.

Best place for them. Gossip is damaging. Only the truth will do, only honesty can save us now.

Desperately, she launched into a run, scrambling down the path, sending stones scudding left and right as she slipped and slithered and nearly fell a dozen times. Thanking the heavens for her fitness, she called again, 'Marta! 'Stop!'

Marta jumped onto the causeway. This hadn't worked out the way she had hoped. She'd meant this morning to be a reunion, a meeting of friends. Instead, Jane hadn't come at all and she and Carrie had argued bitterly.

Her mind was still reeling from Carrie's revelations – how could she have betrayed Jane like that? It was unthinkable. As for that Bed Buddies site ... Marta was still paralysed by shock at the concept. Where was morality? Where was affection? Where were feelings and respect and companionship? It seemed so clinical and calculating, not to say dangerous.

'Marta!'

Far behind her, she heard a call. For a fraction of a second, she hesitated, then grimly strode on. She couldn't bear any more revelations.

'Marta!'

Something in the tone slowed her this time. Reluctantly she stopped and turned round. Carrie was sprinting towards her, a small frantic body with arms and legs flailing as she tried to cover the ground between them.

'I didn't know. Marta, I didn't know about Jake. I'm so sorry. Christ, I'm sorry.'

Carrie hurtled across the last few yards between them, tears streaming down her face as she flung herself at Marta and wrapped her arms round her in a ferocious embrace.

The hug was sweetly unbearable. Marta had been bereft of love and deprived of the comforting support of her lifelong friends for weeks and she clung onto Carrie as though she were a lifebelt in a stormy sea. She could feel Carrie's slight body shaking. It was the first time she'd seen Carrie cry since ... maybe since Simon Small had given her the heave all those years ago, but she was weeping as much as Marta as they sank onto a rock at the side of the causeway and huddled together.

Carrie said, 'Tell me about it. What's happened?'

'You and Jane weren't the only people Tom Vallely has messed with,' she managed, with a croak. 'He had me hoodwinked completely. Jake didn't trust him, but I couldn't see past the charm. He stole things from us. Money. Jake's iPod. A rather valuable brooch of mine too, I think. But worst of all, he made himself so much at home that Jake felt sidelined – and I didn't even realise.'

Marta dabbed ineffectively at her face with a tissue already soaked with tears.

'I can't believe how *stupid* I've been. *Blind*! I knew Jake hated losing his job but I just kept being my usual optimistic self instead of really listening to how he was feeling. Bringing Tom in ... how idiotic could I be – just opened up an even bigger gap between us.'

'Where is he?'

'He's taken a temporary job in London.'

'Temporary? That's all right, surely? I mean, you've not separated? As in marriage on the rocks?'

'He said some awful things to me, Carrie. Like I was bossy and overbearing, that I never let him make any decisions. He said I was trying to run his life and he needed space.'

'Needed space. Oh Marta.'

'Yes.' Marta pulled a face. 'That old line.'

'Why didn't you tell me? Oh, right,' Carrie added, realising, 'I wasn't answering your calls.'

'I so wanted some support.'

Carrie's smile was rueful. 'I didn't think about that, I'm sorry to say. I was angry with you. At least, I thought I was angry with you.'

'It was all my fault,' Marta sniffed. 'I'm so, so sorry.'

'No. How could you know about Tom and me? No-one did. Anyway, I was only hurting myself by not answering your calls. I was feeling so ashamed, I couldn't bring myself to talk to anyone. And that was just stupid, because I've had some bad news and I've been desperate to talk about it.'

'More bad news? What?'

'I didn't get the partnership.'

'*No*! Why ever not? You *deserve* it.'

'I thought I did. I took my eye off the ball.'

'Carrie, you never stop working. How could they fault you? I don't understand.'

Carrie shrugged. 'I haven't brought in enough business, apparently. It's a key requirement.' She gave a ragged sigh. 'I could have done more. All those evenings I was having fun playing with my Bed Buddies, I should have been out networking.'

'You can't work non-stop. Other people have families. You need some down time.'

Carrie scrambled to her feet. 'Come on. It's cold and my bum's wet. Let's walk, shall we?'

She tucked her arm through Marta's.

'Are we friends again? Please tell me we're friends.'

'Forever, Carrie. Please God.'

'And Jane?'

'You tell me. She's so angry with me about Emily. I don't blame her. She asked me to talk to Em, you know. She was worried about her behaviour. I took her out for a birthday treat and ... oh God.'

'And what?'

'I'm *hopeless*. I've been getting everything so wrong recently. Emily wanted to get her hair coloured. She said it would be fine with the school. I was thinking maybe a shade lighter or some highlights but—' She groaned.

'But? Come on, Marta, you can't stop there. What happened?'

'I left her at the hairdressers. I never thought for a minute that she'd ... I thought I'd just have a quick look round the shops and when I got back, she'd gone a hideous platinum blonde and the last six inches looked as though they'd been dipped in a bucket of purple dye.'

Carrie burst out laughing. 'Is that all?'

'It was *terrible*. I knew Jane would kill me.'

'No-one died. Emily's just a teenager, pushing at the boundaries. Remember what we were like?'

'I was supposed to be in charge. If I'd stayed it would never have happened. Anyway, that's not all.'

'What else?'

'The last time I saw Emily she was in a hospital bed and I haven't dared call Jane to find out how she is.'

'Hospital? Why?'

'She sneaked out of the house and got blind drunk at a party

199

in Portobello. Her friend Suzy phoned me in the middle of the night. I called an ambulance and rushed round to try and help. When Neal and Jane caught up with us at A&E, Jane jumped to all the wrong conclusions and somehow the whole episode was my fault.'

'How could it have been your fault?'

'Try telling her that.'

The walked on in silence.

'Where did you leave your car?'

'Silverknowes. You?'

'The same.'

'What are we going to do, Carrie? I've been worried sick about Emily.'

'Well, I'm not exactly flavour of the month either, not since Tom ratted on me.'

They walked along the shore path in silence. The wind had risen fiercely and was whipping the sea into a creamy foam. They had to battle against the force of the gale.

'Tell you what,' Carrie suggested when they finally came to a halt by her car, 'I'll try to get hold of Neal. It'll be easier talking to him than Jane.'

'Would you? That would be fab. I'm off on tour up north next week. Let me know as soon as you hear, OK?'

'Course. Marta—'

'Mm?'

'—I'm so glad about today. Fresh start?'

'Fresh start.'

Business must go on, despite everything. Marta, as professional in her own field as Carrie was in hers, woke the next morning feeling fractionally less miserable than she had since Jake had gone to London, but also feeling distinctly nauseous.

Nothing sat well in her stomach. She trifled with some cereal, before pushing it aside and retreating to bed. This was worrying.

Drew McGraw was flying in at any moment and she was due to dine with him that evening. In another twenty-four hours his colleagues would arrive and they would all depart for the Highlands.

At lunchtime, she called Carrie.

'I'm feeling grim and I need help,' she said. 'I need you to play hostess for me tonight.'

'You wouldn't be trying to matchmake again, would you?'

'Not on your life. I've never even met the man. You might find it useful though. You know you were saying you needed to bring in more business? Well, Drew might just be your man. He's looking to set up in Scotland.'

'Okay. What's the deal?'

'Thanks, Carrie. Just meet him at the restaurant and be nice, that's all.'

'What's up, anyway? Are you going to be alright to travel?'

'I'll have to be,' Marta said grimly. 'I must have eaten something. I'm sure I'll be fine tomorrow, let me know how it goes?'

'Will do.'

'I'm so glad we're friends again, Carrie.'

'Me too. Take care, petal.'

'Bye.'

She was tired. So very tired. Closing her eyes, Marta sank into slumber, wishing more than anything in the world that Jake was there to cuddle her.

Chapter Twenty-five

Drew McGraw was younger than Carrie had imagined he would be and well built but not fat. She could sense the muscles beneath the impeccably cut suit. His wide, pleasant face was topped off with a huge mane of thick, blond hair, which fell rather cutely into his eyes as he stooped to meet her gaze.

A lion nose to nose with a kitten.

'I hope you don't mind me standing in for Marta?'

Carrie had spent the afternoon being uncharacteristically anxious. Should I meet him at the airport, she had asked Marta, who had already covered this by booking a private car.

What should I wear?

What should I talk about?

Are you sure you want me to stand in for you?

So many questions, until Marta had growled and said, 'Carrie, if you don't stop I'll have to get up and do it and I really do not feel up to it, so be a sweetheart and just go and be yourself, hey?'

So now she was standing in the plush surroundings of Martin Wishart's Michelin-starred restaurant in Leith, her small hand in Drew McGraw's great, warm clasp, smiling up at his ruddy face and feeling suddenly irrationally elated.

'Delighted to meet you, Ms Edwards, delighted. Sorry about Marta, of course, but so long as she's okay for tomorrow—'

'I'm sure she will be. And please call me Carrie.'

He was still holding her hand between his two huge paws, but now he withdrew them, beaming. Carrie, who had tried on half a dozen outfits before selecting a black Armani cocktail dress, simple pearls and her favourite Jimmy Choo heels, was satisfied with her choices. Simple, classic, timeless, smart. Gradually, her self-confidence began to reassert itself.

'I'm sure you're tired. Shall we eat?'

Fine dining is an art form. Each mouthful is to be savoured, dwelled upon, analysed. Marta had suggested they go for the tasting menu and this proved to be a good choice. Each small but delicious course was complemented by wine specially selected by the sommelier for its aroma and bouquet, its length on the tongue or its lingering aftertaste. Drew McGraw, it quickly became clear, was a man who enjoyed his dining. Despite his obvious tiredness, they did not rush the meal.

Carrie diligently discussed his journey, the weather, his home town of Houston and the food. Talking to Drew was easy. If this had been a Bed Buddies date, she thought, she would scarcely have waited until the last course before she suggested taking a room. If only...

'...So you see, I need to establish myself quickly, and open an office.'

Carrie jerked her thoughts away from her fantasies. Behave, she rebuked herself. This man is out of bounds.

'Tell me about your business.'

'I'm an entrepreneur.' He laughed. He laughed from the belly, an easy, infectious laugh that had Carrie smiling at once.

'Is that funny?'

He shook his head. 'Not in itself. I was thinking about George W. Bush.'

Carrie was mystified. 'I can see some people would think that was funny,' she said cautiously, uncertain of Drew's political allegiances.

'Oh man,' he was laughing again. 'He was so prone to gaffes. "The trouble with the French", he once said, "is that they have no word for *entrepreneur*".'

Now Carrie was laughing too. 'Did he really say that? Really truly?'

'What line of business are you in?' she asked, setting her glass down and reaching for the water jug.

'I look at scientific research, try to seize on things that might have practical application, invest in them, and turn them into a commercial proposition.'

'Sounds interesting.'

'It can be very satisfying. It puts money back into science and gets the good things out there for folk like you and me to benefit from.'

'So why Scotland?'

'You have some terrific scientists, that's why. Hi-tech innovation, bio-technology, all sorts.'

'Have you got a legal team?'

'Sure.'

Carrie gave a small sigh.

He said, 'Why do you ask?'

Carrie smiled, 'Was I that transparent? I'm a lawyer. I work for a big firm here in Edinburgh. I guess I was hoping you'd say you needed some help.'

'It would do you good to introduce a new client, huh?' Drew asked shrewdly.

Carrie nodded. 'Yes. But that's not why I'm here,' she added hastily, 'I've been a friend of Marta's forever, I'm just helping her out. Honestly.'

Drew finished the last morsel of his dessert and laid down his spoon with a contented grunt. 'I never thought anything else, Carrie. And as it happens, I do have a great legal team back in the States, but I have a suspicion that here in Scotland the law is rather different, huh? My guys gave me some contacts to talk with – Grant Morrison? Abercrombie's?'

He had named two of Ascher Frew's big rivals. 'Not Ascher Frew?'

'Is that your firm?'

'They're good. Just as big as the ones you've been told about. Better.'

205

He finished the last mouthful of wine in his glass. 'How about I get my guys to check them out? If they're as good as you say, I'll be happy to meet with them when I get back from this trip to the Highlands.'

'Really? You would do that?'

'Why not?'

She decided to go for it. 'Would you let me be the person to introduce you?'

He met her gaze with an easy frankness. Drew McGraw was unlike anyone Carrie had ever met. She was drawn to his warmth and straightforwardness. She wanted him to like her – and not only to like her, but to admire her as well.

What would he think of Bed Buddies? Carrie had a horrible feeling that he would not approve.

'Honey, of course I will let you introduce me. Just let me make a coupla calls first is all I ask. Now, I guess I should be sensible and get to bed. But I hope you'll let me see you home first?'

Carrie hesitated. Was 'see you home' a code? Surely not. And yet ... over the course of the evening, she had felt the connection between them intensify. Surely she wasn't wrong? Surely there was desire in his eyes as well as the alert, intelligent interest that characterised everything he said and did? Did she desire him? No question. No question about that at all.

Some instinct held her back.

'There's no need. I can easily get a cab.'

'Please. It will be my pleasure.'

'Thank you, then. I'm quite central.'

'You'll come up? My flat has fantastic views.'

'Can you make cocoa?'

'*Cocoa*?'

Again the deep, relaxed laugh. 'Just joshing, honey. If you had a glass of whisky, now...'

'Whisky I can do, cocoa would be more of a problem.'

'A quick one, then, thank you.'

What was she thinking of? As Drew paid off the taxi, Carrie's head was spinning. She had never asked anyone up to her flat, it was a fixed rule. This was her space and her privacy here was sacred. Marta had been here, of course, and so had Jane, but no men. Bed Buddies were never invited home.

So what was she doing, asking Drew up?

'You lived here long?'

'A couple of years.' She'd bought it in expectation of a partnership at work. The mortgage was ferociously high, she couldn't really afford it, and now that she had failed ... but she couldn't confide that to Drew. It had been difficult enough telling Marta.

She opened the door, but didn't flick on the light. Across the living room, the huge glass wall opened onto an astonishing cityscape. Edinburgh Castle, lofty on its rock, was illuminated so that its ancient walls rose, lofty and commanding, above a sea of city lights. Beyond was a ribbon of blackness – the dark waters of the Firth of Forth – behind that, the lights of the small towns of Fife, twinkling and distant. It was almost better than the daytime view.

'Come in,' she said, standing aside so that she could watch his face.

His reaction was all she could have wished for. He sucked in his breath sharply, then let it out again in a low, soft whistle. Four long strides and he was across at the glass.

'Wow,' he said slowly. 'That is some view.'

'We can go out.' She slid the door aside. The night was cool and, up on the seventh floor, the breeze was brisk. Carrie shivered.

Noticing, Drew said, 'Cold?' and before she even thought about it, he had slid his arm across her shoulders and tucked her close in beside his body as he gazed admiringly around him.

It was a casual gesture. A thoughtful act, nothing more. Be still my beating heart.

'So what am I looking at?' Drew's voice was unchanged, still steady, still relaxed.

He was just being kind.

'The Castle, of course. George Heriot's School. The Camera Obscura – those coloured lights there – the Bank.' As she described the view, Carrie fought for self-control. She no longer knew how to behave in the context of a relationship and the thought brought her to the brink of tears.

'I must go.'

'You haven't had your whisky.'

Disappointment bit deep and she realised she had been praying that he would make a move, that all she would have to do would be to follow.

'Can I take a rain check, honey? I'm real tired.'

'Of course.' She led him back inside and reached for the light switch. Brightness flooded the room and brought with it commonsense. Of course he hadn't kissed her. He was a stranger, he was her friend's client. And that was all.

'Thank you for being such a fabulous hostess, Carrie.'

'My pleasure. I hope you have a good trip north.'

'I'll be in touch when we get back.'

'About your legal needs?' Let it be more, please let it be more.

'Sure. I can be your prize catch.' He laughed and made for the door. 'Good night honey. And thanks again.'

'Good night, Drew.'

As the door closed behind him, Carrie stood and looked around her. The space was the same as always: bright, contemporary, smart, stylish. It was all she had ever wanted it to be.

Yet now it felt only empty.

Chapter Twenty Six

Tom Vallely was inside Jane's head, refusing to leave. In the years since he had walked out, her feelings for him had run full circle. Love – obsession – heartbreak – longing – hate. And now she had to add fear to that list.

You never told Carrie about the baby? Such a very big thing in your life, surely?

His voice echoed in her head, that mellow, rich, seductive voice. Seductive? No, not that, never that. Oily. Oleaginous. The word rolled round her head. Yes, that was it. Ol-e-agi-nous. Slimy and greasy and quite disgustingly slick.

How could she ever have loved that man? And yet he inhabited her, even now.

And did Carrie ever tell you about our affair?

At first, she hadn't believed him. He was lying, winding her up, trying to destroy her friendships just as he had almost destroyed her life. Then, as his words bounced round her head, they began to make sense. Carrie had been very evasive when Tom had left. She'd spoken to her, briefly, on the phone, but they hadn't met. There had been no hugs, no tearful confidences, no comforting. She hadn't thought it odd at the time, she'd just concluded that Carrie was busy – but the lack of someone to turn to had been a key contributor to her breakdown.

Now she saw it. And if what Tom said was true, Carrie's betrayal was as big as his.

But the baby... Jane's hands went instinctively to her stomach.

I was so weak, she thought. *I never thought it would be like that.*

She marched round the house, her limbs restless. Settling to anything was out of the question. In the boys' bedroom, she picked up jotters, some Lego, Ross's Nintendo, assorted crumpled and grubby socks, a limp T-shirt. She smoothed the beds, restored a semblance of order, and called Benji, who was nosing at some unidentified spillage by Ian's desk.

In Emily's room, her poster of the cellist Stephen Isserlis stared down at her, the eyes soulful, as though reflecting the music he was creating. She'd added another poster of Paolo Nutini. Jane scowled at the image before it remembering that this was normal teenage behaviour. After all, aged sixteen, she had been into Mark Knopfler and Bruce Springsteen as well as Elgar and Bach.

Emily.

Her firstborn.

No.

Again the wrenching pain in her belly.

No!

The truth was ...

'You're over-protective of Emily,' Neal had said to her a few days' ago when they'd brought Emily back from the hospital, pale, shaky and scared.

'Over p-protective? What are you talking about? She clearly can't be trusted.'

'I know that's what it seems like, love, but perhaps if we treated her a bit more like a young adult – if we show her we trust her – she might take some responsibility for herself. She's sixteen now. She's old enough to get married.'

Jane shook her head violently. 'That's rubbish. She's still a child, Neal. She obviously needs rules – and punishments.'

As Jane closed Emily's door with her arms full of washing, Benji scampered down the stairs, a whisk of pepper and salt on the grey carpet. Perhaps Neal was right, maybe she was over-protective. But then, he didn't know the reason.

She had never told Neal the truth. She'd been on the verge of it so many times. Once, she'd even planned it all out. She'd tell him over dinner. She had the words rehearsed. But that day, he'd proposed and the truth had become unmentionable. Because if he knew—

The thought of losing him was unendurable.

In the kitchen, the television was on. Some hospital drama. She glanced at it as she thrust the washing into the machine. It looked like a repeat of *Emergency Admissions*, a twice-weekly soap the kids liked to watch. With little interest, she brewed herself a mug of tea, and sank onto a chair in front of the screen. Ten minutes' rest would be welcome.

The story line was familiar: three different incidents, seemingly unconnected; three sets of people who would end up in Accident and Emergency; three stories that would link loosely together with the general aim of adding to the store of human understanding and compassion. Nothing new. Exhausted, she closed her eyes. Recently, days had dragged and nights had offered little respite from her turbulent emotions.

'And you were – where exactly?'

Jane jerked upright, her eyes snapped open, and she watched in fascinated horror as a consultant marched in to a small windowless office and confronted Hazel Gunnion, the hapless nurse in the series.

'I ask you one more time, Nurse Gunnion, where were you?'

There was no mistaking the man who was playing the part. Tom Vallely had the kind of face that aged slowly, but with distinction. In another era, he might have been described as a matinée idol. At forty, the looks he had had in his twenties had matured into something altogether more urbane – he appeared suave, debonair, polished. As an actor, he made a brilliant corporate executive or government minister. Or hospital consultant.

'Running an errand for Andy. Honest I was, Mr Darling.'

It was obvious to Jane, as it probably was to the young nurse, that there would be no escape, but she had to follow the script and tried the lie first.

'You're lying, Nurse. That's not what I heard from Harriet Love.'

Jane stared sightlessly at the screen as the row escalated. Would she never be allowed to forget? Reaching out, she found the television controls. In one snap, Tom Vallely and his intimidated staff were despatched to oblivion.

The washing machine was already spinning Emily's clothes, the hum of its motor like a swarm of angry bees in Jane's head. Like some drugged automaton from *The Stepford Wives* she took the vacuum cleaner out of the cupboard, plugged it in and began pushing it to and fro, to and fro, with ragged movements, through the kitchen, the hall, the living room, the dining room. This was good. This was therapeutic. She must do it more often. Jane yearned for order, but three children, a husband and a dog got perpetually in the way.

Benji darted in front of her and she jerked the machine roughly sideways. A wheel caught on one of the heavy oak chairs and Jane cursed as the chair teetered and began to topple towards her cello. Quickly, she dropped the vacuum cleaner and lurched forward to save it.

Too late. It hit the cello case with a dull thud.

Jane stood frozen. There was a mark on the case where the chair had hit it.

No big deal, she told herself, the case had been bashed a few times, inevitably. All the same, I must check it. When did I last open the case? A couple of years ago perhaps? The last time Emily pestered me.

She laid the case on the floor and knelt down to unlatch it. One swift, well-remembered movement and the cover sprang open.

Then there it was. Her Forster.

Jane's hand moved towards it, drawn inexorably to the gleaming wood. She needed to feel the grain under her fingers. Just one touch wouldn't hurt. Her fingers hovered above the old instrument as gently as a hummingbird in quest of pollen. There. She had touched it. Everything was fine. She was still whole.

Put it away, Jane. Now.

She stared at the cello, her heart beginning to pump, her head swimming.

No! Don't do this! Stop.

Impossible. She had to touch the strings again, feel the familiar catgut, make the connection. She watched her fingers drift towards the bridge, unable to stop them. There. But the strings had been loosened for safe storage and the note was dull.

I should look it over thoroughly.

It's all right, no need to do a full inspection.

No, it needs to be checked, the instrument is my responsibility.

It's all right, Jane, how could there be anything wrong?

All the same...

Stop, now.

I'll tune it, just to be sure.

You know what will happen.

I can't...

Stop.

I can't stop.

She lifted the cello out of the case, unable to fight the impulse any longer.

Ahhhh. Yes. Good.

It felt so familiar in her hands, so right. Her arms went around it protectively, like a mother's arms round a baby.

Her cello.

Her connection to the emotions that lay buried so deep within her.

All coherent thought was suspended. Automatically, her fingers wound the tuning pegs – very carefully because it had

213

been so long since it had been tuned – until the strings rang true. She reached for the bow, tightened it, sank onto the music stool and started to play.

At first it felt good. The notes reverberated round the room, sweet and deep and strong. She hadn't forgotten how to command the instrument, her technique was still good. The music was in her fingers, stored in some deeply ingrained memory bank that required only the touch of the strings to unlock it.

Time passed, but Jane gave no thought to its passage or, indeed, to anything. It might have been minutes, maybe hours had passed. Benji lay at her feet, peacefully dozing, his body twitching as he dreamed.

Why had she been so afraid of this? Once or twice she laughed out loud with the sheer pleasure of it as she played, her feelings swelling so that they became one with the sound and the touch and the melody.

The music was all that mattered.

And yet it wasn't.

She thought of Tom Vallely, of the hurt he had caused.

She thought of Carrie, who had betrayed her.

She thought of Marta, stealing her daughter.

She thought of her baby—

Crash!

She drew the bow roughly over the strings in a grating, blaring discord and came to a grinding halt.

My baby!

She should stop playing now. Her fingers began to hurt. It had been so long since she had played that she had lost the calloused pads that had protected the tips.

It didn't matter. Only the music mattered.

She couldn't, in the end, avoid playing the Elgar – but playing it reminded her, as it always did, of school, where she had first learned the piece, and of Marta and Carrie.

She needed her friends. She had always needed them.

The bow moved quicker now, distorting the natural rhythm of the music as Jane's emotions built up.

No!

She drew the bow discordantly across the strings again and pushed the cello away so hard that it crashed against the corner of the piano. She watched in horror as the neck snapped off from the body and it crumpled to the ground.

No!

Something in Jane's mind snapped too.

Blood.

There had been blood when they had performed the abortion, the blood of murder. She was a murderer. The memory of the sin she had committed had never left her. That was a secret no-one shared, only Tom had guessed and he was not to be trusted.

The memory, so long buried, resurfaced like an angry red devil striking her furiously again and again.

Listen to me!

Acknowledge me!

You have done this thing!

Admit it!

She doubled over, clutching at her stomach, clawing at her clothes. Guilt and fear merged and turned to anguish and she kicked out at the bookcase until music scores, homework jotters and books cascaded onto the floor and lay twisted and torn under her lashing feet. She had lost her baby, she had lost her friends, and when Neal learned the truth about what she had done, she would lose him too.

The pain became unendurable.

Blood would be her escape. Blood for blood. A death for a death.

She stumbled past the shattered cello into the kitchen. Despairing, she slid open a drawer. In a shaft of sunlight, a blade flashed keenly.

With one swift movement she drew it across her wrist.

Pain sliced through her.

A cry escaped her and she threw her arms wide to welcome death.

She was going to be free at last.

She slithered to the floor, blood pooling around her, warm and sweetly metallic, and she slipped into unconsciousness.

By her feet, a frantic Benji started to howl.

Chapter Twenty-seven

October brought with it an unseasonable early flurry of snow. To the west of Fort William, in the wilds of the Highlands, Drew McGraw was about to set out for a day's shooting.

'D'ya think it's gonna snow again?' he asked anxiously, peering out at the blue skies, his mane of hair barely visible under a startling sheepskin hat.

Although the hotel felt stuffy, it was freezing outside. The snow was lying a foot deep on the hills, but the sun was bright and the view was breathtaking. Away to the east, Scotland's highest mountain hunched its white shoulder against the wind and tried to make itself look innocent, yet Marta had heard on the news that three men, caught unprepared for the change in the weather, had just died near the summit of Ben Nevis.

Across the road, in front of the hotel, Loch Eil sparkled in the low morning sun, its banks fringed with white satin ribbons studded with diamonds and pearls.

Drew's party of seven, plus Marta, had arrived the previous night, too late to appreciate the stunning scenery.

'No chance.'

It was Jaime Martinez who spoke. A thin, plain-looking woman, her husband Arno was one of the wealthy potential investors Drew was assiduously courting on this trip. She smiled excitedly, pulled her fur-lined waistcoat up round her ears and pressed her nose against the window.

'I wish. It'd be just amazing to be snowed in here. So beautiful. And such a cute hotel.'

Cute? Thick tartan carpets, heavy tartan curtains and dark green and burgundy walls, matched with Landseer prints of deer and McTaggart seascapes was hardly what Marta would call cute. But the hotel was warm, clean, well serviced and designed to appeal to American taste: the ultimate in expensive tartanalia. Marta had chosen it largely for its position, close to where the shoot would leave, but it also had a reputation for good food and wine and the proprietors knew their market. The rooms were spacious and comfortable, the views exceptional.

'The forecast is fine, Drew,' Marta assured her client, comfortable in the knowledge they would be in the hands of an experienced ghillie. 'You'll get a great day on the hills.'

He grinned amiably, his face already aglow.

'Then I guess I'll brave the outside world. You gals take care now.'

Jaime laughed. 'We're going sightseeing, not mountain climbing.'

Drew opened the front door. The cold was pinching, but there was something exhilarating about it too. In the stuffiness that built up again as soon as the door was closed, Marta began to feel slightly nauseous. Then urgently so.

'Excuse me.'

She ran to the nearest Ladies.

Either I haven't got rid of this stupid bug yet, or this is due to last night's supper, she thought, hanging over the porcelain wretchedly. Yet she had eaten the same as everyone else: venison, tender and pink; roast potatoes, crunchy and crisp; green kale, baked with sweet apples; cranachan – cream, toasted oatmeal, raspberries, a hint of whisky. Good, simple Scottish food.

After a minute, she felt better. She rinsed her mouth at the washbasin, scooping cold water up in cupped hands to her lips, tasting its sweetness after the bitterness of the bile.

'You all right, Marta?' a voice said, behind her.

She swung round. Jaime Martinez had followed her into the Ladies. How much had she seen? How undignified, hardly what was expected of a top-class tour guide. She blushed scarlet.

'Yeah, thanks. Just a touch of nausea. Must've been something I ate last night, but I feel fine now.'

Jaime laughed. 'Either that or you're going to give your husband a very happy surprise.'

Pregnant? Marta stared at Jaime.

'I had the same with all my three. It's worth it, I promise you.'

Pregnant? It isn't possible.

But it was possible. Six weeks. That's how long it had been since she and Jake had last made love.

I'm pregnant.

As soon as Jaime said made the suggestion, Marta knew it was true.

Sweet Lord, what am I going to do?

'The minibus is due,' she said, keeping her voice steady, 'we should go. Thanks for your understanding.'

In the lobby, one of the wives was peering out of the window. 'Is that our bus? Gee, I sure hope it's heated.'

'Yes,' Marta confirmed, sternly banishing all personal worries. Only the responsibilities of the day ahead mattered at this moment. 'That's ours. Now, have you got everything you need? We won't be back till after dark and it's very cold out there. Coats, scarves, gloves ...'

'... credit cards.'

They went out into the bright snow amid much laughter.

Pregnant.

Jake would be thrilled. She thought of her husband, of his once-bright pride in her, of the love she had taken for granted. No, she corrected herself, she could no longer assume that he would welcome this news. The truth was, she had no idea how he would take it.

Professionalism took over as the group embarked on a mini tour of the Highlands.

'Gee, will we see the monster?' Jaime Martinez ran down to the shore at Loch Ness enthusiastically.

It was nonsense, but it thrilled them, and Marta found herself smiling at their childlike pleasure.

'Is that a genuine ruin?' another woman asked as she stared at Urquhart Castle.

Thirteenth-century stonework was highlighted against the brilliant blue of the loch and the snow-covered landscape. Marta gazed at it through the American's eyes and found something steadying in the immutability of the scene.

A third was horrified as they absorbed the story of the battlefield at Culloden.

'You mean they *slaughtered* the poor soldiers as they lay there?'

In the scale of things, she considered, answering their questions patiently, her own problems paled. It was a good lesson.

Only when the history of the land had been wallowed in and its magnificent scenery photographed 'for the folks back home' did she suggest a shopping break. In Inverness, when the group scattered to explore, she was at last able to escape. In a quiet chemist's she bought two pregnancy tests and when they at last arrived back in the hotel and she was finally alone in the oversized, tartan-carpeted bathroom that belonged to her oversized, tartan-carpeted bedroom, she tried both.

She should have been watching the results with Jake. As first one line turned blue, then the other, Marta's heart was sore.

She was going to have a baby. *Their* baby. The child they had longed for.

Surely he would come back to her now? This made everything different.

'Jane's in hospital.'

Carrie's voice sounded distant. Marta strode to the window to catch the best signal on her mobile.

'Say again? I can hardly hear you.'

'Where are you?'

'In the wilds. West of Fort William. Did you say Jane was in hospital?'

'Yeah.'

'What's wrong?'

'She tried to commit suicide.'

'*What?*'

''Fraid so.'

'How? Why? I mean, what happened for heaven's sake?'

'She cut her wrist.'

Marta was struck dumb. Jane's stutter, her crazy accusations about Emily, her erratic behaviour, all stacked up as signs of her increasing vulnerability. But *suicide*?

'Marta? Are you still there?'

'I'm here. Her wrist? You said she cut her wrist?'

'Yes.'

'What was she *thinking* of?'

'I don't know, Marta. I've thought about nothing else since Neal called. Either it was an act of desperation or it was intended as a powerful message. Either way, if Neal hadn't happened to go home she would have died.'

'Oh, Carrie. Dear God in heaven. Tell me what happened.'

'Neal had nipped home for some file he'd forgotten. He says it was as if he was drawn home for some reason. She can't have long done it. She was lying on the floor in the kitchen with Benji going mad. If he'd just been a few minutes later—'

'Don't. It doesn't bear thinking about.'

'There was blood everywhere and she was deeply uncon- scious.'

'Oh God!'

'He managed to put on a tourniquet. The ambulance was there very fast.'

'Christ, Carrie, the kids ...'

'Yeah.' Carrie went quiet. 'There's another thing. Her Forster was smashed.'

'Her cello? I don't understand.'

'She'd been playing it.'

'Really? But she never played it. She's avoided playing it ever since she left the orchestra.'

'I know. Neal wants us to go see her. Whatever is troubling Jane, he thinks it's deep and longstanding. He believes there's something she's not telling anyone.'

'And he thinks she'll tell us?'

'I think he sees us as his last hope. She's not opening up to him. He's tried.'

'Is she still in hospital?'

'They gave her some blood and stitched her up. They're going to send her home later today. '

'Just like that?'

'Hospital's no place to linger.'

'True. Listen, I'll be back in a couple of days. We'll go round when everyone's out, shall we?'

'I think her mother's staying.'

'Oh. Okay.'

Carrie was about to ring off when Marta said, 'I need to talk too.'

'Anything in particular?'

'Oh ... you know.'

'You know is permissible. You know is good. We'll talk about you know by all means. Take good care of Mr McGraw.'

'That's easy.'

'Yeah. Bye.'

'Bye Carrie. Hugs.'

'Hugs to you too.'

Marta sat thinking for a long time. One way or another, her world was turning upside down.

Chapter Twenty-eight

Jane was lying in her bed, half asleep, half awake. On the table beside her a cup of tea was cooling slowly. She'd heard her mother bringing it in, but hadn't been able to rouse herself.

Depression had settled around her, a dark cloud that medication was failing to shift. She had no energy, no interest in anything. She couldn't bring herself to make any effort with her children. Above all, she was still carrying her secret.

And now she had yet another reason to feel guilty: she had tried to commit suicide.

She rolled over and pulled herself up. The bedroom looked much the same as always. The walls had been covered with woodchip paper and painted magnolia many years ago. They'd been meaning to redecorate ever since they'd moved in, but there had never been the time or the money.

One door of the wardrobe stood ajar, revealing chaos inside. The top of the chest of drawers where Neal kept his clothes was barely visible under an avalanche of abandoned ties, cuff links, hairbrushes, paperwork of various kinds, aftershave, a camera, a mug – how long had that been there? The other chest, which she used as a makeshift dressing table, was scarcely better. Earrings vied with make-up for space and the entire contents of a handbag lay heaped in one corner, exactly where she had emptied it out weeks ago. The whole scene was dismal but, even so, there was something reassuring in its familiarity.

How could she have cut her wrist like that? Everything that had been troubling her then was troubling her still, yet she could no more lift a knife and slash her wrist now than walk a tightrope across the Niagara Falls.

She knew the answer – it was the music. The music had breathed air into every ember of emotion, giving it the oxygen it needed to ignite.

'Mum?'

Ross's head poked tentatively round the door.

'Come in, darling.'

He ran across the room and folded himself onto the bottom of the bed.

'Are you okay?'

'I'm fine. I'll get up in a minute. Thank you for coming to see me.'

'I want you to be better.'

'I'm getting better, Ross.'

The door swung open again and Emily slid in, her hair half concealing her face, her thin arms like pale wands.

'Hello darling.'

They used to come in like this, all her children, on Sunday mornings and on special days, jostling and squealing for position on the bed. In recent years, only Ian had kept up the tradition.

Emily crossed her legs underneath her. Her hand went to her hair and she starting twisting a strand of it between her fingers, a sure sign that something was troubling her.

'Em? What is it?'

'Ross and me ...' she started uncertainly, then halted and looked at her brother, biting her lip.

'Is it our fault, Mum?' she blurted out.

'*Your* fault? No, darlings, no, no, no. You mustn't think that, not ever.'

Ross drew in a deep breath. 'I lied to you and Dad. About Em. She asked me to cover up for her and—' he paused, then added with endearing honesty, '—I made her lend me her iPod

226

and promise to buy me tickets for the football. But I didn't think it would end like this.'

'Oh, Ross.'

'I'm sorry. I'm so, so sorry.' He turned to Emily. 'I never thought you'd get like that, you know, in hospital and all.'

Emily said, 'It wasn't your fault, Ross. I did it all by myself.'

'With a little help from Marta Davidson,' Jane added bitterly.

Emily looked at her, her brown eyes wide with surprise.

'Marta? How?'

'Oh come on, Emily. Marta encouraged you to disobey your father and me.'

'No, she didn't.'

'She encouraged you to get your hair dyed, though she must have known we wouldn't have been happy. She bought you clothes she must have known we wouldn't approve of. And heaven knows why she covered up for you after Suzy's party.'

Emily shook her head vigorously.

'No. You've got it all wrong. I told her you wouldn't mind. I told her that it would be all right at school. And I persuaded her to buy me the clothes. She was sweet, Mum, honest. I don't know what I'd have done without her after Suzy's party, I was so scared. And I lied to her – I told her that I'd already texted you to let you know where I was.'

'But why did you do that?'

'Because I knew you and Dad would be furious. I thought if I got home early enough the next day, you need never know.'

'Oh Em. Darling.'

'I'm sorry, Mum. Truly.'

Ross, squirming, said, 'Me too.'

'Listen to me—'

Jane reached out and grasped Emily's right hand, Ross's left. To her surprise, Ross's free hand shot out and grabbed Emily's, so that they were joined in a circle.

'—Your dad and I, we love you. We love all of you, very

much. Maybe we don't do everything right, but we do try. I'm sorry, Emily, if you didn't feel able to talk to us about how you were feeling. Ross, I'm sorry that you felt you had to lie. But there's one thing you must understand.'

She hesitated. How to explain her actions to them? It was so complicated, and so not something that two children should have to come to terms with.

'I haven't been well. There was something – a shadow in my head, if you like – that made me act oddly. It's gone. It has passed. And it was my shadow, nothing to do with you.'

'Honest?'

'Honest. Now, let's move on, shall we? All of us? Family hug?'

As she folded them into her arms, it occurred her that perhaps she needed to think again, that perhaps her friends were not the cause of her woes – that maybe the cause lay within herself.

She stroked Emily's hair. Her daughter was painfully like her. What would her ghost baby have been like?

She had lied to her children. The pain inside her would never go away. But to move forward, she did have to confront it.

When the doorbell rang a few days later, Jane was up and about. Always slim, she'd lost more weight, so that her jeans hung loosely round her hips and the white T-shirt flapped limply around her small breasts. Benji barked excitedly and ran to the door. Jane, following him reluctantly, caught sight of herself in the mirror. Her face was pale and there were dark circles around her eyes. Her hair looked lank and lifeless. She was in no state to receive visitors.

Carrie and Marta stood together on her doorstep.

'Hi, Jane, can we come in?'

'We need to talk.'

'Hi,' Jane said, her voice weak with surprise.

In the kitchen, she made tea, but didn't touch her own. She

228

stared down at her hands instead, twisting them round each other, first this way, then that, kneading the fingers, rubbing the knuckles.

Carrie spoke first. 'We were so shocked when Neal called to tell us. How are you feeling?'

Jane gave a quick, sidelong glance at Carrie's solemn face.

'Why did you do it, Jane?' Marta asked, extending her hand and touching Jane's arm lightly.

She gave a low moan and buried her face in her hands. Her body was beginning to tremble. Someone – Carrie? – shoved back her chair. She heard the scraping on the floor, then felt arms around her.

All her emotions were replaced by anger and she pushed Carrie away fiercely.

'Don't pretend to care, Carrie. It's so hypocritical.'

'Jane, don't.'

'We were supposed to be friends, weren't we? Friends forever, that's what I thought. But you *stole* T-Tom. I loved him then, more than anything, and you stole him. How could you, Carrie?'

Carrie sat down abruptly.

'No,' she said quietly. 'It wasn't like that.'

'He *loved* me. He loved *me*. He loved me until you came along.'

'No, Jane. Listen to me. Tom swore he'd already told you he was leaving. I promise you, Jane, I swear it on my own life. That's how it was. I would never have stolen him from you. Your friendship meant everything to me. It always has. Tom told me that you had been growing apart for ages, that he was looking for somewhere else to live, that you and he agreed.'

'It's not true,' Jane's voice cracked as anger and hurt battled with a yearning for resolution. 'I had n-no idea.'

'Well, I guess that doesn't surprise me,' Carrie said. 'Tom Vallely is a lying, cowardly, manipulative bastard. Do you know

229

something, Jane? He deceived both of us. He made me believe he was in love with me, that he was just waiting for the right moment to tell you he was leaving – and then he went off and married someone else. I couldn't believe it. I was so angry, I could have strung him up. I couldn't even talk to you about it because you'd disappeared.'

She paused and glanced briefly at Marta. 'Did you know that it was because of Tom Vallely that I decided I wasn't going to get involved in a serious relationship again?'

'You're joking.' Jane stared at Carrie in surprise.

'Nope. I decided I'd concentrate on my career for a while, then I discovered that actually, I quite liked being in control of my life.'

'I'm sorry.'

'Don't be sorry, Jane, it's just the way it happened. My punishment, if you like, for cheating on you.'

'He's even more of a b-bastard than I thought he was.'

Marta leaned forward.

'It's my fault. I was totally taken in by him. I didn't know any of this, only that you'd split up – amicably I thought – and it seemed like a fun idea to stage a reunion.'

Jane said slowly, 'No, Marta. It's brought it all to the surface but maybe that's not a b-bad thing. There's something I've never told anyone. I didn't think I ever would but Tom—' she stopped, then said softly, 'Tom is threatening to tell Neal and I don't know what to do.'

'Tell Neal what?'

'You can tell us, Janie.'

Jane stood up and walked across to the window. She straightened the bottle of washing-up liquid, spotted a mark on the sill, took a cloth from the cupboard and scrubbed at it, replaced the cloth, then finally, unable to find any more jobs to do, turned to face them.

'When Tom left me,' she said, 'I was p-p-p-pregnant.'

'Pregnant?' Marta asked, bewildered.

Carrie said softly, 'Oh Jane – is that why you went off radar?'

Jane's laugh was sour. 'When I found out, I thought it might bring Tom back. Not a chance, of course. He didn't want to know. He even questioned the p-paternity. I got desperate. I didn't know what to do. I'd let down my p-parents. They'd sacrificed so m-much for me and I'd thrown it all away. I decided to go ahead and terminate. I thought that would solve everything.'

'You went through all this on your own? Oh Jane—'

'Someone in the orchestra gave me names, contact details, phone numbers. I called one, visited a clinic, went through a mind-numbing series of talks and consultations, and made a d-decision.'

Marta muttered something.

Carrie was more audible. She said, 'Jesus.'

'I lied to the clinic when they asked me if someone was meeting me. I didn't think it would be that bad. It was just a simple operation.'

She buried her face in her hands. 'I thought that termination would solve all my problems but I couldn't have been more wrong.'

She fished in her pocket for a tissue and scrubbed roughly at her eyes.

'It haunted me. I guess I had a kind of breakdown, only I didn't know that. There was no-one to tell me ... no friends...'

'Oh Jane—'

'I handed in my n-notice at the orchestra.' She flashed a crooked smile at Marta. 'Worst thing I could have done, I suppose, but I was in no state to make rational judgements, I just wanted to hide. From everybody.'

'I wish—'

'I left my cello with one of the flautists, packed what I could in a suitcase and posted a letter to my p-parents telling them I'd been offered work abroad. Then I hopped on the first train I saw – it went to M-Manchester.'

'How did you *live*, for heaven's sake?'

Jane shrugged. 'I found a room in a small hostel and a job in a supermarket. That was it. I went to ground. I was hardly functioning, I wasn't talking to anyone, I didn't go anywhere. I was barely existing.'

The silence stretched on forever.

Marta, sitting with her hands on her stomach, as though she was feeling the loss herself, broke it first. 'How did you manage, all alone?

'Why didn't you tell us, Jane?' Carrie asked.

Jane began to cry.

Carrie crossed to where she was standing and folded her into her arms.

'You poor, poor thing.'

'I killed it, Carrie. I've never forgotten what I did. I m-murdered that baby.'

'Ssshh...'

Carrie tried to soothe her. Marta was hugging herself tightly. She looked drawn and pale.

'I killed it because I couldn't cope. I couldn't put my p-parents through that. They never knew. I did it to avoid the shame. How could I have d-done it, Carrie?'

The words were barely audible, they came out as strangled sobs.

'I've never told anyone. I kept thinking it would go away and I'd get better. But it didn't, it got worse and worse and when I saw T-Tom again—'

'Ssshh...ssshh...'

'I couldn't stand it. I simply couldn't ... I'm so sorry, so sorry... so...'

Her words were muffled in Carrie's chest as she curled forwards and buried her head in the warmth of her friend's sweater.

'The darkness closed round me again, like it did when I had the abortion. It all came back, every detail. All those months in that ghastly room in that grim hostel in Manchester, all those months working my guts out in that shabby supermarket, and not able to play my m-m-music any more, not able to even listen...'

'Ssshh... it's all right, Jane. We know now. We understand. We still love you.'

'And the worst thing is,' her voice rose to a wail, 'I've never told Neal. He's always been so against abortion. I can't b-bear to think of what he'd say.'

'He'll understand, Jane. Neal loves you.'

'I've never wanted to risk it. It might change the way he feels about me and I couldn't go on if he left me.'

'I'm sure he won't leave you.'

'And now T-Tom is threatening to tell him.'

'Tom Vallely is a vicious, blackmailing, sadistic, barbaric sociopath and he has to be stopped,' Carrie spat.

'Stopped from telling Neal?'

Carrie took her hand.

'Jane, darling, you should tell Neal about this. He's desperately worried about you. You can't go on keeping this secret; it's eating away at you. I doubt if it'll make the slightest difference to his feelings. Maybe it seems like he's uncompromising on this, but all he wants is for you to be all right.'

'He needs to understand why this happened, Jane,' Marta said.

'I suppose you're right. I don't want to think about it at the m-moment. What did you mean about stopping Tom?'

'I meant, he mustn't be allowed to carry on doing this. He blackmailed me, you know. He made me pay over cash to stop him telling you about our affair – then he told you anyway.'

'Oh my God—'

'So we have to think of something, don't you agree? Marta?'

'I do.' Marta hesitated. 'Jane?' she asked in a tentative voice.

'Yes?'

'How's Emily? I've been so worried about her.'

'She's much better. Thanks for asking.'

'I didn't mean to ... I never ... I only ever wanted to help, you know.'

'Yes. I know that now. I'm sorry I was so m-mad at you.'

'I'm sorry if I did anything wrong. I love Emily dearly.'

'I know you do. And I said something terrible to you – about not knowing how to bring up children—'

'Because I'd never had one of my own. That hurt, Jane, I can't pretend it didn't.'

'I was lashing out because I was angry. I'm really sorry.'

'It's okay. And anyway ... this might not be the most tactful time to tell you—'

Jane caught on at once. 'You're p-pregnant?'

'You're *pregnant?*' Carrie squealed.

Marta's eyes were shining. 'I can't pretend the timing is the best. Jane, Jake's gone to London. Things aren't good between us at the moment.'

'Oh my God! Does he know?'

'Not yet.'

'I never thought ... I thought you and Jake were solid. What happened?'

'Who knows? Tom happened. Not an affair,' Marta said hastily, 'he just made himself rather too much at home and Jake felt edged out. Being out of work for so long made him more vulnerable than I'd realised. His self-esteem had plummeted. I can't believe that spotting Tom that day in the café has caused so much damage.'

'As Carrie says, Tom Vallely,' Jane spat out the name as if it were a curse, even managing to avoid the stutter, 'has to be stopped.'

They looked at each other.

'But how?' Marta asked.

234

Chapter Twenty-nine

'And if I ever find you anywhere near that cupboard again—'

Tom let his voice trail off threateningly. He turned his profile to the camera, clenched his wrist just a little too tightly round the young actress's wrist (simply in order to inject a little real drama into her insipid acting, naturally) and half closed his eyes menacingly.

Conscious of the camera zooming in for a close-up, he held the look, allowing the merest flicker of the lids for added effect.

The young nurse looked at him, fear writ large in her huge, dark eyes.

'I won't. I promise!' she quavered.

'Because that smart young husband of yours just might not be quite so doting if he heard that—'

'Don't tell! Please don't tell! I'll do anything!'

Tom let go of the girl's wrist with a fierce thrust that sent her banging into the wall.

'Cut! Thanks Tom, Joy – you were both great. Right, let's take a break for lunch, back in an hour.'

Tom Vallely was having the time of his life. He had established his character, Mr Charles Darling, an arrogant and egotistical consultant, as one of the core characters in the soap and *Emergency Admissions* was beginning to soar in the ratings. He liked to think of it as the Vallely Effect. He was looking forward to the regular pay cheque, but there were snags. The first cheque might be safely in the bank but it didn't even begin to cover his debts – and he was already running up big bills to fund the lifestyle he was determined to enjoy.

The young actress playing the nurse he had just threatened was in the canteen when he arrived. He glimpsed her by the till, talking to one of the runners and rubbing her wrist. She caught sight of him and turned away quickly. Silly bitch. She'd flirted him into bed when he'd joined the cast but after just one shag she'd refused to see him again.

'You're really hot, Tom,' she explained, painfully sincere, 'but a bit too hot for me. Sorry.'

Tom didn't take well to rejection. In any other situation he might have pursued the matter, but when you were working with someone every day it didn't do to fall out too seriously. Instead, he took it out on her in small ways – a snide word here, a joke at her expense there and if, like today, he got the chance of physical contact, he played up to it. Subtly, of course, so that no-one else saw.

She'd better not snitch.

He glared at her across the room, staring fiercely at the back of her head, sure that she would know he was looking at her. He watched her hand come up and rub her neck as if it was sore.

Result.

At the canteen he helped himself to salad, a brown roll and a glass of juice. Must watch the figure. Wouldn't do to pile on the beef.

Ann Playfair was in today. He spotted the middle-aged scriptwriter at a table by herself. Looked like a dyke. Good writer though, she came up with some excellent storylines for Mr Darling and, in fairness, she had been useful in helping him to land the role.

'Afternoon, Ann. May I join you or is someone sitting here?'

Turn on the charm, Vallely, you never know what's round the corner. He smiled his best smile and summoned warmth to his eyes.

'Hello, Tom. Please,' she indicated the vacant chair, 'do sit. How's it going?'

236

'Brilliant. Loved that last script you did, Ann, the one where my character pulls off the impossible and saves the lad who was mangled in the farm machinery. And the "Will they, won't they" line with Harriet Love is sheer genius.'

'You're getting on well with Hayley?'

'Doesn't it show?' Tom had shagged Hayley Dearborn, who played Harriet Love, a couple of times. He knew he'd get her into bed again, too, despite her protestations that she had a husband and kids in Chester and she really shouldn't be...

'And the rest of the cast?'

He shrugged. 'They're okay. Yes. Good bunch.'

'You don't think your character is a little too arrogant?'

'Hmm. Self-confident, wouldn't you say, rather than arrogant?'

'It's a fine line.'

'I can only go on the scripts I get, darling.'

Ann put aside her plate and started on her dessert. Jam roly poly and custard, no wonder she was so fat. Tom sipped his water and bit his tongue. Wouldn't do to get on the wrong side of a scriptwriter.

'Sometimes actors bring out the best in a character, sometimes the worst. And scriptwriters pick up on that as well as feed into it.'

'Are you saying I should tone the character down a bit?'

'I wouldn't presume to advise you, Tom. That's the director's job.'

'Well, she seems very happy.'

'That's good.'

Tom let her finish her pudding, then asked, 'Any good storylines coming up for Mr Darling?'

'Tom. You know I can't say. That's not my job.'

'Worth a try though.' He grinned at her artlessly and was rewarded with a smile in return. 'Any news from the girls? Marta?'

'Aren't you in touch?'

He put on a shamefaced look. 'Should be, of course, but it's been manic round here.'

'Right.'

'So...?' he prompted.

'Marta phoned me last week. Jake's in London, she says, on a temporary contract. She sounded a bit down, but on the plus side, she's been very busy with a certain Mr McGraw, an American.'

Tom's ears pricked up. 'Is that the guy who was on the news the other night? The one who's poured millions into setting up some new business venture in Dundee?'

'Apparently, yes. Marta's been running tailor-made tours for some of the Americans he's bringing over, real up-market stuff. She's been enjoying that. And Carrie – you know Carrie?'

Did he know Carrie? Tom nearly laughed out loud. Instead he simply nodded encouragingly and waited.

'Carrie Edwards has been seeing this man, it seems, this Mr McGraw. Marta says she's a changed woman, like a teenager in love.'

Really? Caroline Edwards in love? Well, well.

'How wonderful.'

'Jane Harvie, though, the third of the friends – I take it you know her as well? Jane is seriously depressed. Marta didn't say why. If you're concerned about the girls, Tom, maybe you should get on the phone. Didn't you stay with Marta and Jake in Edinburgh? I'm sure she'd welcome a call.'

'Of course. Sure. I'll call today. Nice to chat with you, Ann darling. I'll have to move though. An actor's work and all that.'

'Yes, of course. Bye Tom. Nice to see you are prospering.'

Prospering? Up to a point, but not enough. Worth a phone call, for sure.

Chapter Thirty

The flurry of snow that had been so widespread across the Highlands didn't touch Edinburgh, but the weather had turned autumnal.

Forced into the garden – Jake's domain – to tidy up the falling leaves, Marta grew thoughtful.

Jake was due home today. She glanced at her watch. His train would be pulling in to Waverley Station any time now. He had refused her offer to meet him – 'Don't be silly, Marta, I'm perfectly capable of catching a bus' – so it would be at least forty minutes before he got here.

Jake didn't know about the baby. She'd been tempted to tell him a dozen times, but as soon as he'd told her he was coming back for a weekend, she'd decided that this was something better done face to face.

'Coming home? Oh Jake, how lovely,' she'd said, thrilled.

'Just to pack up more of my things.'

'Oh, I see.'

They'd been talking more and more on the phone – getting closer. The stilted conversations of the days just after his departure had mellowed into a comfortable familiarity.

'It's going really well here.'

'I'm glad,' she lied. That is, she *was* glad for him. He sounded so much like the old Jake, telling her about the projects he was working on, enthusiastic again. She just wasn't happy that he was in London, not in Edinburgh. Once he was here though ... once he knew about the baby...

She bent again, picked up the bag full of leaves and crossed to the compost bin. There, that looked neater. Under the apple tree, the first of the crop had dropped. She would make a crumble for supper.

He rang the doorbell.

Rang the bell. In his own house.

Instantly, Marta felt uneasy. Why had he done that? He still had a key.

'Hi, Jake.'

She hadn't anticipated the impact his physical presence would have on her. There he was, her Jake, her husband, so deeply, dearly familiar, and yet so obviously out of bounds. He made that clear at once, bending forward and to kiss her cheek with polite formality. He defined the limits he wished to maintain.

'Journey alright? It's so lovely to see you.' Christ, she sounded like a stranger, or at least, a passing friend. 'Oh Jake—' she extended her arm, reached out to him impulsively.

'Bang on time,' he said cheerfully, ignoring the outstretched hand. 'May I come in?'

Biting her lip, Marta stood aside. She'd worked hard in the cottage to make sure everything was perfect. A large vase of hydrangeas stood on the hall table, perfectly lit by the ceiling spotlights. She had put coffee on to brew and the smell was wafting along the corridor to where they stood. In the small living room, pale autumn sunshine streamed pleasingly in through the window, highlighting the bronze sculpture of the sleeping woman they had bought together in a gallery in town as a Christmas present to each other.

Two years ago. That was all. Two years, and yet it seemed like a lifetime.

On the far wall, the sunlight picked out a print Jake had given her for her thirty-fifth birthday, so that the freshness of the green and the intense blue of the Himalayan poppies glowed like gems.

'Is that coffee on offer? I could kill for a decent brew.'

'Of course. Want it in here?'

'Thanks.'

He could have walked in and helped himself. That would have been the natural thing to do, not to sit and wait for her to bring it, like a guest. She bit back her comments and went to fetch the coffee, pouring a glass of juice for herself. She had gone off coffee completely.

If he notices, I'll tell him now.

But Jake didn't notice. He talked, instead, about London, about the job, about life in the south.

'Getting the Tube every day, that's the worst bit. If I could afford somewhere a bit nearer, I'd love to be able to walk, but it's so expensive. I'll keep looking. Maybe I'll get lucky and find a room somewhere.'

'I'm sure it's tiring. What's the place you're in like?'

'Doesn't compare with this.' He gestured round the room. 'You've always made things so nice.'

Come back then. Come home.

'Thanks.'

He finished his coffee.

'I'll take my bag up to the spare room, will I? I can pack my stuff up tomorrow. You don't mind me going into your room to do that?'

Marta's heart plummeted. This was horrible. It was worse than not having him here at all. She'd thought – what? – that he would fall back into bed with her? Perhaps not, that was always going to be unlikely, but still, the reality was a shock, like getting into a bath you expected to be warm and finding out that it was icy.

'Sure. No problem,' she said dismally.

Worse was to come. He glanced at his watch. 'Then I'll have to get going, sharpish. I'm seeing my mates for the Hearts match.'

241

'Oh!'

She'd expected they would do something together, go for a walk on the beach, visit a gallery, go to the cinema, perhaps.

'What about later?'

She'd already made the crumble.

'If you don't mind me using my key, I'll just let myself in. That alright? I wouldn't want you to stay up for me.'

'Sure.'

'It's great being able to see the guys again. I'll catch up on the news, do the town.'

He was smiling, relaxed, apparently happy – indeed, happier than she had seen him look for some time.

Marta's expectations were comprehensively punctured. She felt her lip quivering and tears stinging her eyes, but pride made her summon the will to hold them back.

At the door, he turned back to study her. 'You're looking well, by the way Marta. Positively glowing.'

'Thanks.'

'See you in the morning. I'll try not to disturb you.'

'See you.'

And then he was gone, swinging along the path and down the road, and Marta was left feeling far, far worse than she had felt in all the weeks he had been away.

She couldn't let him leave without telling him, because once he knew, it would change everything. In the morning, he appeared in the kitchen looking cheerful.

'Brilliant match. And Hearts won.'

'I saw the result. How were your friends?'

'In great form. Iain's missus is expecting again.'

Now. Now was her opportunity.

'That's nice. Jake—'

'Is that porridge you've made? Excellent. You always were a fine homemaker, Marta. Do you mind if I take sugar on it?'

'I've already put it on the table for you.'

'So you have. This is tasty. I've missed having porridge.'

The moment was slipping away. She had to say something. Perhaps start with something less dramatic? Like an apology?

'Jake, I've been meaning to say, well, I'm sorry. About Tom, I mean. It was really stupid, bringing him into the house like that, not even asking you.' She bit her lip. 'If you'd been a bit more honest about it, earlier on … I mean, perhaps I could have—'

'So it's my fault, is it?' Jake broke in, his tone edgy.

'No! No, I didn't mean that. I only meant … you've always been so easygoing, I didn't realise how you felt about him until it was too late. That's all.'

'I did try to tell you. You kept defending him.'

'Did I?'

'You wouldn't listen, Marta.'

'Oh.'

'Your trouble is, you always see only the best in people. It's not the worst fault anyone can have, but sometimes it can cause real problems. It certainly did this time.'

'Then I'm doubly sorry.'

This was not going well.

'I wanted to tell you that, Jake. And I wanted to tell you … I've been thinking … I'm really proud of you.'

'Proud?'

'Of the way you dealt with being unemployed. Tom – well, he was a sponger and a thief. I know that now. On the other hand, you did everything you could, you wrote all those letters, phoned people, even got that temporary job in the Assembly Rooms—'

'All pretty much organised by you.'

'I only encouraged you. You did it.'

'Yes. Well. Thanks for apologising, Marta.'

Jake pushed aside his bowl and ran his hand through his hair.

'I'd better go and start packing. My train's at eleven.'

Time was slipping away. Do it now. Tell him now. You have to tell him.

Marta laid her hand on his arm, detaining him. Jake, half rising from his chair, sank down in response to her touch and looked at her.

Say it.

'There's something I have to tell you, Jake. I'm pregnant. You're going to be a father at last!' she smiled.

'Bloody hell.'

Jake's mouth fell open. She'd anticipated surprise – but she'd foreseen pleasure too, not this blankness.

'It's happened at last.'

Again she smiled, more tentatively this time.

'Bloody hell,' Jake said again, but this time there was a note of irritation in his voice.

'Aren't you—' she faltered, 'aren't you pleased?'

'Well, the timing could hardly be worse, could it?'

'But your contract will be up in February and the baby's not due till mid-May.'

The silence seemed to go on forever.

Say something, Jake. Tell me you're happy. Tell me this is all a big mistake. Tell me you really love me.

'I'm not planning on coming back, Marta.'

Shock paralysed her. She could hear the kitchen clock with its faint tick, tick, tick, marking out the moments of her bewilderment. Jake's face was set. She could feel the grain of the oak table under her fingers, ripples of time across the years. At last she found her voice.

'You can't mean that. You're going to be a father, Jake. It's what we've always wanted.'

'It's what you've always wanted.'

'*Jake!*'

'I've never been able to work out what our lives would be like if we had a baby, Marta. I was just too much of a wimp to tell you.'

244

'I don't understand.'

'You're an organiser, Marta. A very good one. You organised our home, you organised your work. And you organised me. You made all the decisions in our lives. Where we lived. Where we went on our holidays. What I wore.'

'You were happy to let me.'

'Yes. That was my fault. I allowed habit to take hold and as my irritation grew, I became less and less able to admit to it. But a baby, Marta?'

'Our baby—'

'I can see what would happen. Everything would be organised round the child and by some magical art, I would be organised into some level of the family hierarchy so deeply invisible that I would barely exist.'

'*No*, Jake! How can you say that? How can you *think* that?'

He shook his head.

'Sorry, love, but I'm finding I like making decisions for myself. It's not always easy, and I make mistakes, but they are *my* mistakes. And anyway ... I've started seeing someone else.'

Marta gasped. So soon?

'Her name is Jenny and she's in the public-relations team in the firm where I'm working.'

She did not want to know this.

He gave a short laugh. 'Ironically, she's a single mother. She has a child of three, a boy.'

'You mean, you can become a father to someone else's child, but not to your own?' she asked incredulously.

'Hang on a minute, Marta, you've only just told me about being pregnant, it's not exactly something I've been factoring into my decisions. Anyway, it's early days'

'How could you even *think* of taking on another family when you've got one of your own on the way?'

'I didn't say I was going to "take on a family" as you put it.'

'Well it sounds remarkably—' Marta bit her tongue. A row wasn't going to help. She swallowed miserably.

'All I'm saying,' Jake said, 'is that at the moment, I can't see my way to coming back to you. A baby?' He raked his hair. 'Christ.'

'Jake—'

Jake pushed back his chair and stood. 'I won't abandon you, Marta. You know I'd never ... Jesus.'

He turned on his heel and headed for the stairs.

Her heartbeat slowed and became sluggish, so that breathing became difficult and her limbs grew cold. She started to shiver. There must be a way round this. She would talk to Jake again when he came downstairs. That was it, yes, she would talk to him again.

'I'll phone you,' he called from the hall.

'You're not going already?'

He dropped his bag on the floor and pulled her into an embrace, but as her heart lurched with hope he said quietly, 'My train's in fifty minutes, I have to go or I'll miss it.'

'Darling—'

'Listen, love, you've dropped a bombshell. You're going to have to let me digest the news.'

'If you don't want to come back to Edinburgh, I could come to London—'

He released her sharply. 'Don't use this pregnancy as blackmail, Marta. That's not your style at all.'

Her hands flew up to her face to cover the sudden heat in her cheeks.

'I'm pleased you're pregnant, Marta,' he said more gently, 'for your sake. I know how much you wanted a baby. But babies can't heal broken relationships, they never could.' He bent and kissed her cheek again. 'We'll talk soon, I promise. We'll work something out.'

He closed the door behind him.

He had gone. And now she was alone.

But not, this time, completely alone. Her hands shaking, she picked up her phone.

'Carrie,' she said, her voice trembling, 'I need you. Please, please help me—'

Chapter Thirty-one

Carrie left Marta's cottage a couple of hours later, exhausted with the effort of trying to stem her friend's emotion.

Of course Jake would come round. In time he would warm to the idea of fatherhood.

Jake loved her, he'd always loved her, anyone could see that. In the meantime, she and Jane were there for Marta, any time.

Difficult was too mild a word to describe the scene. Soothing Marta, Carrie inwardly wept for her. Reassuring her about the future, she had no idea what lay in store for her friend. Life as a single mother was almost certainly on the cards.

Who could have predicted it? A few months ago they had seemed the most comfortable couple she knew, in their beautiful little cottage, with their settled lives and their good jobs.

'Bye, darling. Call me any time. And Jane.'

She waved to Marta from the gate and drove away, but stopped just around the corner. She couldn't wait to dial the now-familiar number.

The reception inside the Mercedes was clear as a bell. 'Hi. It's me.'

'Hi, Carrie darling.'

The booming sound of Drew McGraw's voice filled her with undiluted joy. She ached to be with him, to be holding his huge hand. Since that night at her flat, she'd gone out with him a dozen times, maybe twenty. He'd been true to his word. He had brought his business to Ascher Frew, and Carrie's standing at the office had rocketed. Surely now, surely soon, she would get the offer of the partnership? But her world had rocked and its axis no longer tilted from the office towards success. Its magnetic pull was elsewhere.

'Hi love.'

It was all so new. Not since she had been knocked out by Tom Vallely all those years ago had she surrendered herself so completely to her feelings. It wasn't that she felt safe, though she was sure that Drew would not hurt her intentionally. He was no Tom – but neither had he made clear his intentions towards her in any way. It was simply that she was unable, this time, to help herself.

She had fallen in love.

Yet Drew, larger than life and twice as generous, had made no move on her. Carrie was beside herself with lust. Every inch of soft tissue ached for him. Her hands longed to stroke him. Her breasts tingled for want of his touch. She desired, more than anything, to take him inside her, to lie with him, limb to limb, skin to skin. Drew, though, had done nothing more than hold her hand. It wasn't natural. It wasn't what she was used to. But, by heaven, it fired her up.

'You free now?'

'I'm free.'

'How's Marta?'

'Not good,' Carrie said in a tired voice, 'I'll tell you when I see you.'

'Right-o.'

He had taken an apartment in Queen Street for the duration of his stay. Carrie had offered her spare room (hoping that, once he was there, he would swiftly migrate to her bedroom) but he had gently turned the offer down, pleading pressure of work and odd hours.

'You wanna dine out? Or I could have something sent here.'

'I'll come round to you.'

Was there any choice? Eating out, she would only ache to play with his feet under the table, hold his hand across it, she

250

would have no appetite, no eyes for anything except him. In his apartment, even though she would not initiate any move, contact would be easier – and perhaps tonight (the thought kept her going) – perhaps tonight they would at last end up in bed.

'How long will you be?'

'Twenty minutes. Half an hour if I can't get parked.'

'Indian, Chinese or pizza?'

'Anything you like.'

She wasn't hungry. All she wanted was Drew.

'Hurry slowly, then.'

He meant, keep safe.

'I will.'

Love you, she wanted to say, love you darling Drew – but she couldn't. That had to come from him and though she knew he liked her, liked her a lot, she didn't know how much.

She met the delivery man on Drew's doorstep.

'Here. I'll take it. What do I owe you?'

She paid the bill and rang the bell.

'Hi gorgeous.'

'Hi,' she grinned, flooded by happiness at the mere sight of him. 'I bring goodies.'

'Aw, honey, did you pay? You shouldn't have. Here, let me.'

He stooped to take the bags from her.

Carrie loved it that he was twice her size, that she only came up to his shoulder and that she was like a wisp next to him. She loved it that his appetite for food, as for life, was hearty.

Over the naan and the dhal, the tandoori prawns, plump and pink with their bright red coating, and the lamb korma – Drew had not yet acquired a taste for hot spices – she filled him in on the situation with Marta.

'That's too bad,' he said, tearing off another strip of naan. 'She's a great gal, she doesn't deserve that.'

'No. She doesn't.'

'I've been thinking.'

'Is that unusual?' Carrie teased him. Drew was always drifting off into some dream or other, usually planning ways to make more money, build up his business. His answer surprised her.

'Unusual – yeah. Thinking the kind of thoughts I've been thinking, at any rate.'

'Go on then, spill the beans.'

'Beans?'

He looked puzzled.

'It's an expression, Drew. It just means, tell me.'

He surprised her again by taking her hands across the table.

'I'd like for you to come to the States with me when I go back next week. Think you can get away? I would like to introduce you to my folks.'

Carrie's heart started hammering.

'Why Drew! What a lovely invitation. Thank you.'

'You know how I feel about you.'

No, actually, I don't. Tell me.

'I really care about you, Carrie. I haven't felt this way in a long time. A very long time. You're real special – clever, sassy, full of energy and ambition. I'd like for us to spend more time together. Maybe—' he broke off. 'Well, honey, what d'ya say? Will you come?'

'Well now, you have surprised me, Drew.'

'Yeah? You must know I really fancy you.'

His thumbs were stroking the insides of her palms. Carrie felt as though she was melting inside.

'Come here.'

He tugged at her right hand, released the left so that she was able to slide round the table and sit on his knee.

'Carrie, honey, do you think ...'

His words faded to nothing as his lips came down on hers in

a kiss more gentle than she would have thought possible from such a bear of a man. Then the kissing turned more urgent, more insistent, and she felt his hand creep up inside her sweater. *Yes! Oh yes!* His fingers were on her breasts, tugging at her bra, pulling it down urgently so that they could seek out her nipples. He stood, swiftly, scooping her up in his arms and carrying her effortless towards the bedroom.

'Carrie? You all right with this?' he whispered as they neared the bed.

She didn't answer. She just turned her face up towards him and sought his lips again, her tongue finding his tongue, her breathing quickening as her hands found the smooth warmth of his skin under his shirt.

'Don't stop, Drew,' she whispered at last, as he surfaced for air. 'Please don't stop.'

And then they were one. She felt him slip into her, heard his long 'Aaaah' of pleasure, heard her own sigh of delight.

'Honey – is it safe?'

'Fine, yes,' she said, her hand stroking the length of his back, feeling the muscles of his shoulders, the hollow in the small of his back, the round firmness of his butt. It felt as though they had always known each other, were made for each other, fitted together as sweetly and as perfectly as though God above had designed them as a pair.

Later, after they were both delightfully sated, he repeated his question.

'How about the States, Carrie? Whad'ya think?'

'I'd have to ask for time off.'

'I could say I need you with me. Consultations with my US lawyers.'

Carrie grinned. 'Why Mr McGraw!'

'I could even make that true.'

'Ah.'

'So you'll come?'

253

'Of course I'll come, Drew.'

'Great. That's great.'

And he showed her just how great he thought it was in the most personal of ways.

The call Carrie least wanted to take came the next morning. She had got into the office early and, at nine, had already been at her desk for an hour. She needed a caffeine fix.

'I'm off for a coffee, Sally,' she said to her colleague. 'Want one?'

'Oh, yeah, great, thanks. Large latte please.'

'I'll get the money when I get back, don't worry.'

She picked up her bag and as she did so, her mobile started to ring. She hesitated. Work or personal, that was the question. If it was work, she should stay and deal with it. If it was personal, she might as well get on her way and talk as she went. Taking a chance, she headed towards the door, answering as she went.

'Hi, Carrie here.'

'Darling D.A. Delight. Hello.'

Carrie nearly dropped the phone. *Tom. Christ.*

'What do you want?' she said ungraciously, signalling to Yvonne as she passed that she'd be back shortly.

'Charming. Not even a "How are you"?'

'Tom, I think we both know that you are unlikely to be calling me simply to pass the time of day. I take it life's a beach, now that you've hit the small screen?'

'Oh yes, a blast. Wine, women and song. Or to put it in a more contemporary way, sex, drugs and rock 'n roll, baby.'

'So to what do I owe the honour of this call then?'

Tom sounded pained. 'Can I not just phone for a chat?'

'You never have before.'

His laughter rang out down the line.

'How well you know me, Caroline dear. I heard a little bird tell me you're in love.'

Carrie's heart skipped a beat.

'In love? Moi?' she parried helplessly.

'Toi. Little Carrie. Or should I say 'Lil Miz Caroline.' He said it in a deep drawl. 'In love with a very interesting American, by all accounts.'

Damn and double damn. How had he heard about Drew? She didn't reply.

'Yes. As blithe as a schoolgirl, was what I heard. That fairly sent my pulses racing, I can tell you.'

The laugh was laden with innuendo.

'Shut up, Tom. You're disgusting.'

'Oh, so now I'm disgusting, am I? So what's changed so suddenly, huh? From bed buddy to the sweet innocent, is it? I'm guessing dear Mr McGraw would be quite interested in that. I'm guessing a respectable businessman from the American South might be a little, shall we say, surprised to hear about the sexual predilections of the new-found companion of his heart.'

'Shut it, Tom. You know nothing about it. Anyway, I've already told him.'

'Then a confirmatory call from me will come as no surprise, will it, darling?'

'What's wrong, Tom? You can't be broke, surely. Not with your new status as a television star.'

'Well actually, darling, now that you mention it, a little top-up of the funds would come in quite useful.'

'Don't expect it from me,' Carrie said, her anger almost uncontainable. 'The last time I contributed to your *funds* I discovered you hadn't even kept your side of the bargain.'

'Ah. You found that out, did you? A little time slip, that was all. I promised you I wouldn't say a word to Janie after our conversation, and I didn't. Actually, I'd told her before I called you.'

Carrie was seething. 'You're a fucking bastard, Tom.'

'I can be,' he said. 'Oh I agree, I can be. But I do assure you,

'Caroline darling, you have my *absolute* word for it, that if you contribute to my funds this time I will say nothing at all to your delightful new man about your unalloyed obsession with sex with any and every stranger.'

'That is *so* not what it's like!' Carrie exploded. She was outside the deli now, but she could see heads turning her way, expressions curious, from inside the shop. She stepped away and said in low voice, 'You know it's not like that, Tom. You *know* it's not.'

'Ah, but will Mr McGraw? That's the question, I think.'

Carrie was pacing up and down the street, thinking furiously. If she could just pay him off this time, keep him quiet, soon they'd be in the States, away from his reach. And besides, she'd have got closer to Drew, taught him to trust her, love her. He would never believe Tom then. She could laugh him off as a mere troublemaker. But right now, she couldn't risk it.

'How much?'

'Five grand.'

'*Five*—! You must be joking.'

'Would I jest about a thing like this, Carrie darling?'

'Where am I going to find money like that?'

'You'll find it,' he said easily. 'Look on it as an investment in your future. Now listen, darling, I must go. A working man and all that. Give me a call when you've got everything in place. But don't leave it too long. Tomorrow afternoon will be fine.'

'*Tomorrow*! Ha ha.'

'No joke, Carrie. Bye.'

And he was gone.

Carrie, still shaking, was back at the office before she realised that she hadn't been to the deli.

'Where's my latte, then?' Sally asked expectantly.

'Shit. Sorry. I forgot.'

'Carrie. Christ. If that's what love does to you, give me less of it,' Sally groaned. 'I'll go myself.'

'No, I'll go back. I need the air.'

Chapter Thirty-two

A week after Ross and Emily made their joint confession to Jane, Emily made another, even bigger one, to her mother.

'Mum? Can I tell you something?'

They were on their own in the house. Gran Porter, her presence required less as Jane's health improved, had retreated to her own flat. 'I'll just have a quiet wee evening to myself, Jane, if that's all right with you.' Neal had taken the boys to a school football game and as Jane tackled a pile of ironing, an unusual sense of calm prevailed in the Harvie household.

'Of course, d-darling. Here, sit down.'

Jane swept a pile of crumpled clothing off the chair nearest to her onto the slightly hairy floor to make room for Emily. She picked a shirt off the top of the pile and stretched it over the ironing board.

'What is it?'

Emily settled onto the chair.

'I'll fold these for you.'

She picked up some towels and began to smooth them half-heartedly.

'Thanks. What is it?'

'You know Robbie?'

Jane frowned. Robbie Jamieson was not her favourite topic of conversation.

'Yes?' A series of serious discussions with Emily about her recent behaviour had led to an agreement that she would stop seeing him. It hadn't been a difficult agreement, Emily had been surprisingly acquiescent.

'That night – the one when I ended up in hospital?'

'What about it?'

'I slept with Robbie.'

Jane's iron hovered in mid-air, then landed heavily on the shirt. Both her hands flew to her mouth as she stared at her daughter.

'Oh, Emily. Why? Why did you d-d-do that?'

'Don't be angry with me. I loved him. At least, I thought I did. I guess I thought it would tie him to me. But it wasn't really very nice. Is that shirt all right?'

'Oh!' Jane seized the iron and placed it upright on the end of the board. She looked at the shirt ruefully, then bundled it up and tossed it to one side. 'Never mind that – Emily, d-d-dearest – are you all right? My baby...'

She squatted down beside Emily and put her arms round her.

'Are you? I mean, you're not likely to be p-pregnant?'

Surely history would not be so unkind?

'No, of course not. I may be stupid but I'm not that irresponsible. I just wanted to tell you, that's all. I thought you should know.'

'Thank you Emily. You know, sleeping with someone should be a very special thing. You should wait until you are really ready.'

'I know that now. It hurt. And it felt a bit dirty. I didn't want to listen to Suzy, but she was right all along. Robbie didn't care about me much, I can see it now. I've already told him I don't want to see him again. I've decided to leave the orchestra.'

'Leave the orchestra? Emily, no, surely not.'

'I *hate* it.'

'Because Robbie goes?'

'I suppose.'

'You mustn't let it rule your life. It was just the once, wasn't it?'

'Yeah. It wasn't all Robbie's fault. I mean, Suzy's right, he *is* a *really* selfish guy and all that, but I did throw myself at him. And now I can't stand even looking at him.'

'Emily, sweetest.' Jane hugged her again, 'What a shame you d-did it for the first time with ... well, it's done now, I suppose. But you're only sixteen ... wait a bit, eh? Wait until you meet someone you really care about?'

Emily nodded. 'Yeah. I will.'

She stood up.

'All right if I go and practice my cello now?'

'Of course. Maybe you can join the orchestra again next term?'

'I'll think about it.'

'And Emily—'

'Yeah?'

'When my Forster is mended, why d-don't you start playing it?'

Emily swung back, her face aflame with delight.

'Do you mean it? Really?'

Jane nodded. She had no more fear of the cello. Her fears had moved on.

If Jane had thought she was going to have a quiet evening with the ironing, it seemed that she was mistaken because just as Emily began her cello practice, the doorbell rang. She sighed. Hopefully it would be just one of the Mormons who called round from time to time, squeaky clean, trying to convert them all to their cause. A quick, polite, 'No thanks, we're Presbyterians' would see the back of the young man.

But it wasn't a Mormon, it was Marta.

'I'm sorry, Jane, I know I should have called, but I just ... I was out just driving around and I... Please—'

'Come in.'

Jane's irritation flew to the skies as compassion took its place. She knew about Jake's visit, and what had happened, but when she'd related the events of the weekend, Marta had been matter-of-fact, very calm, hopeful of a good resolution. The Marta in front of her now was a wreck, her normally immaculate blonde hair was bedraggled and limp, she wasn't wearing any make-up, and her hands were visibly trembling.

'Sweetheart, come into the kitchen. Here, I'll get t-tea. Sit.'

She indicated the chair just vacated by Emily.

Marta collapsed onto it as though someone had hit the back of her knees.

'I'm sorry,' she said.

'For what?'

'For troubling you. For coming in unannounced. I can hear Emily practising.' She cocked her head in the direction of the music room and managed a shaky smile. 'How is she?'

'She's getting a lot b-better, thanks,' Jane said firmly. 'Here.' She ladled two spoons of sugar into the tea – her mother always maintained that the best thing for shock was hot, sweet tea – and put the steaming mug down in front of Marta. 'T-tell.'

Marta lifted the mug, but she seemed to have some difficulty in taking a sip.

'It's just hit me, Jane. That's all. I feel so...' she searched for the word. 'Empty. And *stupid*!' She snapped out the word angrily. 'How could I not have seen what was happening? How could I not have understood my own behaviour better? Or read our relationship more accurately? How could I have been such a *fool*?'

Jane abandoned all thought of ironing and found another chair. 'Are you sure it's as b-bad as you think?'

Marta groaned.

'Jane, I replay what he said over and over and over in my head all the time. I pick apart his words until they make no sense at all. I don't know. I think so. I think it's probably worse. He's seeing someone else, you know.'

Jane did know. Marta had told her a dozen times already.

'Really?' she said sympathetically. 'P-probably just enjoying a bit of freedom.'

Marta talked, Jane mostly listened. The conversation was circular.

'I should have seen it coming and done something about it.'

'That's easy to say in retrospect, M-Marta.'

'If only I'd...'

When Marta's mug was empty, she put it down and stared at it unseeingly for a minute then said, in an unexpected twist of conversation, 'Have you told Neal yet? About the ... you know.'

Jane was caught off guard. 'N-no, not yet.'

'Oh Jane, why not? You must tell him, you know, and the sooner the better.'

The truth was that Jane, fearful about Neal's reaction, was still in two minds. It was a long time ago. She'd been young. She'd been alone, unable to talk to friends about it. Times were very different then. Excuses chased round her head, each justifying silence. Besides, Marta's ideas – always well intentioned – all too often ended by backfiring. She couldn't be sure. And if she couldn't be sure, she couldn't take the risk.

Marta, perhaps seeing the look of doubt on Jane's face, said earnestly, 'You have to talk, Jane. I didn't talk to Jake, that was what the problem was.'

Jane sighed. 'I suppose you're right.'

'I'd better go and let you get on with your ironing. Thanks for the tea and sympathy.'

At the door, she said again, 'Tell Neal, Jane. You won't regret it.'

Whether she would have told Neal or not, Jane was never to know, because the next morning, after the house had cleared of husband and children – Emily and Ross cheerfully bickering again, a good sign – the telephone rang. Expecting her mother, wanting to discuss arrangements for the day's visit, she answered it quickly.

'Hello?'

But it was not Evelyn Porter. It was Tom Vallely. At the sound of his voice, Jane nearly dropped the phone. It felt as though the receiver had suddenly burst into flames in her hand. Pain shot up her arm, along her left side, and started to make her ear burn and her head throb.

'What is it?'

'Don't sound so suspicious, Janie darling. Just calling to hear how you are.'

'What d-do you care?'

'Oh Janie, Janie, Janie,' he said reproachfully, 'I cared for you for years, don't you remember?'

She tried to remember. Perhaps there had been a bit of caring, early on, but the truth was that she'd always wondered why charismatic, sexy, popular Tom Vallely had stuck with her, plain Jane Porter. He could have had anyone in those days.

After they'd split up, she did suspect that he had been unfaithful more than once. Thinking back, she remembered small incidents, the faintest scent on his clothes, a blonde hair on his sweater, things she had not even considered or which he had airily explained away.

'You d-don't care for me now,' she said. 'Anyway, I'm fine, thank you, so you have no need to worry.'

'Good, good. That's not what I heard, but if you say so.'

'Heard? What did you hear?'

'Oh, I heard you were really depressed. I didn't like to think about that, Janie darling. I thought you might be a bit worried, you know, because of Neal not knowing about the abortion. It occurred to me that you might be concerned that I would tell him.'

'You wouldn't!'

'No. Of course I wouldn't,' Tom said reassuringly. 'Only the thing is, Janie darling, I find myself a little short of cash right now. Maintaining my new lifestyle is a little more expensive than

I thought it would be. And I thought you would be so relieved to know for sure that Neal would not be hearing anything from me once you help me out a little.'

'Help you out?'

'Money, darling. I need some money. And then Tom will disappear. Simple! Except, of course, you will have the extreme pleasure of watching me three times a week on your television screen.'

'I haven't g-g-got any money.'

'Poor darling Janie, that stutter's getting worse, wouldn't you say? I think you'll find some money. Oh, I think so. And then all your problems will go away.'

'T-Tom, don't do this to me.'

'I've got to go now. Rehearsals beckon. A star's life is not an easy one.' His laugh made her shiver. 'I'll call tomorrow. Tell you where to send it,' he said cheerfully. 'Because I'm sure your children wouldn't like to know what you did either, would they now? Bye darling.'

The fire on Jane's left side had been quenched by an icy glacier. She felt numb, sick, filled with helplessness and despair. She sank onto the sofa and buried her face in her hands. She'd find the money somehow. She would do whatever it took to protect her family from the knowledge of what had happened. But would she be able to live with herself afterwards?

Chapter Thirty-three

For the first time, Carrie made an excuse not to see Drew.

'I'm shattered, darling,' she told him when he phoned in the afternoon. 'I was in the office really early this morning, I think I've been overdoing it recently. I don't have your unquenchable energy,' she said lamely. It wasn't true – her energy levels were generally off the top end of the scale.

'We could just cuddle up together?'

'You know we wouldn't just "cuddle up" Drew. If I'm with you I can't sleep for looking at you and marvelling that you care for me.'

He gave his big, easy laugh.

'Right then, honey, I'll let you off just this once. Take care of yourself now.'

'And you.'

She ended the call, her heart heavy. But how could she face him? She had to get Tom off her back. Then, perhaps, everything would settle down and she could put all this aside.

Earlier in the day she had reluctantly telephoned her broker and asked him to cash in some of the shares she had inherited from her father – money she had been keeping for a rainy day. Resentment wrestled with anger, first one emotion uppermost, then the other. Still she had not called Tom back.

After work, she headed to the gym. She tackled the rowing machine first then headed to the treadmill. Carrie liked running. She liked to push herself harder and harder, a bit longer this time, a bit faster the next. Tonight she tried both – further, faster. The pain in her legs was nothing to the hurt in her heart.

Tom bloody Vallely. Tom bloody Vallely.

The words echoed round and round to the rhythm of her pounding feet. Sweat was pouring off her. She had no idea how long she had been running, but after some time she knew that even if she paid him the money, Tom was not going to go away. Why would he, if he thought that all he had to do was threaten her and she would stump up? It was so obvious she couldn't imagine why it hadn't occurred to her before.

I can't win. I can never be free of this.

She slowed her pace. The treadmill slowed. She stopped running.

Enough. She couldn't run any more.

The views from her penthouse windows gave her no pleasure tonight. The clean open space of her living quarters, usually so cherished, did nothing now but emphasise her loneliness.

In the bathroom, feeling the need for further punishment, she turned the shower to cold and stood under it. The water cascaded down her back, splashing onto the marble tiles behind her. She scrubbed at her skin. If only she could wash her past away, if only she had found Drew years ago, if only Tom hadn't come back into her life, if only ... if only ... if only ...

Clarity seemed to come with cleanliness. She couldn't allow Tom Vallely to capitalise on this and besides, she could spend the rest of her life being held to ransom by the loathsome man.

She turned off the water and dried herself roughly. She had reached a decision and her resolve was steely.

'Hi, who's there?' Drew's voice boomed down the intercom.

'It's me. Can I come up?'

The night had turned icy. There would be a frost later. Carrie was chilled to the bone, but half the cause was fear.

'Hi!'

He flung the door open and reached out his arms delightedly, ready to scoop her up in them.

266

Carrie stepped back, out of his reach.

'Don't, Drew. Don't touch me.'

He was all concern.

'Why, honey, what's wrong? You sick?'

She shook her head. 'Can I come in? I have to tell you something.'

'Sure, sure, come on in.' He opened the door wide, a look of bewilderment on his face. 'But I don't understand—'

'Drew. I have to tell you this because you're a good man, a wonderful man and you think I'm a good, clean-living person, that I share your values.'

She drew a long, juddering breath and went on, 'I haven't been the person you think I am, Drew. I haven't had simple, monogamous relationships, in fact I have deliberately steered clear of any kind of relationships for many years, because I wanted to be in control of my life and in charge of my feelings.'

'Honey, that's okay—'

'No.' She held up a warning hand. 'I haven't told you yet. Listen. I don't mean I haven't had sexual relationships. The truth is, I have had as much sex as I wanted, when I wanted, with whoever I wanted.'

Carrie couldn't look at Drew, she just had to get this out.

'I met people first of all through advertisements in the newspaper. If I liked them, I slept with them. If things threatened to turn serious, I got out, moved on, found another partner. After the internet took off, I found a site called bed-buddies.net. I became a member. I made appointments with men through the site and met them for sex.'

She stopped. 'That's it. Hardly the sweet, wholesome kind of woman I imagine you're looking to share your life with.'

He took half a step towards her, but again she held up her hands, warning him off.

'I wasn't going to tell you, Drew. The truth is, for the first time in my life, I have fallen in love. And because of that I can't hide my past from you. It wouldn't be fair, it wouldn't be honest and I simply cannot live a lie.

'I can't come to the States with you, Drew, not that you'd want me to come now anyway. I can't meet your family. Now that you know what I've been like, you'll despise me and I can't handle that. It doesn't matter that I've changed. It doesn't make any difference that I would never go near anyone but you now. It doesn't matter that I've finally discovered what it means to love someone. The past cannot be undone. I plead guilty, m'lud.'

Tears were near the surface and she fought them valiantly, though her voice became choked.

'I love you, Drew. I've not said those words to anyone for years and years and I swore I would never say them again. But that's the truth of it. I love you and I can't do that to you.'

She turned her face to him and could hold back the tears no longer.

'Goodbye, Drew. I hope, when you think back on this time, you won't think too badly of me.'

This is unbearable. I can't stand it.

As he began to move towards her, she turned swiftly and ran to the door. She had to get out of there. Fast.

Across town, Jane had come to exactly the same conclusion as Carrie. Tom Vallely could not be allowed to blackmail her. All day she had wrestled with her thoughts and in the end it was Marta's voice that kept coming back into her head.

'Tell Neal, Jane. You won't regret it.'

For years now, she had shied away from her past. She had pushed the abortion into the deepest recesses of her mind, convinced that if Neal ever found out he would hate her, or leave her, both of which were unthinkable. But now, she could avoid it no longer.

As the day turned into evening and the evening into night one fact began to make itself clear in Jane's brain: Tom Vallely had pushed her into a corner and there was no escaping from it

Even if she found the money to buy his silence, she could never be free from her memories.

And when you're in a corner, all you can do is turn and fight.

The children were in bed. Neal had come back from his choir practice. It was the time when, usually, they sat down in front of whatever was on television with a cup of tea and a biscuit. Sometimes they chatted inconsequentially, commented on an item on the news, made some remark about one of the children, raised the question of whether they could afford a holiday this year and if they could, where they might go. Tonight, Jane made the tea and brought it through to the front room, but in a change to their usual pattern, she stood next to the television, controls in hand, and asked, 'Are you watching this specially, Neal? There's something I'd like to talk about.'

'Sounds ominous,' Neal grinned. 'Not our Em again, I hope?'

'Not Emily, n-no.'

She flicked the standby button and the screen went black with a small 'pop'.

Nerves were kicking in. Jane had spent most of the evening wondering if she could go through with this, but every time she came to the same conclusion: she had no other option.

She crossed to the sofa, where her husband of sixteen years was lounging, relaxed, one leg draped half along the cushions, the other resting on the carpet, propping him up. She lifted the leg and sat down, replacing it on her lap. Familiar movements, a familiar body. What would he be like when she told him?

'I've got a confession to make.'

'Broken something? Not Ian's precious candlestick I hope?' Neal grinned again. Last year, at school, Ian had crafted a crooked and odd-looking candlestick on a lathe. It was thick in parts, and so thin in others that it would have been easy to snap the wood.

'N-nothing like that.'

There must have been something about her voice, because Neal lifted his leg off her lap and swung to an upright position, suddenly alert. 'What is it, poppet?'

'I'm frightened to say.'

'Why?' He took her hand between his own. 'Talk to me, darling. Tell me what's bothering you.'

'I'm frightened you'll be angry. I'm afraid that you'll hate me.'

She was shaking now, from head to foot. This was even harder than she had anticipated.

'Jane? Sweetheart? I'll always love you, surely you know that?'

She shook her head. 'Not when you know what I did.' Then she collected herself and asked him a question. 'When I met you, Neal, what did you think of m-me?'

'When I *met* you? I thought you were the sweetest, shyest, most vulnerable, person I had ever met. I wanted to take you in my arms and protect you. I wanted to kiss the hell out of you and make you smile.'

'You never asked about my b-background.'

'I waited for you to tell me. And you did. You told me you'd been playing in an orchestra, but that you'd become depressed and had to get away.'

'That was t-t-true. Up to a p-p-point.' The stuttering was becoming almost unmanageable. 'The truth is, my b-boyfriend had just walked out on me.'

'Darling kitten, I guessed that. I loved it that you learned to trust me.'

'But that's not all.' She inhaled deeply. 'Neal, I'd just had an abortion.'

She looked at him, her gaze steady now. It was out. For better or worse, she had told him and whatever happened now, happened.

Astonishingly, the relief was instantaneous. The secret was out and whatever her punishment was to be, it could not be more than she deserved, nor worse than she had imagined.

'An ... abortion.'

'I know what you'll think of me, Neal. I'm sorry. But I was at my wit's end. I was terrified. My parents had given up so much for me, I felt I couldn't let them down – though of course, in the end, I did, because I couldn't carry on with my music.

'I was going to tell you. I wanted to tell you, then you proposed and I wanted you to keep on loving me so much that I found I couldn't. I was terrified you'd leave me because I know how strongly you felt about... Then as time went on, there was never the right time to bring it up.'

Neal hadn't said a word during her whole confession, he'd simply looked at her – but his hands, holding her trembling ones, were rock steady.

'And then that evening, at Marta's. Abortion's a sin, you said. There are no circumstances that justify abortion. I felt ... terrified ... all over again—.'

'Oh my love, my love,' Neal drew her close and hugged her to his chest. 'I'd had a few drinks, darling. I was enjoying a good argument. That was all. And I hated the way Tom was so casual about it all, I just went to the other extreme.'

'You didn't mean it?'

'I ... of course I did. Up to a point. It's not something I would advocate as a form of birth control, nor even approve of in a general way. But I would concede that every case is a case to be decided on its own merits. Was Tom the father?'

Jane nodded.

'I'll kill him! I didn't like the man from the moment I met him and now I know why. He didn't stand by you?'

'He told me he wouldn't support it. Or me. That he was getting married to someone else and that if I said anything he'd kill me.'

'What a bastard!'

Her man was protecting her. Something indefinable in Jane shifted and eased.

271

'He can't hurt me now, Neal. Not so long as you stand by me. Will you?' she added anxiously.

'What did you think I'd do? Walk out on you and the kids? Darling, listen: I always knew you had a secret. I was waiting for you to tell me. I'm just sorry that I made it so difficult for you to confide in me.'

Jane looked at Neal and she saw again the small ghost of her unborn baby. But now the pale, blurred face seemed more peaceful, as if it knew it was finally being laid to rest.

She would carry the child in her heart always. But the shard of glass that had been buried deep inside her felt as though it had been pulled through her skin, leaving only a raw wound that would, given time, begin to heal.

'Have you noticed something?' Neal asked at length.

'No, what?'

'Your stammer. It seems to have gone.'

Jane smiled her lopsided smile.

Perhaps – could it be true? – the healing had begun already.

Chapter Thirty-four

<FFE 2 CI CoW 11.00 2morrow.>

Marta received the text from Jane around midnight, Carrie a few minutes later.

Jane was calling a Council of War.

Jane?

Jane had always been the last of the three friends to initiate any event or any idea – and yet she was doing so now? When she was so low?

The last time Marta had walked across to the island, she had stowed her walking shoes in the wardrobe in the spare room. Now, as she went in to fetch them, her gaze lit on the notebook that Jake had handed her. Tom's notebook. She'd completely forgotten it again. Funny that he'd never phoned to ask for it back.

She picked it up and riffled through it. Notes, names, numbers, seemingly random, jotted here and there, some with initials, some marked out with complicated doodles. Receipts slipped in between the pages. Larger pieces of paper, folded to fit. She smoothed one out and scanned it quickly. Her attention quickened. She unfolded another. And another.

Interesting. Very, very interesting.

Marta had no idea what Jane was considering as the subject of her Council of War, but she slipped the notebook into her small backpack anyway. She was quite certain that the others would find it fascinating.

'The subject of our meeting is "Retribution",' Jane announced solemnly.

The three women were sitting on the top of the hill on Cramond Island, well wrapped up against the October chill. The day was clear and cold and, as was the established custom, each had made her own way across the causeway to the rendezvous.

Marta and Carrie glanced at each other, then looked at Jane.

'Say that again, Jane,' Carrie commanded.

'The subject of our meeting is "Retribution".'

'What's happened to the stutter?' Marta asked.

Jane beamed. Marta couldn't remember her looking this relaxed in a long time.

'It seems to have gone again. Brilliant, isn't it?'

'Yes, sure – but why do you think it's stopped? And so suddenly?'

'I told Neal last night.'

'Oh Jane, that's *great*. I mean, I'm sure it was hellish but by the way you're looking, I'm guessing he took it well?'

'He was fantastic,' Jane said. 'A real hero. You were right, Marta, to encourage me to tell him. But there was another reason I had to – I got a phone call from Tom.'

Carrie bridled. Marta groaned. 'Will that bloody man never go away?' she said. 'What did he want?'

'Let me guess,' Carrie said grimly. 'He wanted money, to stop him telling Neal about the abortion.'

Jane looked at her, surprised. 'Yes. He did. How did you know?'

'Let's just say it's a pattern of behaviour that's familiar,' Carrie said. 'So, you were left with no option, huh?'

'That's how I saw it. I didn't have the kind of money he wanted and anyway, I had this awful feeling he would come back again.'

'That's what I thought.'

'You?' Jane asked, puzzled.

'He was playing that game with me too, Jane.' Carrie grimaced. 'There's a large slice of my past I would rather people didn't know about, Drew in particular. Tom was playing on that. I was just about to make the money available for him when the same thing occurred to me. And besides, I realised that I couldn't deceive Drew. So I told him. And now we've broken up.'

'Carrie, *no*!'

'Oh Carrie, surely not? You seem so fantastic together.'

'Listen, can we not talk about it right now?' Tears glistened in Carrie's eyes and she changed the subject quickly. 'Jane, tell me instead about this retribution idea. I have a feeling I'm going to like it.'

'Okay. If you're sure?'

'Yeah, yeah,' Carrie said impatiently. 'Go on.'

'Well, this is my thinking. We need to get our own back on Tom Vallely. And we need to stop him doing this to others. I've no idea exactly how, that's why I've asked you here. But there's one thing it seems to me is more important than anything—'

'What?'

'We have to do it together. As a team. As friends. The past is past, our friendship has to be held together.'

'Agreed.'

Marta added her voice. 'Agreed. And I have something that might help.'

'Really? What?'

Marta pulled Tom's notebook out of her pocket. 'Take a look at this,' she said. The book fell open at a well-thumbed spread.

'My God!'

'He said that about Anya Merton!'

Carrie squealed. 'Kate H? D'you think that could be Kate Herdman? On the early breakfast show? Jeez! I always thought she was so *proper*.'

'Angela? Isn't that his agent? I have a feeling she'd drop him like a hot brick if she knew he thought *that* about her.'

275

'Yes, but look.' Marta unfolded one of the pieces of paper that had been tucked inside the notebook.

'What is it?' Jane asked curiously.

Carrie took the paper. 'Looks like a pawn ticket. It's that shop in town, isn't it? This is a ticket for a signet ring.'

'There's a clutch of them,' Marta said, unfolding another, then another. 'I didn't think too much of them, till I got to this one.'

She passed the paper to Carrie.

Jane, peering over Carrie's shoulder read out, 'One brooch, late eighteenth century, eighteen carat gold set with pearls, rubies and sapphires, in the form of a bow.'

'That sounds like your great-grandma's brooch, Marta,' Carrie said slowly. 'The one you keep for very special occasions.'

'Yup.'

'It's gone?'

'Yup.'

'When did you find out?'

'Just after Tom left.'

'You didn't go to the police?'

'There'd been no break in, it would have been a bit difficult to prove Tom had taken it, especially if he'd already got rid of it. Anyway, I wasn't in a fit state to think about anything very clearly.'

'Well, he's clearly pawned it. What a scumbag. What can we do? Can you get it back?'

'Hopefully. I've got a photo of it, for insurance. I can't think there'll be too many brooches like that around, and because Tom stayed with us, I think he'd find it quite hard to make up a convincing story to clear himself – not with this ticket made out in his name.'

'So will you go to the police now that you've found this?'

Marta said slowly, 'I was wondering if there might be another way. I thought maybe we could have a bit of fun of our own –

and put a stop to Tom's horrid little tricks. Fancy joining me in a bit of sweet revenge?'

Carrie grinned. 'Do I ever!'

'Just try me,' Jane said. 'What did you have in mind?'

'Well... What do you think about this?'

Cramond Island had been the scene of many a Council of War in years past, and as her friends listened eagerly to her scheme, Marta managed to forget all her other problems for a blissful half hour.

The plan was to play on Tom's weak point: his greed. Carrie's part in the plot was key, but it was going to take some courage. She didn't tell the others just how difficult it was going to be. It's my penance, she thought doggedly, as she steeled herself to make the essential honeytrap call.

'Tom? Hi, it's Carrie.'

'Well hello, darling. Got the money?'

Come straight to the point, why don't you?

'I've got it,' she lied. 'But Tom—'

'Yeah?'

'I thought it would be nice to give you it in person. You know—' she made her tone coy and dropped to a whisper, '— maybe as Bed Buddies? One last time?'

His laughter was spontaneous.

'Carrie darling, what can I say? Can't give up the old ways, huh? So our Mr McGraw isn't so very special after all. I'm tempted to increase the fee ... but no,' he pondered, 'now that I come to think of it, I'll be happy to accept another shag in lieu.'

Bastard.

'I'll look forward to it. Can you make it back to the old stamping ground? The Salamander Hotel? Wouldn't that be nice – revisiting old haunts? Can you get a weekend off?'

'As a matter of fact, we're not filming this weekend. And as it happens, I have some unfinished business in Edinburgh anyway.'

I bet you have, you sneaky rat.

Carrie knew he could never resist a free meal. 'Great. Dinner first then? On me?'

'See you there.'

Chapter Thirty-five

Jane and Marta took their seats at a table for four, set for dinner, in the recess beside the large fireplace in the hotel's modest restaurant, and waited.

In the bar itself, Carrie's nerves were clattering. Her fingers tapped restlessly on the granite counter top. It seemed hard now to think that she had found Tom Vallely irresistible the last time they'd met here.

The memory of Drew's hand, curled protectively and lovingly around her own caused a hurt that was almost physical. She could hear his full-throated laugh and ached for the joy of his company.

'Hi D.A. Delight.'

Carrie jumped. Tom had a nasty habit of appearing from nowhere.

'Oh! Hi. Drink?'

He took off his leather jacket and fedora and hung them on a coatstand, then turned and kissed her on the lips. Carrie strained every muscle not to flinch away. She thought he was going to whisper some sleazy compliment, but instead he whispered, 'Got the money, darling?'

'Calm down, Tom,' she said amicably, sounding more relaxed than she felt. 'We'll get to that. Dinner first. Then upstairs. The money's in my room anyway.'

'How about we go upstairs first?' His hand was on her thigh.

She shook it off. 'Now, now, if you've got that much of an appetite you can munch your way through three courses in anticipation.'

'I'm only hungry for one thing, darling.'

'Well, you're going to have to get me in the mood over dinner, all the same. I'm ravenous.'

This was hard work, but she had to get him through to the dining room.

Tom sighed. 'Okay. Let's skip the drinks though. I'll order some some champagne for the table. If there's any left, we'll take it up with us. Or get another bottle.'

Yes, because you think it's on my bill, you bastard.

'Fine.'

'You're looking particularly fetching tonight, Caroline darling. Is that a Mary Quant dress?'

It was Mary Quant. 'Top Shop,' Carrie said curtly.

'You carry it well, then.'

'Thanks. I've reserved a table. Let's go through.'

Marta and Jane looked up at the sound of Carrie's voice. Tom stopped abruptly, grabbed Carrie's arm and swung her round to face him.

'What's up, Carrie? You're plotting something.'

There was a nasty edge to his voice.

'Plotting? My dear Tom, whatever makes you think that? A little reunion of friends, that's all.'

He let go of her elbow and tried to turn to the door.

'Oh, Tom,' she said, sidestepping smartly to block his way and relieved to see the door blocked by the waiter coming in with champagne glasses and a bucket of ice, 'what about the money?'

He turned back reluctantly.

'This had better not be a set-up, Carrie darling, or—'

'Or what, Tom? Just sit.'

'How lovely to see you, Tom.' Marta stood up to let Tom past her. She pointedly kissed his cheek while Carrie barred his retreat. They'd decided not to let him sit next to Jane. Despite her new-found confidence, she was still far too fragile to be any nearer to Tom than the other side of a dining table.

280

'Marta. Looking beautiful, as always.'

You had to admire him, really, for the professionalism. A lesser bastard would have let the mask slip. Marta ushered him past her, into the depths of the recess, then sat down again, blocking his exit. There was to be no easy escape.

'So how's life on *Emergency Admissions*, Tom?'

'Fantastic. A real blast, darling.'

'Get on with the others, do you?'

'Getting *on* is what I do best,' he smirked.

'Ha, ha.'

'We ordered oysters for you, Tom,' Jane said. 'We know how you like a little lift.'

She giggled.

Tom stared at her.

'What happened to you Janie darling?' he asked curtly, surprise making him lose all his usual affectation. 'What happened to the st-t-tutter?'

He exaggerated the word, cruelly mimicking Jane.

'Finally came to my senses, *darling*.' Jane laughed out loud at the sight of Tom's astonished face. 'And don't think you'll get any cash out of me, Tom, because that little scam has been thoroughly knocked on the head.'

Tom said nothing but his gaze flickered away from her, down at the table, then to Carrie. He was looking more than a little uncomfortable.

Marta was enjoying herself.

'Have some champagne.'

She filled up his glass, splashing a little onto the tablecloth.

'Oops. Mustn't waste it. But hey, then again, why not? We're in a celebratory mood, aren't we, girls?'

'I don't know what you mean,' Tom mumbled.

Carrie leaned forward. 'Let me spell it out for you, Tom. You won't, I'm sorry to say, be getting a nice large cheque from me. And you won't be getting a big fat payoff from Jane either, because both of us have had a little heart-to-heart with our men, and we've told them everything. We have no more secrets, from them or from each other. There's nothing else you can blackmail us about. And by the way, I have unsubscribed from Bed Buddies, so that's an end to that.'

She took a gulp of champagne.

'Oh – and Marta has some good news as well – don't you, Marta?'

Marta smiled and leaned down to pick up her handbag.

'I do. In fact, I'm very pleased about this. You see, Tom, I thought I had lost a brooch of mine. A very special brooch that belonged to my great-grandmother. I couldn't understand where it had gone, because I kept it quite safe. In my underwear drawer, to be precise. So I wasn't best pleased when I discovered that someone had been rifling through my knickers.'

A look of alarm had spread across Tom's face.

'I can't think what you're talking abou—' he blustered.

Marta interrupted him. 'Oh I think you know very well. You see, you left something behind at my cottage.'

She drew the notebook from out of her handbag. Tom, seeing what she held, gave a yelp and snatched at the book. Marta, quicker, held it out of his reach.

'I was puzzled, you see. I had to be sure who the notebook belonged to. So I took a little look inside.' She opened it up. 'There's quite a lot of interesting jottings in here. This one, for example. "Auditions for Richard Curtis film next week. *Bugger* AC." That would be Angela Cutler, I'm guessing? Your agent? Little tiff perhaps? Maybe she didn't think you were quite up to the role?'

Tom snorted, but Marta was relentless.

'Then there's this one, just next to it: "Had to shag AC tonight; business before pleasure".'

Tom turned puce.

'Hmm, not terribly flattering. I wonder what she would think of that?'

282

'You don't know what you're talking about.'

'No? It's really terribly interesting. Snippets of gossip. Scrib-
lings with your opinions of people. What seems like a star
system next to names. Could that be anything to do with how
you rate them in bed, I wonder?'

Jane, almost helpless with laughter, took the book from Marta.

'Not very sensible, Tom, keeping a notebook like this, is it?'
she asked brightly. 'I guess you see this as your kiss-and-tell
book, do you? Some overblown idea of another way to make
money at some point? For when you get famous? Blackmail,
or publish and be damned?' She said the words mockingly. 'Or
maybe you simply can't resist keeping some sort of record of
your conquests? Tamara-Jane Halliday 06017 321 ... Would that
be *the* Tamara-Jane Halliday? The celebrity model, married to
our world-famous heavyweight boxing champion? Hmmm, I
wonder what Ricky Halliday would think of this little entry?
Only two stars out of five, too.'

'Give it here!'

Keeping it well out of reach, Carrie took the book. Short of
making a major scene, it was impossible for Tom to snatch it.

'Here's another note. "Ann Playfair = sharp writer/hardbitten
old bitch." Oh, and a phone number too, though I'm guessing
she is not one of your conquests, because that would be the Ann
Playfair who suggested you audition for the role, would it?'

'Give it to me. You've no right—'

'The little drawing is quite good,' Carrie went on, studying
it. 'A bit lewd, I would say. Could she really get in that position
with a donkey—'

'Carrie, for pity's sake—'

Jane gave him a withering glance. 'Pity? What do you know
about pity, Tom Vallely? Here, Carrie, give me one of those
bits of paper.' She unfolded one. 'Seems to be a ticket for a
pawnshop. "One gent's signet ring, gold." And the date. Gent's
signet ring, Tom? I wonder who that belongs to?'

'Here, give me—'

'And this one.' Marta unfolded another. 'This one's really interesting. "Eighteenth-century brooch, eighteen-carat gold set with pearls, rubies and sapphires." ' She looked up at him. 'Strange. The date is early September this year. When you were staying with me, in fact. And it does sound remarkably like my brooch.' She folded the paper up again. 'Do you know, I think the police might be interested in this.'

'Give it here. That's my property.'

Tom lunged for the book again. This time, Marta let him get it. He pocketed it swiftly, gathering up the pieces of paper they had unfolded and stowing them away with great haste, as though the air might cause them to self-destruct.

'You're welcome.' Carrie smiled.

There was a short silence. Tom looked at them uneasily.

Carrie lifted her glass, sipped again at the champagne.

'You don't think we didn't take a copy of every page in that journal, do you? It's all recorded, every single entry, all on camera and on video, and—' she leaned forward earnestly, '—if you think we have given you back the *original* pawn tickets you're very naive indeed.'

Jane, still giggling, sobered up.

'We've had enough, Tom. Enough of your nasty little habit and your weasel mind. And we're quite sure that there are a lot of women out there who are rather tired of you too. You no longer have any hold over us, but we *do* have a hold on you. So here's our threat: if we *ever* hear of you getting up to your little tricks again, the video we made is going straight onto YouTube.'

'And I want my brooch back, Tom. If I have the slightest problem in getting it, I'll be going to the police,' Marta added. 'You see, it's heavily insured and properly photographed. There will be absolutely no problem in proving it's mine.'

Tom began to splutter.

Marta leant over and stared at him.

'Don't you dare say anything. Just don't you dare. You don't deserve this, Tom. We should be turning you in. But in spite of all the hurt you have caused, we're not malicious. We've decided, the three of us, that we are going to treat you a whole lot better than you have treated us. Tomorrow morning, we are going to go to the pawn shop. I will give you the original ticket and you will go inside, pay any outstanding interest and redeem the brooch. We will all be waiting outside, where you will hand me it. Understood?'

Tom sat speechless and open-mouthed, all bluster and bravado gone.

'Because if you don't, you can be absolutely certain that my first call will be to the police, I promise you that. Got me?'

There was a small space of time, during which Tom appeared to be calculating the odds. Was there any way he could wriggle out of this? At length he nodded reluctantly.

'Good.' The three friends rose to their feet.

Jane said, 'Bye Tom. Enjoy the oysters and the champagne. We told Tim and Stella Morrison that you are settling tonight's bill.'

'Bye Tom,' said Carrie. 'By the way, I added a comment about Star Turn on Bed Buddies before I unsubscribed. I'm afraid it is rather personal. My own "Star" rating system, if you like.'

'Bye Tom. Oh – I've got a present for you.' Marta fumbled in her handbag and brought out a pair of lace-edged scarlet knickers. 'Seeing as you like looking at other people's knickers, I thought you'd like these.'

Quickly, she turned and slipped them onto his head. As they headed for the door, they heard a murmur of amusement bubbling up in the room.

'Brilliant,' Jane said at the door. 'Fantastic.'

'Well done, girls,' Marta punched the air triumphantly.

Carrie spotted the fedora, hanging on the coatstand where he had left it. 'Here's looking at you, babe,' she called across the room, slipping the hat onto her head and tipping the brim to Tom.

He had snatched the knickers off his head and was sitting, looking bewildered, clutching them in his fist. Was it her imagination, wondered Carrie, or were his fine looks fading?

They skipped out of the main door. At the foot of the steps, a stone lion guarded the way. Carrie tossed the hat onto its head and watched as it slipped rakishly across one leonine eye.

'If he's lucky, he might find it there,' she said.

'If not, he could always try the pawn shop,' Jane giggled.

Marta reached out her hands and took Jane's in one, Carrie's in the other.

'Friends?' she asked, smiling at them.

'Forever,' they chorused.

Chapter Thirty-six

'Jake's coming back this weekend. And he's promised to be with me for the birth.'

It was mid-December and Marta, now almost five months into her pregnancy, smiled at her friends. They were sitting in Henderson's vegetarian restaurant in Hanover Street, sheltering from the cold. Jane pulled off her kingfisher beanie and tossed it into her shopping bag. Carrie unbuttoned her Max Mara overcoat and draped it on the back of her chair. Marta, her long legs cased in Ugg boots and black jeans, was wearing a sheepskin bomber jacket, buttoned under her growing stomach. She undid it.

'Has he talked again about coming back after this contract is up?'

'He's not committing himself,' Marta admitted as she sat down on the wooden chair. 'But I still think he'll come round after the baby's born.'

'It's good that you're still talking to each other,' Carrie said, though she did wonder whether Marta – ever the optimist – was deluding herself.

'Still no word from Drew?' Jane asked sympathetically.

Carrie sighed. 'He's left messages a dozen times, Jane, but I can't talk to him, knowing I can't have him. Maybe in time, the pain will go away, but the idea of "just being friends" is completely unthinkable. I've had to excuse myself from the McGraw contract at work, of course, and everyone's been wondering why.'

'Any word of the partnership?'

'Oh yes.' Carrie sounded half-hearted. 'Talk about irony. Henry Frew did hint that the McGraw business might swing the scales in my favour. I may even know before Christmas.'

'That's fantastic!'

'Maybe. On the other hand, withdrawing from handling his business might set the whole thing back again.'

Carrie's eyes, usually so bright and alert, seemed dull. Normally crackling with energy, her movements were listless. She stirred her tea round and round, round and round, watching the whirlpool she was creating, but she didn't drink any.

'You know, I keep thinking that perhaps I shouldn't have told him after all. Perhaps I could have somehow got through it without having to say anything.'

'You're forgetting two things,' Marta chimed in. 'First – you wouldn't have been able to live with yourself for long and second – there was the small matter of Tom Vallely.'

'Ah yes, Tom. Hey, did you know there are rumours in the gossip sheets about him falling out with all and sundry at *EA*?'

'And Ricky Halliday did lash out at him at that night club,' Jane giggled. 'He must've found something out about Tamara-Jane. He was lucky just to get away with a black eye.'

'It wasn't you, was it?'

'Wasn't me what?'

'Who dropped a hint to the guy.'

'No! As if I would!' Jane pondered for a minute. 'Though actually, if I'd thought about it—'

Marta said, 'One of the actresses playing a nurse did a piece in *Heat* last week. She says he's arrogant, self-regarding and a ruthless womaniser.'

'We could have told them that. Anyway, at least you got your brooch back.'

Marta groaned. 'Don't remind me. Please. That's over now.' She looked thoughtful. 'You know, if things go well with Jake this weekend, maybe it will be a case of "all's well that ends well".'

'Meaning?'

'Meaning, if it hadn't been for Tom, things might have drifted on with Jake without me ever realising how bad they were. I've learned a whole lot of lessons and I intend to make sure he knows it.'

Jane admitted, 'I was mad at you, Marta, for bringing Tom back into my life. But if you hadn't done that, I would still be burning up with my secret – you know ... the baby ...' Jane still found it hard to talk about it. 'I wouldn't have told Neal and it would still be eating me up.' She stirred her hot chocolate and took a sip. 'It hasn't been easy, but we're much closer now.'

'All the same, if it hadn't been for Tom, I might still be with Drew,' Carrie added regretfully.

'Yes.' Jane looked thoughtful. 'You know, it strikes me that Project Retribution is not yet complete.'

'What do you mean?'

'I'm not sure.' She finished her glass of wine. 'Leave it with me. Shall we go? I'd better get home to Neal. He's been holding the fort for ages.'

They climbed the steep steps from the basement outside Henderson's. The weather, if anything, was worse. There had been a fall of snow while they'd been inside and the pavements were sugared with white. The temperature had plummeted and between the pockets of sugar, dark slabs gleamed ominously under the street lights.

'Careful now, these pavements are slippery,' Carrie warned, just as a small boy came running full speed down the hill and launched himself into a long slide.

'Watch out, Marta!' Jane shouted.

Marta reached out a hand to grab the iron railing at the top of the steps, but it was too late. The boy cannoned into her and sent her flying. She crashed down on the pavement.

'Kevin, come here!' The boy's mother, hot on her errant son's heels, scolded him. 'You all right, hen?' she asked.

Marta, shaken, rolled onto her knees and picked herself up.

'I'm fine. Don't be cross with him, please. He was just having fun.'

Jane, rushing to help, asked, 'You really all right, Marta?'

'I think so.' She was shaking.

Carrie waved frantically at a passing cab. 'Taxi! You're going home. No more late-night shopping, no doing the housework when you get back, you hear? Go straight to bed and get your feet up. Do you want me to come with you?'

'No, thanks Carrie, I'll be fine. I'm okay, you can stop fussing.' Marta assured them. 'But I will head home, if you don't mind.' She opened the taxi door. 'Bye, darlings.'

'I hope she *is* all right,' Jane said as the cab drew away.

'So do I. Let's meet soon? Love to Neal.'

'Will do, Bye.'

The cramps didn't start till the early hours of the morning. At first, Marta woke with mild discomfort and put it down to indigestion. As the pains increased and became intermittent, but rhythmical, she began to fret; and when, around four, she discovered she was bleeding, she panicked and called Carrie.

'Marta?' Carrie mumbled sleepily. 'What's the time? Four thirty?' She said sharply, 'What is it? What's wrong?'

'I'm bleeding,' Marta said, her voice high and breathless with panic. 'And I'm having contractions.'

Carrie took immediate control. 'Stay right there. Don't move. I'll be with you in twenty minutes.'

She made it in fifteen. 'Hospital. No arguments.'

Marta didn't argue. She was white and shaking and looked very frightened.

'I'll need to get a bag, just in case.'

'You sit there. Tell me what you need.'

Carrie packed efficiently and quickly and they were at the Royal Infirmary twenty minutes later.

Marta was aware that she was curled in a tight ball, yet it felt as though she was scaling a cliff – a sheer black cliff with no edge and no base. Her fingertips ached with the effort of hanging on, her legs screamed with the agony of retaining a grip on the fragile footholds. She longed to get to the top, yet when she got there she knew that there would be something terrible waiting for her. If she didn't get there, she would surely die, but if she did, she might be thrown back into the black abyss. There was no escape from the dilemma.

The cliff blurred and dissolved. Now she was in the garden, looking at her roses. This was more pleasant. But wait – one rose had withered. Marta, spiralling slowly towards the place where the subconscious mind met with wakefulness, could see the petals, pale, pale pink like a baby's skin, yet brown round the edges.

Dead.

Like her baby.

She must get Jake to dig it out. The bush is getting old.

There is no Jake.

The petals are brown.

The rose has withered. You have to cut the dead heads off.

Marta's stomach ached with emptiness. Her eyelids fluttered as the pale winter sun edged low across the horizon and fell across her face.

My baby is dead.

As she floated nearer to consciousness, the thought turned itself into a bright, sharp thing. Someone was speaking. Who was it? The voice was familiar. The speaker stopped and a strange, other-earthly moan filled the silence. That sounded familiar too, in a curious way. Her mouth was dry. She closed it and the mewling stopped. Could it have been her?

'She's waking up.'

She recognised Jane's voice.

'Here, Marta. Drink this sweetie.'

291

Carrie?

'Where—?' Her eyes were open now. The sunlight hurt. Everything hurt..

My baby is dead.

She squeezed her eyes shut, as though closing them might make reality disappear.

'You're at home, Marta. We're here. Jane and I. Look, I've brought you some tea. Sit up love. Drink. It'll do you good.'

'You sound like my gran,' Marta smiled weakly. 'I bet you've even put sugar in it.' She rolled herself into a sitting position.

'A spoonful,' Carrie admitted.

Marta could see the relief in Carrie's eyes. Marta's sounding more human, they were thinking, thank God.

It had been three days since Carrie had brought her back from the hospital. Three days of unspeakable heartache. She had lost the baby. All these years of trying, then the miracle. But now there was no baby.

'What did Jake say,' she asked, 'when you told him?'

She'd been sipping the tea, but as she lifted her head she caught the look that flashed between Jane and Carrie.

'No-one's told him,' she observed flatly.

'Marta, love, we've been so concerned about you, we didn't think—'

'Christ, Marta, I'm sorry—'

Marta's gaze travelled to the clock on the far wall. Three thirty.

'What day is it?' she asked.

'Saturday.'

There was a moment's silence.

'Saturday. Oh shit,' Carrie said.

'Do you think—?' Jane started, but the sweet chime of the doorbell cut her short.

Jake picked up the glass ornament, its severed tail in his left hand, the heavy bird in his right. A gleam of sunlight caught the broken edge of its body and sent a sparkling cascade of light up and down the far wall. The red glass inside the bird looked like a fractured heart.

Marta stared at it dully. A few months ago she had spiritedly rejected the crass symbolism of the accident. I'll mend my broken friendships, she had vowed, I'll fight to save my marriage.

Where was that spirit now?

'What happened?' he asked, waving the broken glass.

The light bounced off the edge again and this time dazzled her. She held up a hand to shield herself from its reproachful glare.

'I'm so sorry, Jake. I meant to tell you. It was an accident.'

'Why didn't you chuck it?'

'I couldn't do that!'

'Why not? What's the point of keeping it? You can't mend a thing like this, you'd see the crack.'

The symbolism swamped her.

'I know you loved that bird,' she said mournfully.

'Loved it?' he said, turning round and replacing it on the mantelpiece. 'I loathed the damn thing.'

'Really? It was your grandmother's.'

'I loved *her*. But the bird was a really naff bit of 1960s design. I only kept it 'cos she used to look for it when she came – what's wrong?'

Marta realised she was staring at him, eyes wide, mouth agape. She said slowly, 'You loved her ... but you hated the bird.'

'Yeah.' He sounded puzzled. 'So?'

'There was no connection between the broken bird and your love for your grandmother.'

'Of course not. What are you talking about, Marta?'

Marta started to laugh. The noise erupted from deep within her, bubbling up in a small giggle, then turning to an unstoppable wave. It proved contagious. Jake's mouth twitched, the corners turned up into a smile, and he joined in, puzzled but infected by her mirth.

'What? What is it?' Jake kept asking, before lapsing back into chortles of amusement.

At length they subsided.

'Now can you tell me?'

'It's not really funny,' Marta said, which set them both off once more. When it finally struck her that her laughter was more hysterical than healthy, she stopped abruptly, blew her nose and wiped her eyes, and explained. 'I got hung up on it as a metaphor. Remember Tom Vallely's play? *The Glass Ornament*? It was about broken friendships and not being able to mend them.'

'But that's bollocks.'

'Up to a point. I did finally realise that I could do something about my friendship with Carrie and Jane – and I have done. But ridiculously, I still felt – probably because it was *your* ornament – that I'd been responsible for breaking our marriage. The symbol became reality. Then when you said that, you know, about your grandmother ... I began to wonder whether—'

Marta broke off awkwardly and bit her lips fretfully.

'When I lost the baby, Jake—' she said in a low voice. '—how can I say this so that you understand? I would never blackmail you, I hope you believe that, but all the same, I couldn't stop hoping that you would come back to me when your child was born. And now it's gone.'

Jake crossed the room and sank down onto the sofa beside her. He took her hands in his.

'Listen to me. I'm so sorry about the baby. I'm gutted. Truly. But you have to know that I never saw the baby as a pawn in our relationship.'

Marta had thought her heart could not possibly be any more painful than it had been, but now she discovered that she was wrong. Grief overwhelmed her. She could hardly hear Jake's words.

'Like I said before, I don't believe children can mend broken relationships. If I do come back, it will be because of *you*.'

She was twisting her hands, concentrating on not wailing with anguish.

'I'm loving London, Marta, that's the thing. I'm enjoying working again, doing what I'm good at, filling my head with good stuff, using my experience and my skills. I'm not great at living on my own, but I'm not keen on getting back into a relationship where I can't be an equal decision maker.'

Marta hardly dared breathe. 'What does Jenny think of that?'

'Who? Oh, Jenny. I stopped dating her. Lovely lady, but we agreed it wasn't working out.'

'I'm sorry.'

She wasn't sorry though. Not one bit.

'The main reason was that a big part of my heart was still here,' he squeezed her hands, 'with you.'

Now it was not a question of not daring to breathe, she actually *couldn't* breathe. He let go of her hands and sat back.

'I don't know what the hell to think, Marta. Could we start again? Would it be a good idea? Or have we just grown out of each other? I've changed. Or at least, maybe I haven't changed, I've just discovered what I want to be – and maybe I'm not the man you want any more.'

There was so much Marta wanted to say...

Eventually, Jake had to prompt her.

'Marta? Have we messed everything up completely? What do you think?'

Chapter Thirty-seven

Exercise releases endorphins. It is a proven and effective way of combating depression – more effective, many would argue, than swallowing pills. Carrie Edwards had hated all forms of exercise at school. Marta had been the sporty one. Athletic and tall, she had easily commanded the netball court. With her long legs, she had covered the ground on the track. In the gym, she had thrown herself wholeheartedly into vaulting and performing handstands and cartwheels. And all the while, Carrie and Jane had contented themselves with eternal excuses.

Carrie discovered running after the debacle with Tom, back in London. The headlines had been predictably corny.

'SWIFT WEDDING!'

'AFTER EDEN STAR WEDS SOAP'S SWIFT'

'SWIFT BITE AT EDEN'S APPLE'

Carrie had spotted the first one in the Tube one hellish Monday morning, when the teeming London rain had begrimed everything with a sooty dankness. As she swung belligerently from a strap, cursing commuter hell, she absently scanned the back of a newspaper held by another passenger a few uncomfortable inches from her nose.

She knew of Serena Swift – who didn't? The daughter of a wealthy gadget inventor, she was clawing her way up the celebrity ladder in a cloud of (alleged) marijuana smoke and white powder, starting with a role as a bitchy and slightly scandalous gold digger in one of the popular weekly television soaps. Close to life, the gossip sheets said – except that Serena had a fortune of her own.

Now Serena Swift had married ... Tom Vallely?

A stray elbow jabbed Carrie in the face as she peered at the paper. She pulled back sharply.

'Sorry.' A man in a pin-striped suit breathed a garlic-laden apology. She nodded an acknowledgement as her brain raced. Tom? *Her* Tom? The Tom she was having a hugely passionate affair with, on the serious understanding that he was leaving Jane because he loved her?

Leaving the Underground station she bought a couple of redtops and ducked into a café to scan their contents. There had been nothing wrong with her eyesight, despite the jiggling of the train – the facts appeared incontrovertible. Tom Vallely had dashed into the Chelsea Registry Office on Saturday and married soap star Serena Swift.

Something in Carrie hardened at that moment. Instead of moping, she settled into a deep and dark anger that translated as resolve and became characterised by energy. The energy was unleashed as a storm at work – in one case after another she applied herself unstintingly to complexities and detail. At leisure (when she had any) she became relentless and determinedly pleasure-seeking, gracing one party after another, bedding one man after another.

All of this activity was distinguished by one thing – control. Carrie did not turn to drink or to drugs, that would have been to relinquish power and Carrie had no intention of ever letting anyone have dominance over her emotions again. Instead, she had found solace, unexpectedly, through exercise, mostly running.

In the years that followed, the running remained a constant. Wherever she was in the world, it was usually in good hotels and there was usually a gym. Where she could escape safely into the countryside and weather permitted, she ran out of doors, savouring the freedom and the fresh air. Since Drew had jetted back to the States, she had increased her mileage dramatically, pounding the streets of Edinburgh obsessively.

It was the only answer. The company of men didn't interest her. Drew haunted her. She heard his voice call her name as she walked along the street. In her flat, she saw his big, graceful frame at the window, on the balcony, making coffee – the way he liked it – in her kitchen. Even at work, though she had withdrawn from handling his business, there were so many meetings where the McGraw estate was mentioned that she felt like crawling under the desk.

On Sunday morning her run began as a routine five miler and turned into a mega fifteen miles plus. From her penthouse on the edge of the Meadows it was a short jog into the Queen's Park and thence down to Portobello and the sea. The route took her not a stone's throw from Marta's cottage.

Jake would still be there.

Carrie, breathing evenly but fast, directed heartfelt wishes in Marta's direction, still ashamed that somehow, in the midst of the drama and tragedy, she had forgotten to brief Jake when Marta miscarried.

Please God, she prayed as she took the hill and her breathing quickened, bring those two souls back together again.

And then it was back into the park and up Arthur's Seat, taking the punishment to her slight frame willingly. The second time around, she diverted off the road and scrambled breathlessly up the final steep slope to the summit. The cold of the past week had eased as a warm front arrived from the west and Carrie found herself in the company of half a dozen walkers as she bounded up the rocky path.

'Brilliant views today.' A short man, his black microfibre hat pulled down snugly over his ears, was speaking to her.

'Yes, fabulous,' Carrie acknowledged, scanning the distant horizon. It was indeed a clear day. Along the sweeping blue waters of the estuary, the Forth bridges stood out like a child's drawing, etched against the skyline while sixty miles to the north, the mountains of the Highlands could be seen in shadowy outline.

She paused to take it all in.

'You look fit,' said the man, gesturing at her slight running vest and Lycra leggings. 'Not cold?'

She shook her head. Weirdo. Move on. But the man's eyes were friendly, neutral; one lover of the outdoors saluting another, that was all.

She scrambled the last few feet to the trig point, held out her hand and touched the top. Drew was here. Drew touched this stone. The memory caught her throat and she felt her eyes prick with hot, salty tears. Stop. Ridiculous. And yet the recollections crowded in. They had climbed here together one afternoon.

'I could be happy here,' Drew had said. 'My kinda place.'

And then he had looked at her, smiled with his eyes and added softly, 'My kinda girl.'

Carrie's heart had stopped pumping, her breathing was back to normal and the whole point was to run from memories, not to relive them.

The early promise of the day was turning into disappointment as she stepped out of the mini market in Simpson Loan with fruit juice and the Sunday papers.

Carrie shivered. Already she was cooling down and the disappearance of the sun behind thick cloud was not helping. Home for a shower, then coffee, juice and the week's news.

The luxury of living alone is that you can choose. Had it really only been months since she'd thought that? It was still true, of course, but how hollow it seemed, how spectacularly meaningless. Even the full-on luxury of her beloved bathroom afforded her no comfort today. She emerged, a towel round her head, a soft robe round her body. At least the coffee smelled good. She padded barefoot across to the kitchen to pour herself a cup. As she passed the phone, it began to ring and without thinking, she picked it up.

'Carrie here, hi.'

'Hi honey.'

Drew! Carrie's heart, which had recovered from its running rate twenty minutes ago, resumed pumping at full speed. Her first instinct was to drop the phone, but she counted to five and summoned all her courage.

'Hello Drew.' What now? Leave me alone, this hurts too much? Grovel again about my past? She stood rooted to the spot, transfixed by indecision.

'Don't hang up on me, honey,' he said urgently, as if he could see her hand already moving the phone back to its cradle. 'We gotta talk.'

Carrie sighed. 'Drew, please,' she pleaded. 'I've done the confessional. I've scoured my insides till they're bleeding and I can't go over this ground again. I—'

'Honey, listen, will ya?'

Carrie sank to the carpet and leaned weakly against the sofa. The towel, unwinding, fell down over her eyes and she pulled it off and tossed it to the floor, where it lay damply.

'All right,' she conceded, her voice little more than a mumble.

'Great.' Drew sounded purposeful, but without warning he broke off and exhaled sharply. 'Gee, I had it all planned out, and now I can't find the words.'

'Let me say them for you,' Carrie said dully. 'You're shocked at my behaviour. I'm not the person you thought I was. I misled you cruelly. You had believed that—'

'Stop right there.' The command was back in his voice. 'And get this into that little head of yours. We do not drop bombshells then run away. We talk about things, even if they are difficult things. You got that?'

Carrie gulped but found she couldn't speak. Who was this 'we'?

'Got that?' Drew said again, demanding an answer.

'Yes,' Carrie muttered.

301

'And one thing you gotta understand about me – I like to get to the bottom of things, get the whole story and not some jumbled up part-truth. I don't allow my employees to get away with that kinda behaviour and I don't expect it in my personal relationships either. Understood?'

'But I know you, Drew,' Carrie protested. 'I know your values. You're a great guy, an honourable guy, I could tell that from the way you treated me, like a real *gentleman*—'

Drew burst out laughing. 'A gentleman? You mean like some old-fashioned Victorian guy with a top hat and cane?'

'No, I mean—'

'You mean because I didn't jump into bed with you on our first date?'

'Or our second or third or twentieth.'

'Doesn't mean I didn't want to.'

Surprise made Carrie's voice uncharacteristically shrill. 'Did you?'

'Honey, do grizzlies eat fish?'

'But—'

'Baby, I took you seriously. You weren't just some nice piece of ass I wanted to lay. I wanted to get to know you, I respected you, and there's something about delayed gratification ... you know? Makes it all the sweeter.'

Carrie thought, *how shallow my approach to building a relationship must be*, but in a sudden burst of defiance she burst out, 'I'm not ashamed of my private life,' before crumbling and admitting, 'or I wasn't until I met you, anyway. Then I knew that you would judge my behaviour and find me wanting and I couldn't stand knowing that.'

'Judge you? You haven't been listening, Carrie. I make my judgements based on facts and there's a whole bunch of facts missing here, is what I think. Like *why* you had to be in control like that? Why you were so unable to give of your real self in a relationship? Why you restricted your life to the entirely physical and could not give your heart to anyone?'

302

Spot on. Drew's questions split Carrie's hang-ups wide open and laid bare her vulnerability. She started to weep, desperately trying to keep her sobs silent. She grabbed at the wet towel and buried her face in it, willing him to keep talking.

'And then you told me something, Carrie, and left me before I was able to give any answer to it.'

Unfair. Ungentlemanly to mention it.

'You told me you loved me.'

Still she couldn't speak.

'Is that true, Carrie?' His voice was softer now, choosing another way to probe the most tender parts of her soul.

'I ... don't ... know.' She summoned all the strength she could find. Drew deserved someone better than her, so she had to release him. 'No. I don't think, after all, that I do.'

That shocked him into silence. Eventually he said slowly, 'I don't believe you.'

'You should.'

Go. Take your freedom. Find yourself a wholesome all-American princess.

'Carrie—'

'Goodbye, Drew. It was great knowing you. Really.'

And this time, before she changed her mind, she did put the phone down.

Chapter Thirty-eight

Jane's depression was lifting. She had not undergone a miraculous cure, but the combined effect of having unburdened herself and the new sense of closeness with her family was slowly working.

She noticed the burgeoning of maturity in Emily. The Forster had undergone skilled and extensive renovation – the cost, thankfully, covered by the insurance. It was back and sounding as mellifluous as ever. Emily had started playing the instrument and Jane found that not only could she listen to it, but that she was also able to help Emily with her technique. Playing it again herself was a step too far.

'I'm definitely going to rejoin the orchestra after Christmas, Mum.'

'I'm so pleased.' Jane said. 'Is Robbie still in it?'

Emily shrugged. 'Who cares? I've got other friends.'

It was a positive sign. Ross, too, seemed to have changed. He seemed to be fighting with his siblings less and concentrating better at school, to judge by his grades. And Ian, her baby, the sweetest, most loving of all her children – the small anxieties Ian had been showing seemed to have dissipated.

He was in the kitchen now, baking a special cake for her.

'You're not to look, Mummy.'

'How can I not look? I'll have to take it out of the oven.'

She wouldn't let him do that, not yet.

'All right,' he conceded, 'I s'pose. But once it's out, you're not to look. I'm going to decorate it as soon as it's cool – can I use the butter in the fridge?'

'All of it?'

'Hmm, no, maybe not, maybe just half? And some jam?' He was hopping from one foot to the other impatient, as always, to get on with the job in hand. 'Mummy?'

'Ian.'

'Gran says if we set our minds to something, we can usually do it. Is that right?'

'"Where there's a will, there's a way",' Jane quoted back at him, smiling. 'I guess so. If you really want to do something you can work hard to achieve it.'

'I want to be a pastry chef at Langham's then, when I grow up.' Ian had been avidly watching *Masterchef: the Professionals*.

Jane didn't laugh. She hugged him.

'It's a fine ambition,' she said into his hair.

She had been determined, just like him, when she'd been that age. She was going to be a concert cellist, the greatest since Jacqueline du Pré, there had never been any doubt in her mind. And she had worked hard at it, keeping the goal in her sights until...

No, it was not to be revisited. She had come to terms with the past. Whatever had happened, it had shaped her into what she was. And what she was, at last, was a loving mother and devoted wife who had found a sense of peace.

'Don't you let that ambition go. Now, is that cake ready to come out of the oven?'

Later, after the children were in bed, she took a mug of tea and a slice of Ian's delicious jam sponge through to the living room, subsided onto the sofa and stared into the muddy brown liquid.

Her life was definitely mending. Neal's calm support had helped.

She had found a kind of peace. But she had not yet had justice.

She ate the cake slowly and thought about Tom. By deciding not to turn him over to the police they had let him off too lightly. If landing him in jail was a step too far, surely they could still indulge in some form of revenge, by puncturing his insufferable pride, perhaps?

Jane had never been one for initiatives – she'd always left that to Marta and Carrie. But ... Ian's words spun round her head: Gran says if we set our minds to something, we can usually do it. Out of the mouths of babes...

Wiping her hands, she rummaged in her bag for her address book, then picked up the phone and dialled.

'Ann?' she said, proud of the fact that, as she talked to the woman who had first coached her out of it, there was no trace of a stammer. 'It's Jane here. Jane Harvie. I need to talk to you about something. Have you got a moment?'

Chapter Thirty-nine

Tom Vallely strolled into the elegant living room of his rented penthouse. He was wearing a short silk dressing gown and looked as though he had just risen from a pleasant night's exercise. He popped a Nespresso capsule into the machine and set it to work, yawned, stretched, wandered into the hall and came back with the morning's post.

Bills. He tossed them to one side.

A letter. Angela's writing. She'd been trying to call him for days but he'd been busy with his latest shag – the youngest actress to join *Emergency Admissions* and still very impressionable – and he couldn't be bothered with Angela Cutler and her increasingly desperate need for sexual attention. He put the letter aside.

He took the cup and wandered over to the window, cradling it in his hands. He'd always dreamed of a penthouse like this. Smart, contemporary and very, very expensive, just the sort of place for a rising star – and with *Emergency Admissions* now providing a nice little income, he could afford it.

The last envelope was a large brown one, the latest script. He slit it open and skimmed through the papers it contained, slowly at first then leafing through the pages more and more frantically. Finally he reached the end and flung the whole lot down onto the white sofa in a rage. They spilled untidily across the leather as he let out a huge roar of pure fury.

'Tom?' A girl emerged from the bedroom, wearing only one of Tom's shirts. She was petite and waif-like, her hair was screwed up loosely on top of her head and secured with a vivid pink clip. She looked very young. 'What is it?'

She laid a questioning hand on his arm but he flung her off with such force that she spun round and hit the wall. She slid to the floor, looking dazed and shocked.

'The *bitches*,' Tom spat. 'The fucking bitches.'

Chapter Forty

Shortly before Christmas, Jane called Carrie.

'Neal's taking the family out to the panto on Wednesday night,' she said. 'I've given my ticket to Suzy Patterson – Em's delighted. So am I, I can't stand panto. Anyway, *Emergency Admissions* is on. Come on round. We can have a girls' night in.'

Carrie groaned. 'You don't expect us to watch that, do you? Couldn't we just have a gossip?'

'It might just be worth it this week,' Jane said.

Marta was even more reluctant.

'I can't stand it, Jane,' she confessed. 'I feel responsible for getting that man the part. I hate being the agent of his good fortune.'

'It's only an hour.'

'I didn't know you were such a fan.'

'A little birdie tells me it might be interesting.'

'Oh yes? Tell me more.'

'You'll have to come and see.'

They arrived at the same time. Marta brought chocolates, Carrie was bearing champagne.

'Bubbly?' Jane enquired, raising her eyebrows, when Carrie handed her the chilled Bollinger.

Carrie shrugged off her coat and hung it as carefully as she could among the muddle of blazers, jackets, waterproofs and winter coats on Jane's coatstand.

'I'm celebrating. Henry Frew told me today that I'd been given a partnership.'

311

Jane shrieked and Marta enveloped her in a bear hug.

'Fantastic!'

'Brilliant! You must be so chuffed!'

'I guess,' she said, her voice flat.

'Carrie? What's wrong? You've waited all your life for this.'

She smiled. 'Yeah, you're right. Fetch the glasses. Let's drink to success.'

She would not be drawn on what was bothering her.

'Tell me about Jake, Marta,' Jane said as they clinked their glasses and sank into the well-worn comfort of her sofa. 'What's the latest?'

Marta sipped the cold, crisp bubbles and gave a small shrug of her shoulders.

'We're working on it. When he started discussing whether we might get back together, I almost leapt for joy. But it's not that simple. Jake's changing, he's much more his own man and he seems to have really found himself in London. I can't ask him to come back to Scotland.'

'Does he want to stay in London?'

'I think so, though he says he's prepared to think about a move back.'

'What's stopping you? Surely you should be moving heaven and earth to get him back here.'

'There are so many options. If he came back here we'd be back in the same fix – no job, Jake miserable. Maybe it *is* time we went our separate ways, let each other have space to grow and develop.'

'Listen to yourself, Marta. This is *Jake* we're talking about. You're made for each other; you always have been.'

'You think? Even a different Jake, one who's not so...' she hesitated, searching for the right word, ' ...malleable?'

'If a different Marta is prepared to let the man be his own man a bit more.'

She pursed her lips. 'Maybe you're right. But I can't ask him to come back here, whatever he says. His career is in London, he's

312

obviously finding it stimulating. You should see him. He looks so different, like he's really fulfilled. If I want to keep him, I'd have to move to London. And a move to London is a big thought, especially when you guys are closer than you have been for years.'

'There are phones. Text. Email. Trains, planes and auto-mobiles, for heaven's sake. Friendship is forever, wherever. And you'd easily get a job in London.'

Marta's features relaxed into a soft smile. 'Thanks. The main thing is the lines are still open between us. We're talking. In loads of ways we're closer than we've ever been and whatever decision we make, it'll be one we've thought through and decided on together. We might even have one last try at a family. Jake reckons if I don't work for a bit, relax more, there's a chance I might conceive again. The clock's ticking, after all.'

'So what's the problem?'

'I just need to be sure. We both need to be. I couldn't go through all this again, it would kill me.'

'Just go for it, Marta. You know it's the right thing.'

Carrie's mobile peeped and bleeped in her bag.

'Answer it,' Marta urged.

'*Emergency Admissions* is about to start.' Jane stood up and walked across to switch on the television.

Marta groaned. 'Must we?'

'Shush. Enjoy.'

The on-screen romance between James Darling, the surgeon played by Tom Vallely, and Harriet Love, a manager at High Hampstead hospital, had provided the *Emergency Admissions* script with many moments of high drama and not a few jokes at the expense of the two aptly named characters.

Darling, handsome, arrogant, charming and deeply dislikable, ran rings around the good-natured, adoring Love, who had allowed herself to be used as a doormat. In recent episodes, Darling had been conducting a parallel affair with one of the young nurses – and Harriet Love had finally found out.

'What a rat,' Carrie said.

'But he *is* plausible, you have to concede,' Marta argued.

'That's not acting, though, is it?' said Carrie.

'Shhh,' Jane chided.

They watched in fascination as Love confronted Darling with her knowledge. He denied it. They saw her doubt. He seduced her with silky words. They made love (as much as was possible on an early evening show), he got out of bed, his smile irritatingly smug.

'Don't you just hate him?' Marta said.

'Talk about true to life.'

'Shhh,' said Jane.

It looked as though the lovers had patched things up. Harriet Love went out to work, Darling showered, preened, shaved, took a call on his mobile, arranged a dinner date.

Carrie's mobile buzzed again. Again she ignored it.

Darling opened a drawer, rummaged around, shoved aside silky knickers. Marta sat up straight.

'Jesus,' she breathed.

Between the layers of neatly folded underwear, Darling had found a brooch. A beautiful gold bow, encrusted with pearls.

'I don't believe it!'

'How could they have known—'

'Shhh,' said Jane.

The storyline moved on. An accident on the motorway, a multiple pile-up, a major emergency. Harriet Love was at the heart of the action, calling in extra staff, finding empty beds, calling other hospitals, organising what needed to be done. In the midst of it all, she called James Darling. He answered on his mobile, pleaded a sudden feverish chill, refused to answer her plea for help.

He ended the call. The camera panned out. He wasn't sweating at home, he was in a restaurant. The girl he was dining with smiled at him adoringly. On her jacket was pinned a brooch.

The brooch Darling had taken from Harriet Love's underwear drawer earlier.

'Jane?' Marta looked at her friend inquiringly. 'What's going on?'

'Shhh,' Jane said.

Back at the hospital, the action was at its height. But one of the doctors, volunteering for an extra shift, had cut short his dinner – at the very restaurant where James Darling was dining with the young nurse. Thinking Harriet might call on the surgeon to come in, he mentioned it to her. Harriet Love's reaction was intuitive, instant – and rather unprofessional. Handing over command to a colleague, she ran outside and flagged down a taxi. Within minutes, she was standing, framed in the doorway of the restaurant, watching her lover holding hands with her young rival. The camera focused on Darling's profile, then panned to the girl's face, then ... slowly ... to the brooch.

Distress, despair, fury, flitted across Harriet's face. She made a strangled, inarticulate sound. The girl saw her and said something to Darling. As he turned and saw Harriet, she lunged for the door and rushed headlong into the street.

'What's going to happen?' Marta reached for Carrie's hand and gripped it tightly.

It was Carrie, this time, her attention riveted by the action on screen, who said, 'Shhh.'

Darling tore open the door of the restaurant and raced down the street after the figure of Love, who was crossing at a red light.

'No! They couldn't, could they?'

Jane laughed. 'Oh yes,' she crowed, 'I think they could!'

The light changed to green but Darling, intent on reaching Harriet, didn't stop. There was a second when his face was clearly shown, shocked and disbelieving, as a lorry, unable to brake or swerve, mowed him down.

Cut to the A&E department. Darling, covered in blood, on a ventilator, in his own hospital, his own staff clustered around him. The heartbeat stopped, the monitor slipped to a single continuous note. A nurse reached for the defibrillator, but the consultant laid a hand on her arm, shook his head.

The signature tune faded in.

He was dead.

Jane looked at the others and her smile was full of glee and mischief.

'That's it,' she said. 'Justice. At last.' She switched off the television. Marta and Carrie stared at her in shocked silence.

'Jane,' Carrie said at length, her voice deeply admiring, 'how the hell did you manage that?'

In all her life, Jane had never done anything so bold or so imaginative. Pride burst through.

'I read an article in a magazine, an interview with a scriptwriter. I always thought the storylines of these soaps were decided on in committee, by the producers. I hadn't realised that good scriptwriters have the ear of the producers – and when an actor is not popular, the door can be open for writers to make suggestions...'

'Ann Playfair?' Marta said, starting to laugh.

Jane nodded. 'She was fantastic. I went to see her in Glasgow. I told her lots of things about Tom – funnily enough, none of it surprised her. But she seized on the brooch idea. It's so visual, she said it was ideal. She did the synopsis for the episode and pitched it at the weekly meeting. I think the producers had actually seen through Tom's charm – there had been quite a few mutterings among the cast – and they were quite receptive to the idea of killing off his character. Plus, they wanted something dramatic just before Christmas.'

'Jane, you are utterly, utterly brilliant,' Marta said appreciatively. 'I would never have thought of that.'

Jane was sitting up very straight. Her eyes were shining, her face had begun to lose the greyness of despair and she looked more confident than she had looked for years. She's changing

Marta thought, a weight has come off her shoulders and you can actually see it.

Carrie bent down and found her phone. 'Back in a minute,' she said.

They watched in silence as she left the room.

'She's not happy, is she?' Jane said anxiously.

'No. You'd think this would be the most thrilling day of her life – getting the partnership and everything,' Marta sighed. 'You know, for years I've tried to get Carrie hooked up with a decent guy – then the first time it happens, it all goes horribly wrong.'

There was a screech from the hall. They looked at each other, startled. Carrie burst in, her eyes luminous.

'What?'

'What's happened?'

'Look!' She handed her phone to Jane. Jane read the text, but simply looked mystified.

'*What?*' Marta urged impatiently, holding out her hand for the phone. She read the message.

<I do believe there's a vacancy for a DA, Stateside. Full time. Interested?>

She looked up at Carrie. 'What does it mean, Carrie?'

Carrie looked mortified, but the embarrassment faded almost instantly to joy. 'DA Delight was my pseudonym on Bed Buddies. It stood for District Attorney, though no-one knew that, or cared. It was my private joke – except that Tom knew, and that's how he sussed me. I had a dream, years ago, to go to the States and study law there. It all seemed so glamorous. The influence of Hollywood, I guess. *To Kill a Mockingbird.*'

'I remember you loved that at school. So—'

'I told Drew. When I confessed about Bed Buddies, I told him everything. He's been trying to get me to talk and last week we finally did. But I felt so guilty that I set him free from our

317

relationship. I thought he deserved someone better than me, so I destroyed everything we had together – or I thought I did. What this means, though—' she danced a little jig on the carpet, '— is that he won't take "no" for an answer. He wants me to be with him in the States. Permanently.'

Jane said, breathlessly, 'But the *partnership*, Carrie. It's all you've ever dreamed about.'

'Bugger the partnership.'

She was so clearly in love that Marta, watching her, felt a momentary pang. The dynamics of the relationship between the three of them was shifting. Jane had become confident and more assertive. Carrie had developed a soft centre and was jettisoning the ambition that had driven her for so long. As for herself ... a choice lay in front of her and it was one that would dictate the direction of the rest of her life. Ever since Jake had left, she had thought there was only one thing she wanted: to get him back. Now it didn't seem quite so simple, and she had to consider what was the right thing for Jake as well as for her. That meant that she had changed as well. All she had to do was work out whether they could still make their marriage work.

'So,' she said slowly, 'Carrie's off to America. It's possible – just possible – that I may go and live in London. Jane's become more independent all of a sudden.' She looked at them both, filled with concern. 'There have been so many awful things recently. We've fallen out, discovered we weren't as close as we'd always believed we were – we've really tested our friendship. I thought we had got through it, that we'd be closer than we ever had been. But now – we're in danger of losing it all again.'

'Come here, you daft doughnut,' Carrie commanded, taking her hand and pulling her out of the chair. 'And you, Jane, come here.'

They stood, their hands entwined, in a circle. 'Friends.'

'Friends—' Jane said, her face shining.

Stuff happens, Marta thought, scanning the dear, familiar faces of her two soul mates.

Life gets you.
Everything changes.
But my friends are a constant.
'—Forever,' she finished.

THE END

Fourthcoming from
Jenny Harper

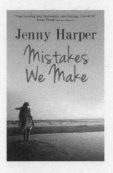

Volume Five of Jenny Harper's acclaimed
Heartlands series

Coming Summer 2016

Other Titles

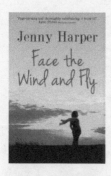

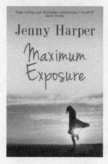

Reading Group Discussion Points

- Each of the three friends has a distinct character, priorities and approach to life. Marta longs for a child and takes her husband, Jake, for granted; Jane has three children and a husband she adores but music is missing from her life; and Carrie has eschewed long term relationships in favour of ambition, and has chosen sexual fulfilment above commitment. Is there any character you would criticise for their life choices? And if so, has your opinion of that character changed by the end of the book?

- Tom is a sociopath who cheerfully manipulates people for his own ends – and simply for pleasure. Do you think his character was well drawn? He can be very charming – did you ever like him?

- Friendship is a big theme in the book. What do you think keeps these three women close, across the years? Does the fact that the friendship survives despite being severely tested by Tom's machinations ring true for you?

- Women's issues – sex, motherhood and the inability to conceive (or the termination of a pregnancy) – all feature largely in this book. Which element resonated most with you?

Reading Group Discussion Points

Reading Group Discussion Points

- Cheerful, organising Marta finds she has never taken true account of her husband's feelings; Jane has been afraid to tell the truth to her husband; and Carrie has repressed her feelings because she wants to remain in control. By the end, each woman has changed in some way. How? And does each journey improve and enrich the character, or not?

- What do you feel about the way in which the women take revenge on Tom? Is their behaviour justified? Petty? Exhilarating?

- What do you think about the men in the book, Jake, Neal and Drew?

- Who in the book would you most like to meet, and what would you ask them?

- Would you have advised any of the women to make different choices at any point?

- Have you read Jenny Harper's other books? If so, do you see any similarities in theme, writing style, structure, or is this one completely different? And will you look out for any more books by Jenny Harper in the future?

For more information about **Jenny Harper**

and other **Accent Press** titles

please visit

www.accentpress.co.uk

http://www.jennyharperauthor.co.uk